DRAGONS
OF
DELTORA

Special Edition
Books 3&4

DRAGONS OF DELTORA

Special Edition
Books 3&4

EMILY RODDA

SCHOLASTIC INC.

New York Toronto London Auckland Sydney
Mexico City New Delhi Hong Kong Buenos Aires

Dragons of Deltora #3: Isle of the Dead, ISBN 0-439-63375-3,
Text and graphics copyright © 2004 by Emily Rodda.

Dragons of Deltora #4: The Sister of the South, ISBN 0-439-63376-1,
Text and graphics copyright © 2004 by Emily Rodda.

Graphics by Kate Rowe.
Cover illustration copyright © 2004 by Scholastic Australia.
Cover illustration by Marc McBride.

12 11 10 9 8 7 6 5 4 3 2 1   6 7 8 9 10/0

Printed in the U.S.A.   23

This edition created exclusively for Barnes & Noble, Inc.

2006 Barnes & Noble Books

ISBN 0-7607-9612-2

First compilation printing, April 2006

for Reuben Jakeman

Contents

DRAGONS OF DELTORA

ISLE OF
THE DEAD

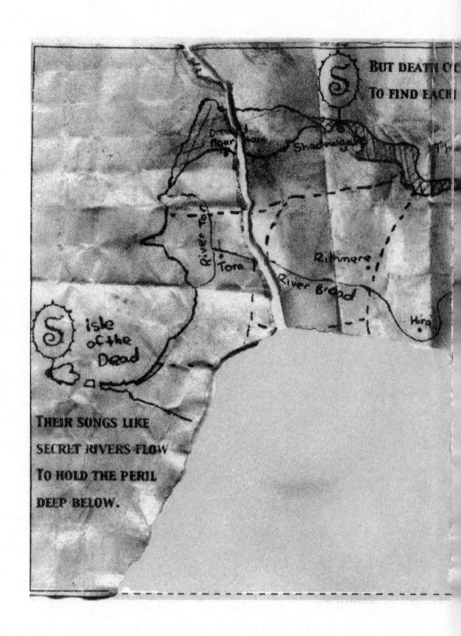

BUT DEATH C[O]

TO FIND EACH [...]

THEIR SONGS LIKE
SECRET RIVERS FLOW
TO HOLD THE PERIL
DEEP BELOW.

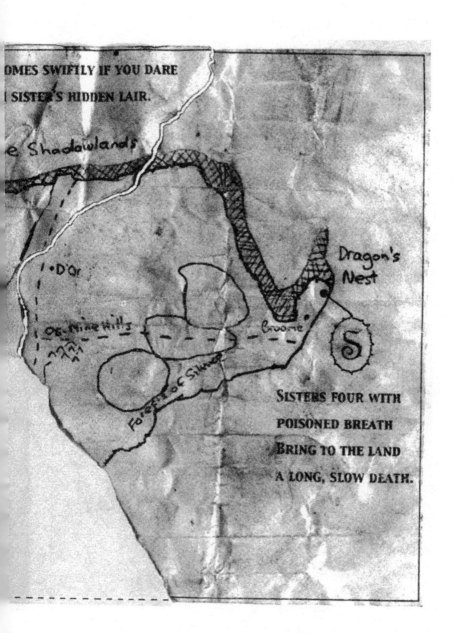

OMES SWIFTLY IF YOU DARE

SISTER'S HIDDEN LAIR.

e Shadowlands

·D'Or

Os-Nine Hills

Forest of Silence

Croome

Dragon's Nest

S

SISTERS FOUR WITH
POISONED BREATH
BRING TO THE LAND
A LONG, SLOW DEATH.

The story so far . . .

Lief, Barda, and Jasmine are on a secret quest to find and destroy the Four Sisters, Shadow Lord creations that are poisoning Deltora. To succeed, they must wake Deltora's last seven dragons, which have been deep in enchanted sleep for centuries. Only when the power of a dragon joins with the power of a gem in the Belt of Deltora can a Sister be destroyed.

Deltora's dragons, fierce protectors of their land, were hunted almost to extinction by the Shadow Lord's Ak-Baba. When only one dragon from each gem territory remained, the explorer Doran the Dragonlover persuaded them to sleep in safety until a king, wearing the Belt of Deltora, called them to wake.

Too late, Doran learned of the Shadow Lord's plan to use the Four Sisters to starve Deltora's people. Once the dragons had gone there was nothing to stop the Enemy from putting the Sisters in place. Doran tried to warn of the danger, but was not believed. Leaving a map showing where he thought the Sisters were, he set out to find proof. He never returned, and his map was marked by the Shadow Lord, torn into four parts, and hidden.

The first map fragment led Lief, Barda, and Jasmine to Dragon's Nest, where, with the ruby dragon, they destroyed the Sister of the East and found a second map part pointing to Shadowgate in the north. Despite the efforts of the evil Laughing Jack, they reached Shadowgate, destroyed the Sis-

Contents

ter of the North with the emerald dragon, and found the third part of the map.

Now they must move on to seek the Sister of the West on the fearful Isle of the Dead.

Now read on . . .

1 ~ The Chase

Doom strolled through the great doorway of the palace in Del, and casually scanned the northern sky. He saw the messenger bird the guards had reported, but his stern, scarred face showed no sign of eagerness, fear, or hope.

Many people were talking on the stairs that led down to the palace lawn and the road beyond. There was much to talk about. For weeks there had been rumors of strange happenings in the east — of dragons flying the skies and crops beginning to thrive.

Now the same tales had begun coming in from the north.

But none of the people on the stairs approached Doom to ask him if the rumors were true. None of them did more than glance nervously at the silent figure by the palace doors. Doom was a legend among them, but they feared him.

With all their hearts they wished their young king would return from his tour around the kingdom. Times were hard, and they missed Lief sorely.

The bird swooped down and dropped its message into Doom's hands. To the disappointment of the people turning to look, Doom moved inside at once. Whatever the message was, he plainly did not intend to share it.

✳

Alone in the palace dining room, Doom tore open the message with a feverish haste that would have very much surprised those who thought he had no feelings.

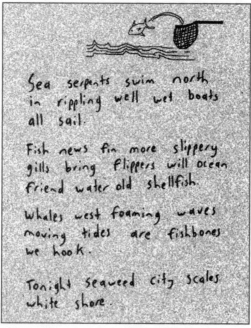

Sea serpents swim north, in rippling well wet boats all sail.

Fish news fin more slippery gills bring flippers will ocean friend water old shellfish.

Whales west foaming waves moving tides are fishbones we hook.

Tonight seaweed city scales white shore.

The note was not signed, but the familiar writing told Doom that Lief, at least, was safe. A tiny piece of brown wood had been folded within the paper. Doom picked it up and smelled it.

"Boolong cone," he muttered, raising his eyebrows. "So — he is on Dread Mountain. And the others?"

He glanced at the sketch at the top of the note, then read each sentence from back to front, leaving out all words that had anything to do with fish.

All well in north. His heart gave a great thud. This could only mean that against all odds the Sister of the North had been destroyed, and that Lief, Barda, and Jasmine were all safe.

Old friend will bring more news. Gla-Thon of the Dread Gnomes, perhaps. There was no one else Doom could think of who might have helped the companions in the north.

We are moving west. So they had found the third fragment of the map of Doran the Dragonlover. They knew the location of the Sister of the West!

White city tonight. At this, Doom leaped to his feet. Tora! Lief, Barda, and Jasmine would be in the marble city of magic this very night! No doubt they were going to ask the Torans to speed them to their new goal. A message sent now would reach them just in time.

Hastily he scribbled a note, then strode into the hallway and turned in the direction of the guarded area where the messenger birds were kept.

As he reached the library he remembered with a stab of irritation that old Josef the librarian wished desperately to write to Lief. His nagging had nearly driven Doom mad over the past weeks.

The library door was open. Inside, Josef's assistant Paff was arranging books on shelves, looking even more harried than usual.

"Where is Josef?" Doom demanded.

Paff jumped, and her pink-rimmed eyes widened. "He — is in the kitchen," she said breathlessly. "He did not eat at midday because — "

"Run to him at once, if you please," Doom broke in impatiently. "A bird is leaving with a message for Lief very soon. This is Josef's chance to send a note, if he makes haste. Take paper and a pen for him."

"Josef always carries a pen and a notebook with him," Paff said, then waited, her mouth hanging slightly open.

"Go then!" Doom thundered.

Paff dropped the books she was holding, shot past him like a startled rabbit, and ran in the direction of the kitchen.

Doom moved on, his face like thunder. In truth, he was annoyed with himself for losing his temper with someone as defenseless as Paff. But the people he passed drew back fearfully, and wished all the more that their beloved Lief would come home.

✳

While Doom was striding through the palace and Josef was dropping his soup spoon and frantically searching for his little notebook, Lief was flying towards Tora in the pouch of a Kin.

A few days before, he, Barda, and Jasmine had been astounded when three of the fabled flying creatures had arrived in Shadowgate to carry them to rest and safety on Dread Mountain.

The Kin were Ailsa, Bruna, and young Prin. Prin had grown very much since the companions last saw her and was now almost as large as Ailsa.

"But — how did you know where we were?" Lief had gasped when the first joyous greetings were over.

"Dreaming Water!" Prin said proudly. "Every night for weeks I have drunk the Water and thought of you, so I could visit you in my dreams."

"We have all been so afraid for you," sighed Bruna. "The Dread Gnomes, too — especially your good friend Gla-Thon. She wanted to speed to your aid when you first arrived in Shadowgate, but the old leader Fa-Glin forbade it. He said that if you had wanted Gla-Thon's help, you would have asked for it."

Stunned, Lief exchanged glances with Barda and Jasmine. So their whereabouts had not been secret at all — on Dread Mountain, at least!

"Let us fly!" Prin squeaked. "Everyone is wild to

see you. The Gnomes are trying to make a welcome feast. But how can they make a feast when they have no food but a few old berries and stalks?"

"They should learn to eat Boolong cones, as we do," said Bruna. "There are very many of those."

Lief, Barda, and Jasmine had said no more. But during the next few days, while they rested in the caverns of the Gnomes, and the famous green moss from the Dread Mountain stream healed Lief's wounds, they had talked and wondered a great deal.

Somehow the Shadow Lord had always known where they were in the north. They had not been able to understand why. Perhaps they now had their answer.

Trust only old friends . . .

So Doom had said in his last message. And the Dread Gnomes were old friends, just as the Kin were. But were all the Gnomes of the same mind? Or was there one whose loyalty lay in the Shadowlands?

It would only take one . . .

They told only Gla-Thon of their fears.

"Much as I wish to, I cannot swear there is no traitor among us," she said soberly. "There can be one bad berry in any bunch, however sweet it seems."

And so it was that the companions smilingly put their fingers to their lips when any question about their future travels was asked of them in the caverns of the Gnomes.

So it was that they sent no message to Del until

Gla-Thon could arrange for a bird to fly in secret, the day they left Dread Mountain.

So it was that they asked the Kin to give them all that remained of the Dreaming Water, knowing that the gentle creatures could refuse them nothing.

And so it was that they asked Ailsa, Bruna, and Prin to carry them away, but did not tell them where they were to go until they were high in the air and no one else could hear.

Careful and suspicious people themselves, the Gnomes accepted without complaint the companions' desire for secrecy. Fa-Glin also supplied all manner of goods to help them on their way — including a soft leather bag filled with gold pieces, which Jasmine had tucked securely in one of her many pockets.

"It is nothing," Fa-Glin had sighed when they thanked him. "Gold and jewels we have in plenty. If only we could eat them!"

Now the Kin were flying towards Tora, skimming over the low hills that rolled beyond the mountains. The light was slowly dimming and the wind was blowing across their path, but Lief, Barda, and Jasmine were all sure they would reach their goal by nightfall.

Then suddenly Kree, who was flying beside them, wheeled and screeched. And behind them they heard a distant, furious roar.

They turned their heads and saw a large green shape streaking towards them from the mountains.

Lief felt a thrill of fear. The emerald dragon had joined him to destroy the Sister of the North, but he knew that it felt no friendship towards him. And by the sound of its roars, it was very angry.

Filli squealed and bolted into hiding beneath Jasmine's collar. Bruna and Ailsa screamed, and their wingbeats faltered. But Prin put down her head and made an abrupt right turn.

"Prin, come back!" Ailsa shrieked after her. "You are going the wrong way! You are flying towards the coast!"

"Do you wish to be eaten?" cried Prin. "That is a dragon, Ailsa! A dragon! We can never outfly it unless we use the wind."

"If we can cross the border into amethyst country, it will not be able to follow!" Lief shouted. "Do your best!"

With the wind at their backs, the Kin made good speed. The hills beneath them gave way to flat, barren land, and soon they could see the glittering sea ahead. But every moment the dragon was gaining on them.

We must have crossed the border long ago, Lief thought in dismay. *But it has not stopped — if anything, it is flying faster!*

And suddenly Kree was crying a warning and the beast was above them, bearing down on them, forcing them to the ground.

Sobbing with fright, the Kin thudded to land.

Lief, Barda, and Jasmine rolled from their pouches and at once were pinned down by the wind of the dragon's mighty wingbeats.

Then, abruptly, they could move again, and the pounding of the waves and the cries of seabirds were the only sounds they could hear.

Shakily they crawled to their feet. The dragon was crouching beside them, huge and menacing. Its green eyes blazed with anger. The spines on its back were like quivering spears.

"Do you dare to steal the emerald away yet again from its territory and mine, young king?" it hissed.

Lief felt Barda and Jasmine move behind him, and knew that they were reaching for their weapons, poised to defend him. But his hands remained on the Belt of Deltora. He knew he must show no sign of weakness.

"I must take it, dragon of the emerald," he said. "It is part of the Belt that unites us all. And I must wear the Belt to the Isle of the Dead, in the land of the diamond, to find and destroy the Sister of the West."

"What do I care for the Sister of the West?" hissed the dragon. "The evil in my land is gone, and that is all that matters."

Lief took a deep breath. "The man you called Dragonfriend — the man known to us as Doran the Dragonlover — did not agree with you," he said.

The dragon did not blink. But at the mention of Doran's name a stillness settled over it. Lief knew that he had its attention.

"Doran thought as I do about our land," he went on firmly. "Your territory is all that matters to you, perhaps. But for Doran, the whole of Deltora was important."

He took a deep breath and met the dragon's eyes unflinchingly.

"Doran lost his life because he tried to find the Four Sisters and foil the Shadow Lord's plans," he said. "Now we are risking *our* lives to finish the work he began. You must not hinder us. You must let us go!"

2 - Bone Point

Slowly the fire in the green eyes died and the wicked spines were lowered. "You speak to me as plainly as Dragonfriend spoke long ago when he persuaded me to sleep," the dragon growled. "And though I do not like it, I accept your words, as once I accepted his."

The relief was so great that Lief almost staggered.

"Thank you," he said. "Then we will go on our way."

"If you must," the dragon said coldly. "But I warn you — beware the dragons of the amethyst and the diamond. Emerald dragons are honorable. Others are full of lies and hungry for land and power."

Lief made no reply. He knew it was useless to argue. Jasmine, however, was not so wise.

"You are a fine one to talk of honor, dragon," she

snapped. "You crossed the border into amethyst territory without a thought when you were pursuing us! Yet when the lapis-lazuli dragon entered *your* land, you — "

The dragon bared its fangs. "Do not speak of that small, sly beast to me, girl! If it invades my territory again, I will tear it apart. Its blood will wash my stones. Its scales will fall on my mountains like rain."

"Why, you dragons hate your own kind even more than you hate the Shadow Lord!" Jasmine exclaimed. "I cannot think how Doran persuaded you to trust one another enough to sleep — even to save your lives!"

Steam gushed from the dragon's jaws. "I did not trust the other dragons," it hissed furiously. "I trusted Dragonfriend, whom I loved, and who knew my true name. Your foolishness angers me. I bid you farewell."

With a dull clatter it unfurled its leathery wings.

Kree took flight with a squawk, the Kin cowered, and Lief, Barda, and Jasmine scrambled clear.

The next moment, they were again pinned to the ground by the gale of huge wingbeats. And when at last they were able to raise their heads, the dragon was far above them, a shadow in the dimming sky.

"Jasmine!" cried Lief in exasperation.

"I merely spoke the truth." Jasmine shrugged, as Kree fluttered back to her arm.

"Speaking of truth," Barda said, "I fear it is true to say that we are in a pretty pickle. Look around you."

Jasmine and Lief turned and looked.

They were on a long point of land stretching out into the sea. A narrow road wound to the land's end, where a lighthouse rose, tall, white, and lonely. Wind whistled across the flat earth, bringing with it the sting of salt. Waves crashed against the rocks. A few seabirds wheeled above the foam-flecked ocean, their cries faint and ghostly.

"This is a dreary place, indeed," Jasmine said. Filli whimpered under her collar. All that could be seen of him was the tip of his nose.

"It would help if we knew where we were, Lief," Barda muttered. "You have the map — "

"We do not need the map," Lief said slowly.

His companions glanced at him in surprise.

"I know of this place," Lief went on, staring at the lighthouse. "It is called Bone Point."

"Well, whatever its name is, it is as flat as gnomes' bread," scowled Prin. "We cannot take flight from here. We should never have let ourselves be forced down. Now we are stranded!"

"Better stranded than torn to pieces in the air!" snapped Ailsa.

Barda jerked his head towards the tall white column of the lighthouse. "The lighthouse has a viewing platform at the top. Surely you could take off from there?"

"We could try," said Ailsa doubtfully.

Lief made a small movement, as if he was about to protest. When Barda glanced at him, however, he pressed his lips together and nodded.

"Yes. We have no choice," he muttered. "Even if the amethyst dragon senses the Belt and comes to us, it will not be able to carry us all."

He squared his shoulders and began walking swiftly towards the lighthouse.

※

When Jasmine and Barda at last caught up with Lief, he was standing by the lighthouse door, staring up at the viewing platform. Protected by bright red railings, the platform circled the tall building like a necklace. Above it gleamed the windows of the light chamber, neatly capped by a rounded red roof.

Barda exclaimed in surprise and pointed to an engraved stone set into the base of the lighthouse wall:

THE BONE POINT LIGHT

My light will shine like truth through the darkness.

I was born in the mind of Adin.
I was made by the builders of Raladin.
The magic of Tora protects me.
Sailors in peril will bless me.

"Yes, the great Adin arranged for the lighthouse to be built," Lief said, glancing down at the stone. "It was just after he united the seven tribes and became king. This verse is printed in the *Deltora Annals*. Josef showed it to Mother and me, just before she left for the west."

"Why, it looks as new as if it was completed only yesterday!" Barda said.

" 'The magic of Tora protects me . . .' " Jasmine read, and frowned in puzzlement.

"Bone Point was part of the territory of the Toran tribe," Lief said slowly. "And, as we know only too well, the magic of the ancient Torans was very powerful."

His companions nodded, remembering the disaster that had befallen the present people of Tora when they broke their ancestors' magic oath of loyalty to Adin and his heirs. Their years of exile from their city had ended only when Lief, as king, forgave them for their fault in Adin's name.

15

"Adin asked the ancient Torans to protect the Light," Lief went on. "He feared that the Shadow Lord might plot to destroy it. It suited the Enemy for Deltora to be isolated — for foreign ships to stay away."

"So — the Light signalled welcome to people from lands to our west?" asked Jasmine.

"It did welcome them, no doubt. But its real purpose was to act as a guide and warning," Lief said. "A hidden spine of rock spears into the sea from the tip of Bone Point. It has been the death of many ships that ventured too near it in the darkness of the night."

In silence they all turned to look at the sea.

"The tide is coming in," Barda murmured.

Waves crashed hard on the tip of the point, and to the south of the lighthouse. But on the northern side, close to where they were standing, there was a sheltered bay. Shells littered the bay's smooth half-moon of pale sand. Higher up, the faded remains of a small red boat lay almost buried in mounds of dry seaweed.

"Fish may not be plentiful, but surely it is still worth throwing out a line when food is so scarce." Barda frowned. "What is the lighthouse keeper thinking of, to let his boat go to ruin?"

"There is no lighthouse keeper," Lief said. "Red Han, the man who kept the Bone Point Light in my father's time, was the last. The Light has been dark since the Shadow Lord invaded and the Torans were banished from their city."

"But what of the foreign ships?" Jasmine asked.

"No foreign ships come near us now," Lief said. "Perhaps because of the danger. Perhaps because the people to our west take the darkness as a sign that the Shadow Lord still rules in Deltora. We do not know."

"But the Torans are back in their city now!" Barda exclaimed. "Surely the Light can be made to shine again? And surely another lighthouse keeper can be found? It is lonely work, I daresay, but — "

"It is not that," Lief broke in wearily. "It is something far more strange."

He paused, then met his companions' curious eyes and went on reluctantly.

"Part of the spell the ancient Torans cast was that only the keeper of the Light, the one sworn to protect it, could enter the chamber where it burned. If a keeper became ill, or wearied of the task, he or she was bound to travel to Tora and solemnly resign before all the people. Only then could a new keeper be appointed."

"A foolhardy spell indeed," Barda said grimly.

Lief grimaced. "So it seems. But no doubt it did not seem so dangerous in the time of Adin. The ancient Torans were very sure of their power. And for many centuries all was well."

He sighed. "But eighteen years ago, something

happened at Bone Point. We do not know what it was. All we know is that the Light went out, and Red Han disappeared."

"No doubt he was easy prey for Ols or Gray Guards once the Torans had been swept away, and their magic no longer protected him," Jasmine said.

"No doubt," Lief answered. "And the sudden loss of both the light keeper and the magic of Tora explains only too well why the Light went out."

"Then why — ?" Barda began impatiently.

"Do you not see?" Lief exclaimed. "Red Han never resigned his trust! The light chamber is sealed. The ancient spell still holds. And it cannot be broken — even by the present people of Tora."

"But — " Jasmine frowned. "But — this must mean that Red Han is still alive, for surely his death would break the spell. Why has he not returned?"

"Because he was unworthy of the trust placed in him!" growled Barda. "He broke his oath and ran away when the protection of Tora was lost. And now he skulks in some corner of Deltora, afraid to come out of hiding."

Lief shook his head, frowning. "Zeean of Tora knew Red Han. She says he was a simple man, but a man of good faith. He had been the light keeper at Bone Point for twenty years. She does not believe he would have betrayed his trust."

"But he could not have resigned in the proper way, even if he wanted to, Lief!" Jasmine exclaimed.

"From what you say, by the time he left here, Tora was deserted."

"That does not explain why he is missing to this day," Lief said. "And it does not explain — "

He broke off, and glanced over his shoulder. The Kin were still some distance away, toiling along the road on their short, stubby legs.

"All those who have entered the lighthouse feel — wickedness," he went on in a low voice. "They hear sounds and see things that are not there. Many say that the place is haunted."

Barda snorted. "Wind howls around a lighthouse. Birds cry and the sea pounds. Add to that a room that cannot be entered and a tale of a missing lighthouse keeper, and timid folk might easily imagine ghosts."

"Perhaps," Lief said. "But my mother is far from timid. She has been here, with Zeean of Tora. Both of them saw things that could not be explained. Bone Point has been a place of ill-omen in these parts for a long time, Barda. No one will come near it."

Barda grinned. "Indeed?" he asked. "Well, plainly one soul at least is not afraid. Perhaps you should ask *her* to be the lighthouse keeper."

"Who?" Lief asked, looking around.

"Why, the girl on the shore!" Barda exclaimed. "The girl painting the — "

He turned again towards the little bay. His jaw dropped.

Puzzled, Lief and Jasmine followed his eyes. But there was nothing to see. The bay was utterly deserted.

"But — but she was there!" Barda gasped. "A girl — about Jasmine's age — with long red hair. She was painting a picture. She had an easel and a brush. She was wearing a yellow skirt. It was tossing in the wind. I — I saw her plainly! Where is she?"

He turned this way and that, searching the flat land frantically. But there was no sign of anyone, and no footprints marked the weed-strewn sand.

"I saw her!" he repeated stubbornly.

Lief nodded. "I am sure you did," he said. "Red Han did not live here alone. And he was not the only one to disappear. Red Han had a daughter."

3 - The Lighthouse

Barda stood stiff with shock. He opened his mouth, but before he could speak, Filli popped his head out from beneath Jasmine's jacket and began chattering a welcome. Prin was panting up to the lighthouse with Bruna and Ailsa close behind her.

"What are you looking for, Barda?" Prin asked. "Have you lost something?"

Barda turned like one in a dream. "Only my senses, it seems," he mumbled.

Plainly he was going to say no more, so Prin turned her attention to the lighthouse.

"Oh, it is much larger than it looks from a distance!" she squealed. "And we can all fit through the door easily, I am sure of it! Shall I — ?"

"Wait!" Lief exclaimed. Gently he pushed Prin aside and put his hand on the shining brass doorknob.

"Jasmine and I will go in first," he said. "You Kin

follow, close behind us. Barda will come last. It is very important that we stay together. Do you understand?"

The three Kin nodded, their eyes wide.

"Is there . . . danger?" whispered Bruna, glancing worriedly at Prin.

"The lighthouse is deserted," Lief said carefully. "But we may see or hear things — things that are not real."

"Spirits!" Prin squeaked in excitement.

Bruna made a frightened sound and clasped her small front paws.

"Some say they are spirits," said Lief. "My mother says they are only visions from the past, kept alive by the walls of this place. The lighthouse is very old, and the magic of Tora is in every stone of it."

He sighed. "The builders of Raladin have been asked to try to knock it down so that another lighthouse can be built in its place. But the Torans have little hope that this can be done."

He turned the brass knob. The door opened smoothly, as though its hinges had been freshly oiled.

Inside it was very dark, and cold as death.

"Something bad happened here," quavered Prin, stepping back. "Something very bad. I feel it."

"I, too," Bruna murmured.

"And I," said Ailsa.

"We will turn back, if you wish," Lief said.

"No," said Ailsa in a small voice. "We will go on. Dreams cannot harm us."

Lief and Barda lit their lanterns. As the flames flared up and began to glow, they saw in front of them a spiral staircase winding upwards. Shadows flickered on smooth, curved stone walls.

Looking up, Lief thought he saw a flash of yellow, like the swirling hem of a yellow skirt. He caught his breath.

"It is not real," Jasmine murmured behind him. And he knew that she had seen what he had seen.

On the wall at the foot of the stairs hung a painting framed by polished sticks of driftwood. It was a picture of the little bay and the sea beyond, painted with love and skill.

The sea was glittering in early morning light. A red rowboat was drawn up on the smooth, wet sand, which was marked with a wavy line of shells cast up by the tide. At the bottom of the painting was a signature.

Lief reached out and touched the name gently with the tips of his fingers.

Bubbling laughter floated down the stairs. Lief jumped violently.

"Father!" a high, excited voice called, echoing,

echoing in the tall, hollow space. "A visitor is coming. Someone is rowing in from that ship! Go down to meet him, Father! Make haste!"

Bruna wailed softly.

"I have caught some fish, too!" the voice ran on. "And the water berries by the bay have ripened. Is it not wonderful? We will be able to give him a good dinner, if he will stay."

Visions from the past . . . Not real . . .

Mother, Zeean, and Peel saw only glimpses, and heard only muffled sounds, Lief thought. *They reported nothing like this.*

He touched the Belt of Deltora, hidden beneath his clothes. *The great amethyst, the gem of Tora, the symbol of truth, is in its own territory now,* he thought. *It feels the power in the lighthouse stones. I must expect that we will see and hear more than others have done.*

Gritting his teeth, he set his foot on the first stair and began to climb.

He climbed fast, trying to keep his mind blank, concentrating on the sound of his companions' footsteps close behind him.

Every now and then he would come to another painting fastened to the stone wall. There were paintings of seabirds, shells, the lighthouse from every angle, the sea in every mood. All had plainly been created by the same loving hand, and were signed in the same way. He took care not to touch them.

Verity, he thought. *A girl with red hair who loved*

the birds and the sea. A lighthouse keeper's daughter, who rowed in a little red boat, and fished, and painted pictures of what she saw around her. What happened to her? Why does her shade linger here?

He remembered what his mother had told him of Verity.

"Little was known of her except that she was born in the lighthouse," Sharn had said. "Her mother died when the girl was only one year old. The local folk say that she was raised by her father and the sea."

Lief realized that there was a door ahead of him. He climbed the last few steps and, holding his breath, pushed the door open. Holding the lantern high, he cautiously moved into the room beyond.

His companions crowded after him, the Kin squeezing through the doorway with grunts and groans.

Barda turned to close the door behind him. He stared.

"Certainly, something has happened here," he said. "This door is damaged. It looks as if it has been kicked. And these marks . . ."

He lowered his lantern and bent to peer at the ominous dark smears that stained the dented, splintered wood of the door.

Lief was looking around him. Plainly, they were in the lighthouse keeper's sitting room.

Dim light filtered through two round windows, one looking back to the land, one looking out to sea.

Many more paintings decorated the walls. Two easy chairs sat together in front of an old black stove. There was a bright woollen rug on the floor. There was a small table with wooden benches on either side of it, and a shelf stacked with blue-striped plates and cups.

It should have been a cozy scene, but it was not. Instead, the room chilled the blood. The very air seemed to taste of misery and horror.

On the far side of the room, near the stove, there was another door. Lief knew that beyond it must be a second staircase that led to the bedchambers and at last to the viewing platform.

Yet he could not make himself move. Nor, it seemed, could anyone else. They stood in silence, crowded together. No one was willing to take the first step.

A cold breeze brushed Lief's cheek. He caught a glimpse of movement from the corner of his eye.

He turned his head slowly. He blinked.

The room had been deserted only moments before. Now he could see, as if through a light mist, two men sitting on either side of the table, playing cards.

Cups stood at the men's elbows, and empty stone bottles lay in a jumble on the floor around their feet. The candle flickering between the men had burned down to a lumpy stub, swimming in wax.

Visions from the past . . .

Lief opened his dry lips. "Do you see them?" he whispered.

"Yes." His companions' voices were like the rustling of leaves in the wind. The Kin sounded terrified.

The man facing them had a broad face, dark red hair, and a bushy red beard. His blue eyes were bloodshot and deeply shadowed. His shoulders were bowed. His blunt fingers trembled as he threw down his cards.

"You win again," he said thickly. "It is nearly dawn. I — I will play no more."

The other man nodded.

He had his back to Lief. Lief could see nothing of him but a dark coat and limp black hair pushed behind a pair of large ears. But something about the way his narrow shoulders tensed showed that this was the moment he had been waiting for.

"Then pay me what you owe, Red Han," this man said softly. "And I will leave you."

"I cannot pay," the bearded man muttered. "You know it, Gant! Why, at midnight I told you I was ruined. You yourself urged me to play on, saying my luck was sure to change." He put his face in his hands. "Ah, what a fool I was to listen to you!" he groaned. "Instead of winning back what I had lost, I now owe three times the sum I owed before!"

"You had better keep your voice down, or you will wake your daughter," the man called Gant murmured. "Let her sleep while she can. She will find out what has happened soon enough."

The bearded man gave a muffled sob.

In one smooth movement, Gant drew a sheaf of papers from his pocket and put them on the table.

Lief, Barda, and Jasmine leaned forward and caught a glimpse of the top sheet.

PROMISE TO PAY

I ....Red Ham...... of
Bone Point
............Lighthouse........
owe the sum of 10 gold coins
to Captain James Gant of The
Lady Luck.

By all I hold dear I swear to
pay my debt, and to seal my solemn
oath I make my mark below.

Red Han

James Gant flicked through the papers with long, thin fingers.

"Why, it *has* been a long night, my poor fellow!" he said softly. "You have signed ten notes in all, I see. And each is for ten gold coins."

Red Han thrust his fingers through his hair and tugged as if to tear it out by the roots. "I cannot pay!" he repeated. "Where would I get a hundred gold coins?"

The thin man shook his head. "You should have thought of that before," he said regretfully. "You signed the notes. You swore a solemn oath to pay."

"It was madness!" groaned Red Han. "Madness!" He looked up, glaring at his visitor with haunted eyes. "You — you encouraged me! You filled out the notes and gave me them to sign. You made it so easy!"

His visitor shrugged. "I was merely trying to help," he said. He paused, then leaned forward, clasping his bony hands on top of the pile of papers.

"Perhaps — perhaps there is something I can do for you, even now," he said, raising his voice to a normal tone for the first time. "There is nothing I like better than helping those less fortunate than myself. Why, I *live* to do good. And you seem such a worthy fellow."

Lief went cold. Those words . . . that voice! He heard Jasmine draw a sharp breath and knew that she, too, had recognized them.

Why had he not seen it before? This vision from the past, this man calling himself Captain James Gant . . . was the man they knew as Laughing Jack.

4 - A Matter of Honor

Jasmine clutched Lief's arm. "Laughing Jack!" she breathed. "I did not know him! He reminded me of someone, certainly, but before he spoke I was racking my brains to think who it was. His hair . . ."

"He is younger," Lief whispered back. "At least eighteen years younger. What we are seeing happened before the Shadow Lord invaded. Red Han was still keeper, and the Light was still burning."

The lighthouse keeper's face had filled with hope. "You will forgive me my debt?" he exclaimed.

"Oh, no, I cannot do that," said his tormentor calmly. "It is a matter of honor — and of business, which is even more important. But . . . perhaps you could do me a service, in exchange for what you owe."

"Anything!" Red Han gasped. "Anything!"

"Excellent," purred Laughing Jack.

He bent forward and began to whisper, so low that Lief could not hear him.

Red Han's eyes widened. His hopeful expression faded, changing to a look of stunned horror.

"But why — why would you want such a thing of me?" he stammered. "If the Bone Point Light goes out, any ship that sails to this coast will be in danger. Foreign ships will stop visiting our shores."

"No doubt," said Laughing Jack.

Red Han leaned forward, his broad brow knotted. "But those ships come to trade," he said. "And more and more Deltora needs the food they offer in exchange for goods. I do not know why we cannot grow enough food for our own needs. But it is so. Would you have our people starve?"

The thin shoulders were raised in a shrug. "You need not concern yourself with such matters, Han," the soft voice said. "Think only of your debt, which must be paid. And bless the good fortune that made you the only one who can enter the chamber of the Bone Point Light."

Red Han's bloodshot eyes narrowed. "By the magic of Tora, that is true," he whispered. "But how do you know it?"

The next moment, he had leaped to his feet, overturning the bench, which crashed to the ground behind him.

"You are a servant of the Enemy!" he hissed. "You tricked me! You came here with one purpose, and one purpose only! To corrupt me and darken the Light. Snake! Traitor! Get out!"

The other man laughed. "And what of the debt you swore to pay? Swore by all you hold dear?"

"Hang the debt!" roared Red Han.

His visitor laughed again. "Ah, it is not so easy," he said softly. "You will pay. One way or another, you will pay."

Red Han lunged at him. With astonishing speed, Laughing Jack slipped from his bench and twisted aside. Han crashed into the second bench and fell.

The door to the second stairway flew open. A girl stood there, her eyes still blurry with sleep. A mass of curling red hair framed her startled face. A blue cloak had been hastily thrown over her night-gown.

"Father!" she cried, seeing her father on the ground and starting forward. "What has happened? Are you — "

"Verity, go back!" thundered her father, struggling to rise.

But it was too late. With the speed of a striking snake, Laughing Jack's long arm whipped around the girl's neck. In seconds she was pinned against his chest, the point of a knife pressed to her throat.

"One step and she dies, Red Han," snarled Laughing Jack. Dragging Verity with him, he began backing towards the door that led downstairs.

He was moving straight for Lief, Barda, Jasmine,

and the Kin. Barda reached out, but his hands clutched at empty air. Laughing Jack and his captive passed through the companions like a cold wind, leaving them shuddering, chilled to the bone.

The lighthouse keeper stood motionless by the table, his fists clenched, his eyes dark with terror.

"I had hoped we could settle this like gentlemen." Laughing Jack smiled. "I dislike crude violence. But you have forced my hand, lighthouse keeper. You have refused to perform the small service I asked of you in payment of your debt. So I will take what is my due — the thing you hold most dear."

"No," whispered Red Han. "No — I beg you!"

Laughing Jack smiled cruelly. "Then put out the Light," he said.

"What!" cried Verity in horror. "Father! No!"

Red Han's face was drawn with anguish. His voice trembled as he spoke.

"I will never put out the Light. I swore to defend it, whatever the cost. And so it must be."

Laughing Jack's lip curled. "Indeed!" he spat. "Then your daughter will pay the price."

"I am willing to pay it," the girl whispered. "I would rather die than — "

Her voice broke off in a choking sob as the bony arm tightened around her neck.

"From your tower you will have a good view of my ship, Red Han," Laughing Jack said softly, easing the door open. "Keep watch. Know that your daughter's suffering is on your own head. When you have seen enough and the Light goes out, Verity will be returned — in what condition, is up to you."

With that, he slipped through the door and slammed it after him. His footsteps rang on the stairs as he ran downwards.

Sick with rage and pity, Lief watched as Red Han sprang to the door with an anguished cry. Han twisted the knob, but the door would not open.

So Laughing Jack had some powers of sorcery, even then, Lief thought. *Not enough to break the spell set on the Light by the people of Tora. But enough for this.*

Red Han kicked the heavy wood and beat on it with his fists. The door shuddered, but held firm.

"Verity!" he groaned. Great tears were rolling down his cheeks. His fists had begun to bleed, but still he struck the door with all his strength.

"No more!" Lief heard Bruna wail.

And suddenly, the vision of Red Han trembled and was gone.

Stunned, the companions looked around. The table was again bare and empty, and the benches stood primly upright. Bruna's quiet sobbing was the only sound.

"So now we know why the Bone Point Light went out," Barda said heavily.

"No!" Jasmine was shaking her head. "Red Han was strong. And so was his daughter. Neither of them would have given in."

"Yet the Light *did* go out," said Lief. "And the food ships ceased to come, just as the Enemy planned."

"Let us leave here," Ailsa begged. "Ah, I was wrong to say that dreams cannot harm you. I am very sore in my heart."

Barda led the way across the room and flung open the second door. As they had expected, another spiral staircase was revealed.

"So I have seen Laughing Jack for myself after all," he muttered as they began to climb. "He is a nasty piece of work, and no mistake."

He frowned. "I am sure I have heard the name *The Lady Luck* before, long ago. I cannot think where, but no doubt it will come to me."

"It is strange to think that once Laughing Jack was the captain of a ship," said Jasmine thoughtfully.

"Very strange." Barda shook his head. "In my experience, people who work by or on the sea rarely move away from it. Yet Laughing Jack seems to have forsaken the coast for the inland."

"Perhaps he hates the memory of his wickedness here," Ailsa suggested quietly from behind them. "Perhaps he fled out of shame."

"No," said Jasmine shortly. "He has no shame. More likely he had to give up his ship because his crew mutinied and ran away from his cruelty. If only the poor beasts he forces to draw his wagon could do the same!"

Lief was behind her, so he could not see her face. But he could hear the pain in her voice.

Briefly he wondered at it. Jasmine's years surviving alone in the Forests of Silence had taught her that life was often cruel. When she could not change a thing, she normally accepted it and moved on, her mind fixed firmly on the future. Yet plainly the memory of Laughing Jack's horses still stabbed her like a knife.

They reached a landing with two open doors leading into small bedchambers. They passed the rooms quickly and continued to climb.

Soon they reached another landing. It was very dark. Barda moved onto it cautiously. Jasmine, and then Lief, followed.

They could hear the sound of wind whistling around the lighthouse. Straight ahead of them was a red-painted door bearing a large sign.

HALT!
ENTRY FORBIDDEN
TO ALL BUT THE KEEPER
OF THE LIGHT

"The light chamber," Lief muttered. "We cannot go that way."

He and Barda lifted their lanterns high. The flickering light revealed another door, set into the curved stone of the outside wall.

Barda strode to the door, pushed it open, and staggered back as a blast of cold wind hit him in the face. Both of the lanterns blew out. The Kin cried out in panic and pushed forward onto the landing, pressing Lief against the red-painted door.

Lief's skin began to tingle unpleasantly. The wood of the door was warm, and it seemed to be vibrating, as if swarms of bees were crawling on the other side.

The magic of Tora protects me . . .

He tried to push himself away from the door, but he could not move. He felt the Belt of Deltora warming at his waist. And suddenly his mind was filled by a picture of the great amethyst, glowing purple like a great thundercloud pierced by lightning.

I am Adin's heir, he thought suddenly. *I wear the Belt of Deltora. Could that be why fate brought me here? Could it be that I can open the door?*

He put his hand to the doorknob and twisted sharply. The knob turned. Eagerly he pushed. The door . . . began to open!

His cry of triumph was cut short as a hot jolt of pain shot through his hand, his arm, his shoulder. Smoke gushed from the crack in the door, hissing like steam.

Lief's face was burning. He felt as if his hair was crackling. He heard an agonized groan, and realized that the sound had come from him.

The air was filled with hissing smoke. And from the smoke loomed faces, twisted with rage. The face of Red Han — other faces he did not know.

The mouths were gaping wide, shouting. Words were roaring in his ears. "Get out! Get out! Get out!"

Other voices were screaming and calling his name — Jasmine's voice, Ailsa's, Prin's.

He felt himself being pulled away from the door. The searing pain abruptly stopped. But the angry faces were pursuing him, writhing in the smoke.

"They are coming after us!" Ailsa shrieked. "Oh, make haste! Make haste!"

And suddenly cold wind and spray were beating on Lief's face. There was dull light, and the sound of crashing waves. He realized that he had been dragged out onto the viewing platform.

The clouds were boiling and rumbling. The wind was howling. Lightning was cracking the sky.

A door slammed behind him.

"Young fool!" roared Barda's voice.

Lief felt hard hands seize and lift him. Suddenly he was wrapped in warmth, and through his confusion realized that he was in Prin's pouch. He was being rolled and jolted as Prin climbed the railing. The wind was howling like a lost soul.

"It is too wild!" Bruna screamed. "We cannot fly in this!"

"We must!" Ailsa cried. "Oh, they are coming — under the door! Make haste!"

"Go, Prin!" Barda shouted. "Go now!"

Then Lief's stomach lurched as Prin launched herself into the air and was instantly swept away.

5 - The Cruel Sea

Beneath them, the surface of the gray sea heaved like the skin of a vast, angry beast. Above them, dark clouds boiled and tumbled. The Kin struggled against the wind, their great wings beating mightily. But it was hopeless. Every moment the gale was sweeping them farther away from land.

Tossed helplessly in Prin's pouch, Lief watched in bewildered dismay as the slim white shape of the lighthouse grew smaller behind them.

I have caused this, he thought. *It is because I tried to open the light chamber door that we were driven from the lighthouse into the storm.*

But the storm . . . how had it come upon them so quickly?

His heart gave a great thud. Cold certainty settled upon him like a shroud.

The Shadow Lord had found them at Bone Point

and seized his chance. He had summoned up the storm. He had sent the wind racing from beyond the mountains to sweep them away.

Away from the land. Away from Deltora. So that . . .

Horror stabbed Lief as he realized that while his face and hands were icy cold, the Belt around his waist was warming. It was growing hot — hot as fire.

The memory of his father's gentle voice filled his mind.

It is death to take the gems beyond Deltora's borders . . .

Even for me, Lief thought wildly. *Even for Adin's heir. For there is older magic than the Belt of Deltora — older magic than the dream of Adin. The ancient magic that bonds the gems, and the dragons, and the land . . .*

And the Shadow Lord knows it.

The Belt was scorching his flesh. It was as if every one of the gems was a red-hot coal.

Prin could feel it. She had begun to gasp and whimper. Her wings were faltering. And still the wind swept them on, on.

Lief looked down. Surging gray water. White-capped waves.

The tide is coming in . . .

He knew what he had to do. He could not afford to think. He had to act now. Now!

He heaved himself up and over the edge of Prin's pouch. And with her cry of shock ringing in his ears, he plunged down, down, into the sea.

He hit the freezing water and went under. For a

few terrifying moments he sank, blind, deaf, his arms flailing helplessly. Then, his lungs almost bursting, he managed to claw his way up.

As his head broke through the surface a dark shape splashed into the waves beside him. He looked up just in time to see Ailsa, her pouch empty, swept away by the howling wind.

"Barda!" he shouted, and choked on a mouthful of salty water.

Barda's head bobbed up beside him, sleek and dripping. Barda's arm reached for him urgently.

Lief shook his head. "I am all right!" he gasped. "I did not fall. I had to jump. But you — "

"You *jumped*?" Barda bellowed, drawing back his hand and treading water furiously. "Are you mad, boy? Why — ?"

"The Belt . . ." Lief's voice failed him. His body was racked with cold, and at the same time burning with heat. Steam was rising from the icy water around him.

Barda's eyes widened as he understood. Rapidly he looked around him.

"There!" he shouted. "Lief — this way!"

Lief turned in the water. Through the dimness he saw the narrow, pale shape of the lighthouse in the distance and the white froth of waves pounding on the shore. With Barda beside him he struck out, trying not to panic, trying to ride the tide towards the land.

"Jasmine!" he sputtered. "Where — ?"

"We both saw you fall," Barda panted. "Jasmine could do nothing, because she cannot swim. She is still up there somewhere, with the Kin. Worried out of her life, no doubt."

Lief looked up. He could see nothing but racing clouds. The Kin, and Jasmine, had been swept farther out to sea.

They will be safe, he promised himself. *Much safer than if I was with them. The Shadow Lord seems to know my every move, so by now he must know that I jumped into the sea. He will let the wind die, for why would he spend his power to no purpose? Then the Kin will be able to fly back to land.*

The Belt was cooling. He could feel it. He knew that this meant that he had managed to move a little closer to shore.

The relief was intense. But his teeth were chattering. His arms and legs were aching and numbed with cold. More and more often his head slipped below the surface of the surging water.

A wave surged over him. Again he went under. Again he forced his head up to the air, his throat aching. He could no longer see the shore. There was a mist in front of his streaming, stinging eyes.

This cannot go on much longer, he thought grimly. But still he pushed towards the sound of the shore, trying to ignore the aching numbness of his legs and arms. He was determined to get as close to land as he could before cold and exhaustion finally overcame him.

Almost certainly he and Barda would be dead by the time the tide tossed them up on the rocks, or onto the sand of the little bay beside the lighthouse. But the Belt would be found.

He could hear Barda splashing heavily at his shoulder, and his heart smote him.

Barda had watched over him almost all his life. At first he had not even been aware of that steadfast protection. Then he had often resisted and resented it. Lately, he had come to take it for granted that whatever he did, Barda would always be by his side.

But Barda has his own life, Lief thought. *Or at least — he has a right to it.*

A picture of Lindal flashed into his mind — Lindal, standing tall and straight by the gates of Broome, the palms of her hands pressed to Barda's in long, wordless farewell.

Barda could have found happiness, after all the years of struggle, Lief thought. *Instead, he will die with me in this cruel sea.*

"I am sorry, Barda," he choked. "I am so — "

And at that moment, his bare foot kicked against something hard.

Stunned, he turned in the water. And through the mist that filmed his eyes he saw, looming dark above him, the side of a ship.

For an instant he stared, unable to believe his eyes. How could a ship have come upon them so silently? How could he have missed seeing it, even in this strange, misty dimness?

He shouted to Barda, then hailed the ship at the top of his lungs. Barda was soon calling with him. But no light appeared above them, and there was no answering call.

Long oars hung from small dark holes ranged along the ship's side just above the waterline. Gasping, Lief reached for the oar closest to him. But even as his fingers closed on the wet, splintery wood, he knew it would be of little use. The oar was too low to be used as a step to the deck. And the hole it poked through was far too small to admit anything bigger than a rat.

"Keep shouting, Lief!" gasped Barda, moving up beside him. "We must *make* them hear us."

Then Lief felt something brush against his free hand. His fingers closed around thick, wet rope. And as he looked up again he saw with amazed joy a rope ladder trailing over the side of the ship, its base disappearing beneath the foam.

"Barda!" he croaked.

"I see it!" He heard Barda pant behind him. "Go! I am with you!"

Lief seized the ladder in both hands, found a rung with his feet and, gritting his chattering teeth, began hauling himself upwards.

He had climbed only about halfway to the deck before he realized that there was something strange about the ship.

It was riding very low in the water, and instead of tossing from side to side in the swell, as he would have expected, it was gliding as smoothly as a fish. This made his climb easier, but a sense of foreboding was growing within him as he forced his aching body on.

As he neared the top of the ladder he paused, his scalp prickling. He could not rid himself of the feeling that he was being watched. Yet he could see no glimmer of light above him. He could hear no voices. The only sounds were the creaking of the timbers and, now and again, a faint, mouselike squeaking.

He glanced quickly from side to side and noticed, very near to his right shoulder, the remains of some painted words.

The ship's name, Lief thought. *So we must be at the front of the ship — the bow.* He peered at the name, trying to read it.

$$T E \quad A \, Y \quad L \, C$$

So much of the paint had flaked off that Lief could make no sense of the fragments that remained. Yet somehow he felt that he should have been able to. There was something about the pattern made by those last flakes of paint that was familiar. Something he had seen before . . .

"No captain of a working ship would let its name wear away like that," Barda muttered from below him. "This is a hulk — abandoned. And some years ago, by the look of it."

Lief was certain that Barda was right. The ship was drifting. The eerie squeaking he could hear was the sound of the wheel spinning from side to side on the deserted deck.

But someone — or something — was aboard. He knew it. Something had sensed them. Something was holding its breath, waiting . . .

"Keep moving, Lief," Barda growled. "Whatever is up there, we must either face it or drown. And I would rather die fighting."

So Barda senses danger, too, Lief thought. *At least we are prepared.* But forcing himself to climb the last few rungs of the ladder was one of the hardest things he had ever done. His legs felt as if they were made of stone. His whole body was weighed down by dread.

He reached the top. He saw crawling mist, a tangle of ropes and sails, the wheel swinging slowly, with no hand to guide it. He saw the jagged stub that was all that remained of the ship's main mast.

A moving picture leaped into his mind like a flash of vivid memory. He saw the ship tossing in a ferocious storm. He saw giant waves crashing over the deck. He heard the terrible, screeching sound of the mast snapping in two, and the terrified cries of drowning men.

Visions of the past . . .

He slid over the side of the ship, onto the deck. Shivering and panting, he crawled aside to make room for Barda. As he did, something made him look up. His heart seemed to fly into his throat.

A woman in a long blue robe was standing motionless on the prow of the ship. She was staring out to sea, leaning forward slightly, her hands clasped over her heart. Mist billowed around her, but nothing on her stirred — not a fold of her robe or a curl of her long red hair.

Her face, with its stubborn chin, its steady gray eyes, was strangely familiar.

Lief's mouth went dry as he realized who she was. And as Barda thudded onto the deck beside him, he suddenly realized, too, why the fragments of the ship's name had rung warning bells in his mind.

This abandoned, drifting hulk was Laughing Jack's ship, *The Lady Luck*.

And the woman standing so silent, so motionless on the prow was Red Han's daughter, Verity.

6 - Ghost Ship

Lief and Barda crawled to their feet, dripping and shivering. The deck creaked beneath them. Behind them, the wheel squeaked and spun. The figure of Verity did not stir.

"It is not real, Lief," Barda muttered. "See how it leans over the water, as if to guide the ship? It is a figurehead, carved out of wood and painted. Many ships have them. You must have seen pictures — "

"Yes," whispered Lief, through chattering teeth. "But I have never seen a figurehead that looks as real as this. And it is Verity to the life. I think — "

His voice faltered. It seemed to him that the rigid figure on the prow turned its head very slightly, as if it had heard him. Or had his eyes been deceived by the drifting mist? He clutched the Belt at his waist . . .

Suddenly there was a flurry of movement, glaring light, and a roar of sound. Seabirds shrieked. Water

49

splashed. Harsh voices cheered, shouted, and guffawed.

Then they were no longer alone. A crowd of grinning men jostled all around them.

Cursing in shock, Barda reached for his sword.

Lief did not move. He knew that the men could not see them. This was the crew of *The Lady Luck*, as it had gathered on deck eighteen years ago to enjoy the sort of entertainment it liked best.

Two men were tying a girl to a short pole fixed to the prow. The girl was wearing a long blue cloak.

"Verity," Barda breathed.

The men had placed Verity so that she was facing the lighthouse that gleamed white across the water.

"Ah, what a fine figurehead she makes, to be sure!" jeered a rat-faced man in a striped woollen cap.

"Too scrawny for my taste!" bawled a hulking brute with a black patch over one eye.

"She will be scrawnier yet when the birds have finished with her, Beef," a third roared, baring teeth like crooked yellow pegs.

The whole crew laughed uproariously.

The girl made no sign that she had heard them. She did not struggle as loop after loop of rope wound about her, binding her to the pole.

Laughing Jack was standing beside her, peering through a telescope. He stood as still as a tall, thin statue, his bony shoulders rigid, the sharp line of his jaw intent. After a moment, he lowered the telescope and turned to Verity, the edges of his wide mouth curving into a smile.

And just for an instant, as he turned, he reminded Lief of someone else. *Someone I know,* Lief thought in confusion. *Who . . . ?*

Then the smile broadened into the familiar death's-head grin, and the illusion vanished.

"Your father is watching, girl," Laughing Jack sneered. "He is in the light chamber."

Verity made no answer.

Laughing Jack moved a little closer to her. "Sound carries well across water," he said. "Red Han will hear you if you scream. You would do well to begin now. The sooner he gives in, the sooner you will be free."

"My father will never give in, James Gant," Verity said. "And I will never call to him."

Laughing Jack's eyes narrowed. "Fine words," he hissed. "But they will not last. Soon you will be begging for food and water, beaten to rags by the wind and the waves. And then the hungry birds will come. You will scream loud enough when they begin to feast on you, girl, make no mistake."

He turned on his heel and strode away from her, directly towards Lief and Barda. The crew stumbled out of his way, some falling over in their haste.

Lief and Barda stood their ground. Laughing Jack passed through them like a gust of icy breath. And in that moment, the vision vanished, and they stood blinking on the creaking deck, mist floating all around them and the silent figurehead their only companion.

"If ever I have the chance to lay my hands on

that grinning monster, he will know what fear is," Barda muttered at last.

His eyes were fixed on the figurehead. His fists were clenched.

He is remembering the girl he saw painting on the beach of the little bay, Lief thought. *The happy girl in the yellow skirt that fluttered in the wind.*

"We do not know the end of the story, Barda," he said. "Red Han may have given in after all. Verity may have been returned to him. Then they may have fled Bone Point together."

"I doubt it," Barda muttered.

Lief doubted it, too. His mind was seething with questions, but the vision he and Barda had just seen was proof to him that *The Lady Luck* had been the setting for frightful deeds. The ship was haunted by memories so terrible that they would not die.

With a heavy heart he turned away from the figurehead. Whatever he had suspected before, he was sure now that it was only a carving.

The skin of the figurehead was smooth and undamaged, the steady eyes untouched. And the scavenging birds would not have left them so.

After Verity's wasted, torn, and lifeless body had been at last cut down, Laughing Jack had no doubt enjoyed replacing it with a likeness of her as she had been. What better way to torment the father who had refused to do his will?

Lief shuddered all over and suddenly became

aware of just how cold he was. His teeth had begun chattering again. Water was dripping from his hair and clothing. His feet felt like blocks of ice.

"We must go below deck and try to find a way of warming ourselves," Barda said. "I can see no lifeboat. No doubt it was taken when the ship was abandoned. We will have to stay here until the storm ends and the Kin return for us."

"There is no storm here," Lief murmured.

They both looked up. The mist moved softly all around them. They could see no sky, no sea. They could hear no wind, no thunder. It was as if the world beyond *The Lady Luck* had disappeared.

"We must find a way of warming ourselves," Barda repeated stubbornly. "We must rest and regain our strength. After that, we can think what to do."

Plainly he was determined not to let dread take hold in him. He was fighting it back in the way he knew best — by concentrating on practical things.

And he is right, Lief thought. *If we panic, we will certainly perish.*

Together they stumbled towards the swinging wheel, stepping over tangled ropes and the tattered remains of canvas sails. Not far behind the wheel there was a narrow door set into a raised portion of the deck.

Barda put out his hand to open it, then glanced back at Lief.

Lief pulled aside his coat and looked down at the Belt of Deltora.

The ruby was pale. *Danger*. The emerald was dull. *Evil. A broken vow.*

"Are they sensing the present, or the past?" Barda murmured.

Lief did not know.

He saw that the lapis-lazuli, the heavenly stone, bringer of good fortune, still sparkled with points of light like the night sky. It was strong. If dangers still lurked below deck, at least they would have some protection. And it was cold, so cold . . .

He took a breath and nodded.

Barda opened the door. A breath of sour air escaped into the mist. A short flight of steps led steeply down.

They took the steps cautiously. At the bottom they found themselves in a small square space, facing a door made of richly carved wood.

Above the door was a dusty panel of colored glass, etched with words and symbols:

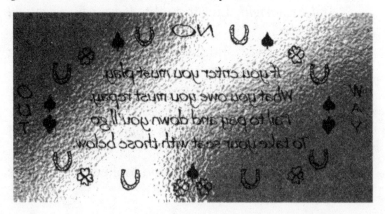

"This is a very fine door for a working ship," Barda murmured. "And it seems to have been a way out, rather than a way in. Well, that does not matter to us."

He peered at the dingy glass panel. "The decorations are all symbols of good fortune. Now why — ?"

Then he slapped the side of his head in annoyance. "Of course! *The Lady Luck!* Now I know where I have heard that name before! I heard a traveller mention it, in my first years of playing the beggar in Del."

He nodded slowly, remembering.

"*The Lady Luck* was a gambling ship — a floating gaming house — that once sailed the River Tor," he said. "It had an evil reputation, though the man I heard tell of it had not seen it for himself. The ship disappeared from the Tor, he said, before the Shadow Lord invaded, and no one knew what had become of it."

"Well, now the mystery is solved," said Lief grimly. "*The Lady Luck* had sailed down the Tor and out to sea. Laughing Jack was following his master's orders. He was on his way to destroy the Bone Point Light."

As he spoke, he was squinting at the small words in the center of the glass panel.

"You cannot read those," Barda said impatiently. "Not in this light, without a mirror. They will only make sense from the other side."

He seized the handle of the door. "Come! The main saloon must be beyond. With luck we will find a stove there. And candles and other supplies, perhaps. Captain James Gant would have made sure his guests had every comfort — while they still had money to lose, in any case!"

Lief hesitated. Something about the carved door made him uneasy.

He looked around and noticed for the first time that another door led off the small space. It was to his left — a thing of plain, flat metal, with a solid lever for a handle.

"Perhaps this leads to the crew's sleeping quarters or the galley," he said. "Let us try it first."

Without waiting for an answer, he pushed down the lever and pulled the metal door open.

Dimness. The sound of water, softly lapping. And a smell so vile that Lief staggered back.

"What is it?" Barda hissed behind him.

Lief was gasping for breath. His eyes were watering, as though the foul air gusting from the space beyond the door was filled with poison.

And at that moment, the mist drifting down the steps brightened, as if softly lit from above.

"The moon is rising," Barda said. "Lief — "

Lief rubbed his eyes and stared into the dimness.

At first he could see only shapes. Then, gradually, he took in the full horror of the scene before him.

He was looking down into the belly of the ship — into the half-submerged cavity where once the rowers had sat, plying their oars.

Where they sat still . . .

Waist-deep in water, half-rotted bodies slumped over the oars. Rusted chains hung like bracelets from their bony wrists. Sea worms coiled around necks and fingers, and snails with speckled shells clustered thickly on the rags that still clung to their bones.

Lief felt the blood drain from his face. He heard Barda cursing softly behind him.

"They were left to die," Barda muttered. "How? Why? What happened here?"

What happened here?

Lief's teeth were chattering. His head was spinning.

He could see . . . he could see a fleshless skull with a black patch still hiding one eye socket. And beside it, a grinning head covered with the dingy, rotted remains of a striped woollen cap.

The soft glow of misty moonlight drifted through the dank, flooded space. Chains clinked softly in the darkness. The slumped horrors seemed to stir . . .

With a cry, Lief staggered back and slammed the door.

"In here!" Barda seized the handle of the carved door and pushed forward. Lief stumbled after him . . .

Into a sudden blaze of light.

7 - Fool's Gold

Stunned, Lief and Barda stood blinking as the door swung softly closed behind them. Whatever they had expected, it was not this.

The long room looked as if it had been deserted only moments before they entered. It was deliciously warm. Thick red carpets covered the floor. A fire crackled in a marble fireplace. Candles burned in sparkling crystal holders hanging from the ceiling. Long, gold-framed mirrors lined the walls, reflecting the room's contents over and over again.

Scattered everywhere were small, polished tables surrounded by comfortable chairs. On some of the tables there were decks of cards. On others there were dice. Still others carried game boards and wheels, games of skill, games of chance. In the center of every table was a gold-edged card explaining the rules of the game, and a tall glass container filled with gold coins.

An open treasure chest brimming with many more gold coins stood to the left of the doorway where Lief and Barda stood. A large notice was fixed to the inside of the open lid.

Do you need a small loan?

The Lady Luck makes it easy!

Take what you need——pay what you owe before you depart.

"It is all an illusion," Barda said, edging away from the chest and drawing his sword. "It must be!"

Lief put his hand upon the topaz. He had learned long ago that the great gem had the power to banish illusions. But nothing in the room wavered or changed appearance.

He crouched and tested the carpet with his fingers. It felt soft and warm. As he straightened, he saw that steam had begun to rise from his wet clothes. They were already drying.

"This is no illusion," he said slowly. "It is real. Somehow, it is real!"

"If we keep our wits about us and touch nothing we should be safe," Barda said. "The moment our garments are dry, we will go back on — "

He broke off, his eyes widening in shock. He glanced down at his feet, then rapidly up again.

"What is it?" Lief hissed. But as the words left his lips, he felt it, too.

Something about the ship had changed. It was no longer simply rocking gently in the tide. It was moving, moving purposefully forward.

And the hair rose on the back of Lief's neck as he heard the sounds that even the thick carpet could not muffle. The rhythmic, creaking sounds of oars.

Without a word he and Barda spun back to the door. The glass panel above it seemed to glow. And now the words etched there could be read easily.

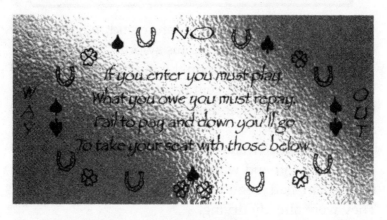

A cold weight seemed to settle in the pit of Lief's stomach. Slowly he looked down.

There was no handle on this side of the door.

Barda snatched his dagger from his belt. He tried to push the point of the dagger into the crack of the door, but the weapon stopped abruptly just short of the carved wood, as if repelled by an invisible barrier.

Barda grunted in surprise and tried again. Still he could not touch the door.

And neither could Lief. For long minutes they both struggled vainly to break through the shield. Whatever they tried, their hands, feet, and weapons bounced back without making contact with the door or the glass panel above it.

"This is useless," Barda panted at last. "The shutting spell is as strong as the barrier that seals the mountains in the Shadowlands."

"Why not?" Lief said bitterly. "The Enemy provided it to *The Lady Luck*, no doubt, in return for Laughing Jack's useful services."

They both looked up at the glass panel. During their vain attack on the door, the ominous message seemed to have grown larger and brighter.

Barda turned his back on it. "If this door is closed to us, we will find another!" he said, and determinedly began to survey the long room.

Lief turned, too, but his heart was heavy. "Barda, I do not think — " he began.

"Just look!" Barda muttered fiercely. "There *must* be another way out. We have only to find it."

The mirrors winked back at them, reflecting chairs and tables, game wheels and boards, coin jars and candles, and their own figures.

But at the far end of the room, directly ahead of

them, there was something that the confusing reflections had disguised at first glance.

It was a painting, the same size as one of the mirrors, and framed in exactly the same way. It was difficult to see clearly, because it gleamed in the light, but it seemed to be a view of land and sea.

"There!" Barda exclaimed. "That painting marks our way out, I am sure of it."

He hurried forward. Putting his doubts aside, Lief followed, dodging through the maze of tables and chairs so as not to touch or disturb anything.

They moved on and on, their boots sinking into the thick carpet. Their reflections walked with them, multiplied over and over again in the mirrors so that it seemed that the grand room was filled with bedraggled wanderers.

"I did not realize the room was quite so long," Barda called over his shoulder. "The mirrors are deceiving."

He began to walk a little more quickly. Lief followed in silence, trying to shield his mind from images of the rotting corpses bending and straightening as they plied the oars. But with every step he became more aware of the relentless sounds of movement below his feet and the faint, unpleasant odor drifting in the warm air.

The minutes dragged by. But their reflections in the mirrors at the end of the room did not grow larger, and the tables ahead never became less.

At last Barda's firm steps faltered, and he stopped. He turned to Lief, his face grim.

"The first line of the rhyme was, 'If you enter, you must play,' " Lief said reluctantly. "I fear that we will not be able to leave until one of us at least plays a game."

Barda clenched his fists. "We cannot play!" he almost shouted. "From what I have seen, the games must be played with gold coins, and we do not have a single one between us!"

For answer, Lief glanced over his shoulder at the treasure chest gaping beside the room's entrance.

"No!" Barda shook his head violently. "We would be mad to fall into that trap, Lief! What if we lose? We will not be able to repay the loan!"

Fail to pay and down you'll go . . .

"We will not lose," said Lief, ignoring the tightness in his chest. "And in any case, we have no choice."

"You have seen for yourself what happens to people who borrow from Laughing Jack, Lief!" exclaimed Barda. "How can you even think of it? Ah, what fools we were not to divide the gnomes' gold between us! It is all with Jasmine, and who knows where she — "

"If you have a better plan than mine, Barda, pray tell me what it is and stop wasting time!" Lief cried furiously.

He did not want to think about what might be

happening to Jasmine. Jasmine, who could not swim. Jasmine, pitching dangerously over the raging sea in the pouch of the smallest and most fearful of the Kin.

He saw Barda eyeing him, and wondered if his companion guessed the reason for his anger.

With a muttered apology he turned away and began hurrying around the polished tables, searching for a game he thought he could win.

It was soon clear that most of the games depended far more on luck than skill. Despite the lapis-lazuli glowing on the Belt, Lief did not wish to trust his and Barda's safety to chance. Yet every game of skill he saw cost two or even three gold coins to play while promising only small winnings, while the games of chance cost only one coin, and success paid well.

"Laughing Jack encouraged his guests to trust their luck rather than their brains," he murmured.

"Of course," Barda said sourly behind him. "That way, he had far more chance of stripping them of everything they had — and more."

Trying to ignore the chill running down his spine, Lief went on looking.

At last he came to a small table at which there was only one chair. On the table, as well as the coin jar and the printed card, was a gold cloth about the size of a handkerchief. The cloth was plainly covering something, but it was impossible to tell what it was.

There were only a few words on the card.

Cage- the- Beetle Puzzle

Test your wits! Arrange the sticks
in time to cage the beetles!

1 player only. 1 gold to play. 2 golds for a win.

"This will do," Lief said. "We have solved puzzles like this before."

Very aware of Barda's eyes burning into his back, he strode to the treasure chest and took a single gold coin. As he was turning away, he found to his surprise that several more coins were sticking to his fingertips.

For a moment he was tempted to keep them, in case he needed to play more than once. Then he realized that he was being lured into borrowing more than he had intended. He turned abruptly and brushed the extra coins back into the chest.

Clutching his one gold piece, he quickly moved back to the table.

"I do not like this," Barda growled. "There is a time limit, Lief. That is clear from the notice. And it is Jasmine who is good at this sort of game."

"Jasmine is not here," Lief snapped. "We are. And surely between us we can see the answer. Especially with the topaz to aid us."

He sat down. Barda stood close behind him and

watched as he slipped the gold coin into the slot at the top of the money jar.

Lief put his hand to the gold cloth. Instantly there was a tiny chiming sound, as if a crystal glass had been tapped with a fingernail. A line on the little card standing by the money jar lit up and began to flash.

1 player only . . . 1 player only . . . 1 player only . . .

Lief's stomach seemed to turn over. He wet his lips. "You will have to move away, Barda," he said. "It seems I must play the game alone."

With a muttered curse, Barda moved back. The words on the card continued to flash. Barda moved away, farther, farther . . .

And suddenly the words on the card grew still and the gold cloth vanished.

"I can see nothing from here," Lief heard Barda call in a low voice. "I cannot help you."

Lief did not answer. He was concentrating fiercely on the objects revealed on the tabletop.

Thirteen silver sticks had been arranged to make six rectangles. Inside each rectangle was a little jewelled beetle. Below the pattern was a small piece of parchment:

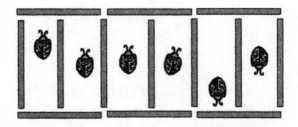

Jack's pet beetles are wild and very
jealous of one another, so they must
have separate cages, all of equal size.
If a thief steals one of Jack's sticks,
how can he build new cages with the
twelve that remain?

As Barda had feared, a small glass timer stood
beside the puzzle. Lief glanced at it and saw that fine
sand had already begun trickling through the narrow
tube that linked the timer's two chambers.

When the top chamber was empty, his time
would be up. The timer was the same size as the one
used in the forge kitchen for boiling eggs, so he knew
that he had less than three minutes to solve the puzzle.

Three minutes to win back what he had borrowed.

Three minutes . . .

Beneath his feet oars creaked and chains rattled.

Fail to pay and down you'll go
To take your seat with those below.

8 - Truth

His heart thudding painfully, Lief picked up one of the silver sticks and put it aside. Now twelve sticks remained on the table, and one beetle's "cage" had only three walls.

With his left hand on the topaz, he hunched forward and with his free hand began moving sticks around, desperately trying to find the solution. But whatever he tried, he could not make six cages of the same size.

What you owe you must repay . . .

The sand was running, running. The top chamber of the timer was already half empty.

Calm your mind, Lief told himself. There is a trick here. A trick! You must relax enough to see it!

He moved his fingers from the topaz to the amethyst — the amethyst that calmed and soothed.

Peace stole through him. His racing mind slowed. And as it did, a thought occurred to him.

If the puzzle was to make cages with twelve sticks, why had there been thirteen sticks in the first place? And why had the sticks been arranged as they were?

To throw me off the scent, he guessed suddenly. *To fix my mind on cages of a certain shape . . .*

He looked at the silver sticks with new eyes. And then he saw the answer.

He glanced at the timer. Only a tiny pile of sand remained in the top chamber. He had just moments left.

Swiftly he rearranged the sticks and put the jewelled beetles in place.

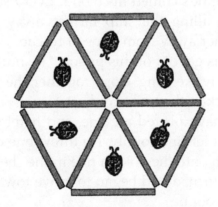

The last grain of sand slipped through the timer. Silently a slot opened at the bottom of the money jar and two gold coins slipped out. Lief snatched them up with a cry of triumph and leaped from the chair.

Barda groaned with relief. Lief swung around to face him, holding up the coins in his closed fist.

"Two coins!" he crowed. "One coin to pay our debt, and one to keep for a souvenir!"

"A souvenir!" Barda called, shakily wiping sweat from his brow. "By the heavens, I could well do without a souvenir of the last few minutes. I believe they took ten years off my life!"

Lief's excitement abruptly died. For a moment, the thrill of winning had made him forget where he was. Now he remembered only too well.

The cursed beings below his feet were still rowing. The sounds chilled his blood. Every stroke of the oars was pulling the ship farther away from Bone Point, further away from hope of rescue.

"Let us get out of this prison," he muttered.

Quickly, keeping close together, he and Barda walked back to the treasure chest.

"We have played a game, and hereby we repay our debt," Lief said loudly. He threw one of the coins he had won onto the golden pile in the chest.

They turned and began to move towards the far end of the room.

This time they made progress, and in moments they were standing before the painting — staring at it in astonishment.

The picture was smooth as glass, but within it a painted sea moved sluggishly and clouds drifted in a red-stained sky.

And rising in the center, unmistakable, was the tall white shape of the Bone Point Light.

Barda drew breath sharply. "What is this? It seems alive! It moves, like a reflection in a mirror. But it is a painting! Only a painting of the Bone Point Light as seen from — "

"From the sea," Lief finished. His scalp was crawling. "I think this *is* a mirror, Barda. Or it *was*. Look at the signature. Verity made this image. It is her view of the Bone Point Light from the prow of *The Lady Luck*."

He rubbed his sweating hands on his coat. "Verity was a prisoner, but no ordinary one, it seems," he said. "Somehow she made an image of what she could see appear in this mirror. She did it with the power of her mind, just as once she used paint and paper to make the pictures hanging on the lighthouse walls."

"It cannot be!" Barda shook his head in disbelief.

"Verity was born in the lighthouse," Lief said quietly. "Toran magic filled the air she breathed from her earliest days. It would not be surprising if she had powerful gifts of her own — though even she may not have been aware of it until . . ."

"Until wickedness and terror came into her life for the first time, in the person of Captain James Gant," Barda finished heavily. "Then, it seems, her gifts woke.

Not soon enough to save her, but in time to leave this image behind, in memory of all she had lost."

Lief nodded, then frowned. Suddenly he was imagining what practical Jasmine would say to that.

"But why?" Jasmine would exclaim. "If Verity could not use her magic to save herself, why did she not spend it on some useful purpose?"

Some useful purpose . . .

Lief looked again at the painting. And this time he saw something that he had not noticed before.

"Barda," he said slowly. "Did you know that the name 'Verity' means 'truth'?"

"Yes," Barda said. "What of it?" Unwilling to abandon his hope that the painting concealed a hidden door, he was running his fingers around the gold frame, vainly searching for a spring or catch.

"There are things in this painting that are not true," Lief murmured. "Do you see?"

Barda paused, glancing at the image. Then he frowned and stepped back a little, to see more clearly.

"For one thing, the viewing platform is missing from the lighthouse," Lief said.

He stretched out his hand and touched the place where the viewing platform should have been. Instantly his fingertip tingled and beneath it something glowed.

Barda gasped, and Lief snatched his hand away. He rubbed his hot fingertip, staring at the painting in amazement.

Where his finger had been, the viewing platform now glowed brightly, its red railings vivid against the whiteness of the tower. And — was it his imagination, or was the Light above a little stronger?

I will shine like truth through the darkness . . .

"The little bay, where I saw Verity first, is missing also," Barda said slowly. "It should be there, on the left — the north side — of the Point. But the painting shows only rocks."

Lief nodded. Again he put out his hand and touched the place. And again, instantly, the painting changed. The Light brightened further, and beneath his fingertip, where only rocks had been before, the little bay glowed, complete with seaweed, shells, and a smashed red boat.

"But the boat was surely not broken in those days!" Barda exclaimed. "Verity used it for fishing!"

"No doubt Laughing Jack wrecked it before he took Verity back to the ship," Lief said. "To prevent Red Han from rowing after them when finally he escaped from the locked room."

As he spoke, he noticed that the sounds below their feet had grown louder, and the movement of the ship less smooth. It was as if the dead rowers were becoming restless.

"The water," Barda said huskily. "It is too still. The waves are not foaming on the rocks. And look! The birds are carrying stems of water berries.

People on the coast use them for food and drink. But seabirds do not. They are — flesh-eaters."

He hunched his shoulders and rubbed the back of his hand over his mouth, as if he wished his last words had remained unspoken.

Lief stretched out both hands. He touched the water at the end of the point, and the berries carried by one of the birds.

He felt a jolt, and jumped back with a sharp cry. This time, with the touch of his fingers, the whole painting had changed.

An entirely different scene was now within the frame. It was the deck of *The Lady Luck* — and it was not a painting. It was real.

Lief felt Barda's hand close on his wrist. Perhaps Barda was speaking, but he could not hear him. His ears were filled with other voices, the calls of birds, and the creaking of ship's timbers.

Figures were moving beneath the smooth surface of the glass — the rat-faced man in the knitted cap, the man with the black eye-patch, and all the rest of the ship's motley crew.

A loop of rope drooped from the rat-faced man's hand. The brute with the black eye-patch was holding a sword. Both were sweating, wild-eyed, and spattered with blood. The rest of the crew were sullen, shuffling, their eyes fixed on the silent figure tied to the pole at the ship's prow.

Verity had plainly been suffering for many days. Her hair hung over her shoulders in a limp, tangled mat. Her cloak and nightgown were stiff with salt. Birds were flying about her head in a swirling cloud.

. . . the hungry birds will come. You will scream loud enough when they begin to feast on you, girl . . .

Lief wanted to turn away, but he could not. The moving image held him fast. And a voice, whispering in his mind.

Look! See! This is the truth of it! The truth . . .

Beyond the cloud of birds, far over the smooth blue water, the Bone Point Light burned defiantly. Red Han had not given in.

The flock of birds parted slightly. Lief's heart thudded as he saw Verity's face clearly for the first time. To his astonishment, it was smooth and unmarked. And as he watched, a bird carrying a tiny branch of water berries moved very close to the girl's mouth and hovered.

Verity opened her lips. The bird pressed the berries into her mouth and held the branch steady as she ate.

They are feeding her! Lief thought dazedly. *Instead of attacking her they are —*

His heart gave a lurch as a harsh voice cried out angrily. He watched, transfixed, as the crew stumbled aside and Laughing Jack strode onto the deck, his teeth bared in fury.

"Did I not tell you to drive the birds away from

her, Scrawn?" Laughing Jack snarled to the rat-faced man with the rope.

The man called Scrawn cowered. "I have been trying, Captain, on my honor," he whined. "My arms fair ache with trying."

He jerked his head at the man in the eye-patch. "Beef tried, too, with me, and a dozen others in turn. But those birds are crafty, Captain. While we fight off one lot, more are sneaking in to her beneath their wings."

"It's not natural," grunted Beef. "The creatures are bewitched."

"And the sea is cursed," called someone from the back of the crowd. "There's been not a wave or a breath of wind since the girl came on board."

"It is true!" The man with the crooked yellow teeth was gnawing his thumb nervously. "Seven long days, and still the witch lives, watered and fed by her creatures. Still the Light burns. And here we rot, with the sails hanging limp as rags, and no slaves below to row us — "

"Silence!" thundered Laughing Jack. His hollow eyes blazed as he stared at Verity, the fluttering birds, and, beyond them, the Bone Point Light.

9 ~ Mutiny

Abruptly the moving picture vanished and Lief and Barda found themselves staring once more at Verity's painting. The pastel image drifted slowly below the surface of the glass, mysterious and full of secrets.

But it will give up its secrets to those seeking the truth, Lief thought. *That is why it is here. We must correct the lies. Reveal what is hidden . . .*

Slowly he became aware of a rising chorus of groans and mutterings mingling with the creaking of the oars beneath his feet. He glanced around him and saw that the light in the great room had dimmed. The candles were burning low.

"How much time has passed since we entered this room?" he whispered. "It does not seem so long . . ."

Barda moved uneasily beside him. "Come away,

Lief," he said. "Whatever this painting is, or how it was created, we should delve into it no further. Through it, the past lives again. The wretched beings below feel it. And they do not like it."

"If that is so, it is because the truth will set us free," Lief murmured.

"No!" hissed Barda. "What is past cannot be undone and is best forgotten. We would be fools to rouse the rowers further, Lief. Soon the candles will go out, and who knows what will happen then?"

Impatiently he shook Lief's arm. "Come away and help me search for the way out," he said. "We have paid our debt, and according to the rhyme at the entrance, we are free to leave. We have only to find the door."

But Lief did not move. "I would rather trust Verity than Laughing Jack," he said quietly.

His eyes were still fixed on the painting. The Light was brighter than it had been before. The little bay and the viewing platform of the lighthouse still glowed in their places. The painting was now more correct than it had been. But there was more to be done.

A fish was flying among the birds in the air. Lief touched it. It disappeared, then reappeared, glowing, under the water where it belonged. He saw that one of the birds was missing a wing, and that there was a second sun in the sky. He touched both errors, and instantly both were corrected.

Eagerly he turned and scanned the great room. But no new door or gap had magically appeared among the mirrors.

What was more, the room had grown even dimmer. The stink of decay was stronger. And the muffled howls of pain and rage from below, the angry clanking and stamping, were louder.

"Lief!" Barda urged, tugging at his arm.

Lief gritted his teeth. "I must finish this," he said. "I must!"

Barda groaned in a fever of impatience. "The rocks at the foot of the lighthouse are smooth, instead of jagged, as they should be," he said rapidly.

Lief touched the rocks. The change was made. Six corrected errors now glowed on the painting. The Light was shining so brightly that it dazzled his eyes.

But when he looked around, nothing had changed.

"There must be another error to find," he muttered.

Desperately he searched the painting. But he could see nothing more that was wrong. Nothing . . .

Then his eye fell on the bird flying alone, high in the sky, at the far right of the image.

The bird was too large — far too large to be real. He stretched out his hand, and touched it.

And at once the painting was replaced by another moving scene — the noisy, crowded deck of *The Lady Luck*, lit by weird red light. The whole crew seemed to be assembled there. Scrawn, the rat-faced man in the striped cap, was among them. So was Beef, with the black eye-patch, and the man with the crooked teeth.

Verity was still tied to the prow, and the exhaustion on her face made it plain that more days had passed. Across the flat sea, the Bone Point Light was still burning. But the men were not looking at Verity or the Light. Instead, they were all looking up, pointing at the vast bird hovering high above the sea to the south.

The giant bird was not an error, then, Lief thought dazedly. *It was not a painted lie, but truth. Like the flat, calm sea, and the birds with the water berries. But what — ?*

His stomach knotted as he realized what the hovering bird was.

"Ak-Baba!" cried Scrawn. His lips were drawn back from his teeth in a snarl of terror. "And here we lie, like chickens waiting to be swooped on by a hawk!"

"What is it doing?" another man wailed. "Why does it circle over the western sea? What business did it have at the Maze of the Beast?"

Lief's heart thudded. He heard Barda grunt with shock.

"For that matter, why is the sky scarlet, so long after dawn?" grunted Beef. "And those clouds to the east — I will knock down the first man who tells me they are natural."

81

"Omens!" wailed the man with crooked teeth. "Omens of doom!"

He tore his eyes from the hovering Ak-Baba and fixed them on Verity. She was staring straight ahead, staring at the Light.

"We are cursed!" the man shrieked. "Thirteen days we have lingered here, and still the girl lives. The whole of nature is taking revenge on us for her sake! Our only hope is to free her. Cut her down!"

He took out a knife and started for the prow.

"Stop!" The voice was like the crack of a whip. The man with the crooked teeth froze, and the others shrank back as Laughing Jack strode onto the deck.

"I have had news," he barked. "Unexpected, but welcome. It seems that we are no longer needed here."

He moved closer to Verity. "Your sacrifice has been in vain, witch!" he spat. "Here is something that you and your idiot father did not count upon. The magic that fed the Bone Point Light has died."

"You lie," the girl whispered.

Laughing Jack's skull-like face split in a humorless grin.

"At dawn this day the Belt of Deltora was broken," he sneered. "The seven gems were scattered. The Ak-Baba you now see in the sky carried but one of them. Like the others, that gem will never be found."

Lief felt a shiver run down his spine. He realized

that he and Barda were witnessing events that had happened the very day of the Shadow Lord's invasion — a time before he was born, when so many lives were changed forever.

His eyes were drawn to the lowering clouds on the eastern horizon. Often he had been told of the darkness that swept over Del with the coming of the Shadow Lord. Now he was seeing it for himself.

He glanced down at the seven jewels shining in their medallions of steel as if to remind himself that Laughing Jack was wrong — the gems *had* been found.

Once lost in the Maze of the Beast, the ghastly domain of the Glus, the amethyst, symbol of truth, now shone on the Belt, bright as a great purple star, fiery as the Bone Point Light.

Verity's voice, husky with pain and disuse, broke through his thoughts. Quickly he looked again at the moving image in the golden frame.

"Del may fall, James Gant," the girl said. "The whole kingdom may fall to the Enemy who is your master. But the magic of Tora is ancient. It does not depend on the Belt. By the will of the Torans, the Light will continue to shine."

Laughing Jack's grin broadened. "Indeed?" he said with relish. "Well, here is something you do not know. At dawn the king and queen fled from Del. They asked help from Tora, but Tora broke its vow of loyalty and refused refuge. As a result the Torans have been swept away, exiled by their own ancestors' magic."

Verity's exhausted face seemed to grow a little paler.

Gleefully Laughing Jack rubbed his hands. "You did not expect that, did you, witch?" he crowed. "And you know what it means, I see. The Light burns now only by the will and efforts of your stubborn father. But unprotected he will be easy prey."

"You touch the Light at your peril, James Gant," Verity breathed.

The man scowled. "The Light is no longer my concern," he spat. "It will die of its own accord once your father is gone, and others will see to him. We are to return to the River Tor."

He turned to the gaping crew. "Man the oars!" he snapped. "We must be away with all speed. I have been warned — "

A high sound split the air. Laughing Jack spun around, his eyes wide with shock. Verity was laughing!

"You cannot deceive me!" she cried. "Your master is displeased with you. You failed him! If the Light dies at last, it will not be because of you, but because the Torans broke their ancient vow. *That* is why he denies you the satisfaction of taking your revenge on my father."

"Silence!" Laughing Jack shrieked.

Flecks of foam had gathered at the corners of his mouth. His eyes were wild.

He snatched his knife from his belt and pointed it at the helpless girl.

"You will pay!" he hissed. "You will pay in pain and blood for every day you have defied me. When we are under way — "

He glanced over his shoulder at his men, as if just realizing that they had not moved.

"Why do you stand gaping there?" he shouted. "I gave you an order!"

The men looked at one another. Scrawn licked his lips, then spoke.

"We are not paid to row, Captain," he said sullenly. "*We* did not choose to sail in haste from the head of the Tor to the sea. We begged you to stop along the way — to replace the slaves delivered to the Gray Guards with new ones to man the oars. But you would not listen."

Lief felt a thrill of horror. So the final fate of the unlucky gamblers who borrowed from Laughing Jack had been even more terrible than he had imagined. They had manned the oars of his ship for a time, certainly. But they had ended their lives as slaves in the Shadowlands.

"How dare you question my orders!" Laughing Jack barked. "The ship is becalmed, you fool! If we are to move, you must row. Get below!"

Beef slowly shook his massive head. "Too many

have died down there, Captain," he grunted. "It is un-
wholesome."

Laughing Jack bared his teeth in fury. "We —
must — get — to — the — Tor!" he hissed. "Or at
least, for now, away from this cursed Point, with its
rocks and shallows, to a safe harbor farther south."

When the men still did not move, he stabbed a
bony finger at the eastern horizon.

"A great storm is coming!" he almost screamed.
"Do you not see it?"

"We see it, right enough," called the man with
crooked teeth. "And whoever summoned it — the red-
headed witch now tied to the prow or the sorcerer you
call your master — we will never outrun it."

He turned to the rest of the crew. "I say this ship
is finished! This ship, and its captain, too."

"Mutiny!" shouted Laughing Jack. "You will
hang for this, Coffin!"

The man called Coffin made no sign that he had
heard.

"We owe James Gant no loyalty," he roared.
"You all know what he is! He supplies slaves to the
Shadowlands, and in return he has this ship, fine food
and drink, and some of the sorcerer's powers he
craves. But is this all he has? Oh, no!"

He bared his peglike teeth. "With my own eyes I
have seen his treasure chest in the gaming room. It
overflows with the gold he cheats from his victims before sending them to the oars. But has he ever offered

to share this bounty with us? No! He has become as rich as a king, while we toil for a pittance!"

"So why should we risk our lives for him?" grunted Beef.

"Indeed!" Coffin shouted. "I say we take the lifeboat and make for the shore — take the girl with us and release her. Perhaps then the sea's vengeance will fall where it deserves — on our brave captain! Let him use his magic to save himself — if he can!"

10 - Deadly Bargain

Most of the men roared agreement. Those nearest to Laughing Jack drew their swords and daggers. His face twitching horribly with fear and anger, Laughing Jack took a step back.

"Wait!" he cried, his voice cracking. "Wait! I will make a bargain with you."

The men hesitated.

"Do not listen to him!" shouted Coffin. "He lies as easily as he breathes!"

"No! Hear me!" shrieked Laughing Jack, clasping his hands. "I have treated you unfairly — I see that now. But I will make it up to you, if only you will help me."

Coffin scowled and shook his head. The other men looked uncertainly at one another, then at the storm clouds rushing towards them from the east.

"Beware!" cried Verity. "Whatever you swear here will bind you. I cannot prevent it."

"What is your offer, Gant?" Scrawn snapped, ignoring her.

"I do not want to lose my ship!" quavered Laughing Jack. "*The Lady Luck* is all that is important to me. So I promise you this: all the treasure will be yours to share if you will man the oars until others are found to replace you!"

He cast his eyes down humbly, but Lief saw that he was peeping at the men beneath his eyelashes, and that his thin mouth twitched at the corners as their faces brightened with greed.

Scrawn wiped his mouth with the back of his hand.

"How do we know you will keep to your bargain, Captain?" he asked gruffly. "How do we know that once the ship is safe you will not break your word?"

Laughing Jack looked up and solemnly placed his hand on his heart.

"All the gold is yours, my loyal crew," he said in a trembling voice. "If I take one piece of it for my own, I myself will take to the oars. I swear it on my soul!"

"I hear your words, James Gant, and they will bind you!" cried Verity from the prow, her voice as shrill as a seabird's call.

Laughing Jack's eyes widened for an instant, then he sneered.

"So!" he said. "According to the witch, my oath cannot be broken. Now, what of you, men? Do not fear, your time at the oars will not be long. Your replacements will soon be found."

He grinned evilly. "You know that the gaming room is a web. You know that human flies blunder into it gladly, and often. And you know that never, unless I will it, do they struggle free. Sooner or later the fools borrow, then cannot repay their debt."

"That is because for every coin they borrow they must pay back three, Captain," sniggered Scrawn. "But that lying sign on the treasure chest says no such thing."

Lief's stomach turned over. He heard Barda give a low groan.

"Why, Scrawn, my little sign does not lie!" said Laughing Jack, raising his eyebrows in mock innocence. "It says plainly, 'Take what you need — pay what you owe before you depart.' It is not *my* fault if my guests mistake its meaning, and assume that the two sums are the same."

The crew laughed uproariously.

"You twist the truth for gain, James Gant!" Verity called. "You use the powers granted to you to revel in lies and wickedness. But I will set my mark upon this ship. I may die, but the truth will live for those who wish to see it, and the truth will set them free."

Laughing Jack's grin did not falter. He paid no more attention to Verity's words than to the shrieks of the swooping birds. His eyes were fixed on his men, willing them to listen only to him.

"So!" he said heartily. "Do we have a bargain?"

The men were grinning, nodding, rubbing their hands. Plainly they were convinced — dazzled by the promise of riches beyond their wildest dreams.

"No!" screamed Coffin. "You fools! You will doom us all!"

Beef's lip curled. His dagger hand jerked forward.

With a low groan, Coffin crumpled and fell lifeless to the deck, blood oozing from the deep wound in his back.

"Very well, Captain," Scrawn said softly, as Beef wiped his blade clean on his jacket. "We will take the places of the slaves until others are found to replace us. Agreed, mates?"

"Agreed!" the men around him bellowed.

"I hear your words, crewmen, and they will bind you!" cried Verity.

And in the blink of an eye, Laughing Jack stood alone on the deck with the captive girl and the sprawled body of Coffin, while from below came the hideous sounds of sliding chains and men shrieking in terror.

Laughing Jack stood dumbfounded, his wide mouth gaping.

Look! See! This is the truth of it! The truth . . .

"Your men are at their oars, James Gant," whispered Verity. "They have taken the places of the slaves indeed, and the chains the slaves bore are their chains now. They are bound by their oath, as you are bound by yours. I warned — "

Her voice broke off in a choking gasp. With a hiss of rage, Laughing Jack had spun around and stabbed her to the heart.

Lief heard himself cry out in horror. Through a scarlet mist he watched as Laughing Jack pulled his dripping knife free.

Seabirds wheeled and screamed above the dying girl's head as her life's blood drained away, flowing down, down over her white nightdress, over her bare feet, down to the sea.

And as the first gleaming red drops touched the water, the sea heaved as though in anguish.

Cool, foaming water sprayed on Verity's twisted body. The healing, loving tide flowed over her. And when it fell back all that remained on the prow was a wooden figurehead, its hands clasped to its breast.

With a roar, huge waves rose and crashed onto the deck of *The Lady Luck*, knocking Laughing Jack from his feet, tumbling him over and over in swirling foam. Coffin's dead body tumbled with him, battered and beaten against the deck.

More waves rose, and more, pounding down as if the sea was a mighty beast trying to tear the ship to pieces. Awash with foaming water, the ship rocked violently, tipping first to one side, then the other. With a groaning shriek the tall mast snapped and crashed to the deck.

Below, the chained men screamed in terror, screamed for release as water poured into their prison and engulfed them. But Laughing Jack paid no attention to them. He did not even glance at the door that led to the rowing bay.

Intent only on his own survival, he was crawling to the lifeboat, tumbling into it, sawing with his knife at the ropes that held the boat above the water.

"Master, save me!" he babbled. "Master, I beg you . . ."

Red-rimmed clouds swept in from the east. The sound of the storm mingled with the crashing of the waves. And in the midst of the storm, a voice spoke, hissing like meat on a spit:

"You are a fool, slave. You deserve to perish. But I still have need of you . . ."

There was a flash of brilliant light and a terrifying clap of thunder. Lief and Barda staggered back, clutching each other, deafened and half-blinded.

And when they looked again, the golden frame was filled once more with the painted view of the Bone Point Light.

The six errors Lief had corrected were glowing still, and the Light was shining like a star. When they turned to look at the rest of the room, however, all they saw was darkness. The candles had died at last.

They stood, motionless, calming themselves,

vainly trying to make out the shapes of tables, chairs, the carved door, and the treasure chest at the other end of the room. But all they could see was the painting behind them, and the small patch of red carpet at their feet. It was as if they were on a tiny island in the midst of a coal-black sea.

"Our time has run out, it seems," Barda muttered.

It was then that Lief became aware that the groans and cries from below had ceased. They had been replaced by a tense, waiting silence that was even more terrifying.

For a moment the silence held. Then Lief stiffened. A stealthy, sliding, brushing sound was coming from somewhere ahead, at floor level.

"What is that?" he hissed. He jumped as he heard the sound again, this time from somewhere to his right.

Suddenly there were brushing, sliding sounds by the dozen, coming from every direction. There were gusts of freezing air, thick with a smell so vile that he could hardly breathe.

And there was the drone of muttering voices.

"Beware!" Barda exclaimed, jerking Lief back.

Only then did Lief see his danger. A square section of the scarlet floor directly in front of him was sliding away, sliding slowly aside with that same faint brushing sound, revealing a yawning pit of inky darkness.

The stench of decay and stagnant water rose from the pit. And, in the darkness, things moved. The painting's soft glow fell first on the mottled tips of grasping, ruined fingers, then on arm bones, reaching, clad in tatters and clinking with chains. Below were the ghastly, upturned faces of dead rowers, hollow eyes burning, grinning mouths muttering, muttering . . .

"My replacement . . . mine, mine . . ."

Lief shrank back as the grasping fingers felt around the edge of the pit, close, so close to his feet that he imagined he could feel the cold breathing from the scraps of flesh that still clung to the bones.

He did not dare speak. His ears were filled with the sound of his frantically beating heart.

He longed to run from the evil-smelling pit, the seeking, clawing hands. But looking out into the darkness, he knew that traps like the one before them must riddle the floor of the room.

He and Barda could not move. One false step and they would be lost.

He touched the Belt of Deltora. The topaz, the gem of faith. The lapis-lazuli, the heavenly stone. The amethyst, for peace and truth.

Faith. Truth . . .

Verity's words seemed to ring in his ears.

I may die, but the truth will live for those who wish to see it, and the truth will set them free.

Slowly, carefully, Lief turned to face the painting.

Without comment, Barda turned, too. Barda knew now that this was their one hope.

They were so close to the wall that their faces were almost touching the image. It was hard to see it. But . . .

Seven errors. Seven . . . there must be . . .

"The road!" Barda whispered suddenly. "The road to the lighthouse is missing! It was neglected and overgrown when we saw it, but surely in the time of Red Han it was — "

"Of course!" Lief pressed his finger on the place where the road should have wound from the hills.

His fingertip grew hot. The painting seemed to shimmer as the road appeared, a snaking, glowing ribbon leading away to the distant hills. And the Light . . . the Light was suddenly blazing like a beacon.

I will shine like Truth through the darkness . . .

Lief spun around. The Light pierced the dark. Its broad, brilliant beam made a bright path over the red carpet, lighting up the black squares that squirmed with grasping fingers. The path led directly to the sealed, carved door.

And the door was opening!

Howls rose from below.

"Run!" Barda roared.

Together they ran along the path of light, dodging the pits filled with claws reaching up to seize their ankles. They reached the doorway and hurtled through it, pounding up onto the deck.

The angry cries of the cheated rowers floated after them. The deck trembled beneath their feet as unseen hands beat it from below. At the prow, just visible through the mist, the figurehead that had been Verity stared forward gravely, hands pressed to its heart.

Both heard the soft voice in their minds at the same time.

Flee this place. Trust the clean sea.

And without hesitation both of them ran to the side of the ship and leaped overboard — plunging recklessly into the cold, dark water.

11 - In the Dunes

Afterwards, Lief and Barda remembered nothing of their time in the sea but that desperate leap, and the black water closing over their heads. When they regained their senses, they were lying on a golden shore in a tumble of shells and seaweed.

They could see by the sky that it was early dawn. Dimly they could hear waves rolling in, regular as a great heartbeat. But where they lay, all was still. The sea had cast them up in the night and left them to sleep.

Stiffly they sat up, staring around them, then at each other. They could not believe that they were alive.

The shore stretched away on either side of them, marked only by the shells and weed of the tide line and the sticklike tracks of birds. Before them was the open sea. Behind them were sand dunes, rising one behind the other as though mimicking the waves.

"We have been swept south, I think," Barda said after a moment, his voice rough with salt. "Far south of Bone Point — beyond the Maze of the Beast, beyond the mouth of the Tor. How could this be?"

"Before we leaped into the sea, the ship was moving," Lief rasped in reply. "It was moving for quite a time. It . . ."

He scrambled unsteadily to his feet. Now that he was fully awake, he was aware of an uneasy, prickling feeling — like a warning of danger. Perhaps he had felt it even as he slept, he thought. He seemed to remember the scraps of dreams, urging him to wake.

He scanned the sea, but saw no sign of *The Lady Luck*. He looked left and right. The shore was deserted. He turned towards the silent dunes. And at once the uneasy feeling grew stronger.

But it was not warning him away from the dunes. It was calling him towards them. Calling him . . .

Quickly he glanced down and even in the half-light saw red and green gleams in the Belt at his waist. The ruby and the emerald were undimmed. They sensed no danger.

And the call was urgent.

"We must go," he muttered. Without even waiting to make sure that Barda was following, he almost ran to the base of the first dune, and began to climb.

The dry sand slipped beneath his feet with a squeaking sound as he struggled upwards. By the time he reached the top of the dune, his legs were shaking.

There was nothing ahead of him but another hill of sand, even higher. He ran awkwardly down the first dune and began climbing the second, again not stopping till he reached the top.

Bewildered, he stared ahead.

Dunes, nothing but sand dunes — pink, mauve, deepening to purple, rising against the brightening sky. There was no sign of movement anywhere. But the call was even stronger.

A wave of dizziness swept over him. His knees buckled and he half fell, half stumbled down the side of the dune, tumbling at last into a heap at the bottom.

He lay there, his head swimming. Sand showered over his legs as Barda slipped down after him. Then he felt a hand lift his head and a water flask was pressed to his lips.

He drank gratefully, then opened his eyes. Barda was crouched beside him, replacing the flask's cap.

"Tell me what you are doing, Lief, and I will follow you more willingly," Barda said wearily. "These dunes remind me unpleasantly of the Shifting Sands. Who knows what lurks within them?"

"I am sorry," Lief muttered, pushing himself up so that he could prop his back against the base of the third dune. "I . . . I felt a call. Very strong. I thought of — Jasmine."

Barda shook his head. "Jasmine could not be here. The wind that swept the Kin away from the lighthouse was blowing west, not south. If Jasmine and the Kin survived the storm, they would have returned to Bone Point, to search for us there."

"*If* they survived," Lief repeated dully. He turned his head away to stare sightlessly along the shadowed cleft that lay between the dunes.

Barda's own heart was very heavy, but doggedly he pressed on.

"We can do nothing for Jasmine. Our task is to take care of ourselves now," he urged. "This call you feel — it may be a trap. The Shadow Lord . . ."

His voice trailed off as he saw that Lief was no longer listening. Lief's eyes had widened. His mouth had dropped open.

Into the sudden silence came the soft sound of falling sand. Barda's scalp prickled. He put his hand to his sword and slowly turned to follow Lief's eyes.

Something was rising from the shadows of the cleft — a huge and terrible head, swaying on a twisting, gray-scaled neck that was still half-buried in the third dune. The beast's fangs were bared in a silent snarl. Its eyes opened — dull, flat dragon eyes.

"Do not move." Barda heard Lief breathe, his voice almost as soft as the whisper of the falling sand.

The dragon's head swayed. Sand showered from its murky scales and poured from between the sagging spines around its snarling jaws.

"Come closer, king of Deltora," it rasped.

Lief climbed to his feet, his face haggard with shock.

"No, Lief!" Barda whispered. "Keep back! This is no real dragon, but a copy, like the false, twisted beast at Dragon's Nest! Its color is proof of it."

Without speaking, Lief looked down at the Belt of Deltora. Following his eyes, Barda saw first the bright gleams of the ruby and the emerald. But then, just before Lief's hand closed over it, he saw that the great amethyst, gem of truth, was flaming like purple fire.

Astounded, he watched as Lief moved forward, one hand on the amethyst, one hand outstretched.

The dragon's eyes seemed to widen as Lief drew closer. Slowly its neck bent, until its head was resting on the sand.

And as Lief's outstretched hand touched the cold, gray ridge of bone above its eyes, the eyes closed, and the dragon gave a great, shuddering sigh.

"You have almost been the death of me, king," it murmured. "Often, in my suffering, I have cursed you in my mind, I confess it. But you have come at last. Now I can only hope that you are not too late."

✳

Hours passed before the dragon spoke again. Lief remained by its side, his hand upon its brow.

Slowly, as the amethyst worked its magic, the dull gray of the dragon's scales changed to mauve, then to purple. Slowly the spines beside its jaws stiffened and its snarling jaws relaxed. Every now and then it struggled, as if trying to free itself. But still only its head and part of its neck were visible above the sand.

At last its eyes opened. Lief saw that they were no longer dull, but gleaming like pale violets.

"You are better," he said.

The dragon snorted faintly. "I am better than I was," it said. "But that is not saying a great deal. Now I know what it is to be as weak as prey. It is not enjoyable."

"No, it is not," Lief agreed.

He hesitated, then decided to take a risk.

"What happened to you?" he asked abruptly. "How did you come to be so near death when we found you?"

"HOW?" thundered the dragon, lifting its head. Lief and Barda shrank back. The dragon coughed, and lowered its head to the sand again.

"I felt you in my land," it said. "I felt the amethyst call me, from far away. It was just as Dragonfriend had said it would be. My oath to him swam into my dreams, and I awoke in my hiding place beneath the sand."

The scales on its head and neck seemed to quiver.

"But the dune had grown since first I buried myself within it," it went on. "The sand was heavy and I was weak with hunger. I began to struggle upwards — then, suddenly, you were gone and I was left stranded, without the strength to free myself."

Its eyes burned reproachfully.

"Just after we crossed your border, we were swept out to sea, through no fault of our own," Lief said.

"It was the Shadow Lord's doing," Barda put in fiercely, as the dragon gave a low growl. "We nearly died ourselves as a result of it, dragon. And it is as well you know it!"

The dragon barely glanced at him. "Dragonfriend said that I would wake at your coming," it said to Lief. "He did not say I might die in the attempt."

"Dragonfriend — Doran — believed, I think, that if the Belt of Deltora was worn constantly by Adin's heir once more, this would mean that the Shadow Lord had been destroyed," Lief said reluctantly. "But, sadly, this is not so. Deltora is free, and the seven Ak-Baba no longer patrol our skies. But the Shadow Lord is still powerful. Even in exile, he tries to destroy us."

"Ah!" The dragon nodded its great head. "Yes. And — I seem to remember that I thought this would be so. I seem to remember telling Dragonfriend that the Enemy would never give in."

Its mouth twitched. "But, of course, Dragonfriend would not listen. Dragonfriend was fiery and impatient. He was intent upon his plan, and did not want to hear objections."

"He wanted to save you," Lief said quietly, then recoiled as the beast's eyes flashed.

"Do not think you have to make excuses for Dragonfriend to me, young king!" the dragon hissed. "Dragonfriend was the best of his kind! He had the heart of a dragon, and he was my true friend. But only fools refuse to see the faults in those they love."

Lief swallowed and nodded, feeling young and clumsy.

Slowly the spark of anger faded from the dragon's eyes.

"Dragonfriend is dead, no doubt," it said, after a moment. "If he was alive, he would have come with you, to find me. And the weight of sand I feel upon me tells me that many years have passed since we said our farewells."

"Yes," Lief said awkwardly. "I am sorry."

"Ah." The dragon grew very still. "And are his bones shut up in some grim place of honor in a human city? Or do they lie beneath a mossy stone in a wild place, as he always hoped they would?"

Lief hesitated. He saw Barda open his mouth to speak, and shot him a warning look.

The dragon was weak and grieving. Now was not the time to add to its burdens. He did not want it to know that Doran had not been honored, but had been thought mad by all his people at the last. He did not want it to know that its friend had died in a frantic, doomed search for proof of the Four Sisters — and died, horribly, no doubt, at the Shadow Lord's hands.

The upstart has the fate he deserves . . .

Lief's stomach churned at the memory of that cold voice hissing from the dying crystal on the forge in Del.

"We do not know where Doran lies," he said at last. "He never returned from — from his last adventure."

The dragon nodded without surprise. "Then, in a way, his wish was granted," it said.

It tilted its head and looked at the sky. "It is strange to think of a world without Dragonfriend in it. Strange and lonely, for after the last of my tribe was gone, he was the only friend of my heart."

Sighing, it lowered its head on the sand once more. "But I will see him very soon, and hear his laughter, where my ancestors fly above the wind," it murmured. "He will be with them, I am sure, for he always said that dragons were more his kin than those of his own kind."

"But — but what do you mean?" Lief exclaimed.

The dragon looked at him with what seemed to be surprise. "I am dying," it said simply. "Do you not understand? You came too late, king of Deltora. Even the amethyst cannot help me now, it seems. I thought perhaps . . . but it is no good. My time of struggle was

106

too long. I cannot find the strength to free myself, and so my place of refuge will become my tomb."

"Do not say that!" Lief cried.

"Why?" the dragon asked. "It is the truth."

"But you have been imprisoned only for a single night, dragon!" said Barda, in the tone he might use to encourage exhausted troops. "Surely you are not so feeble!"

The dragon's eyes slid in his direction for the briefest of moments, then moved back to Lief. "Your friend's ordeal in the sea has addled his brains," it said. "Does he — ?"

Abruptly it broke off. It lifted its head, and its forked tongue flickered in and out, tasting the air.

"Arm yourself, king!" it muttered. "We are invaded."

12 - Surprises

L ief and Barda crawled up the side of the dune and peered cautiously over the top. They were staring straight into the sun, but they could see, shimmering in the distance, a long, wavering shape.

The shape was approaching fast — very fast. Its center was dark, but at each end, bright colors flapped like wings.

Then Lief's dazzled eyes suddenly made sense of what they were seeing. The shape separated into five separate shapes — five figures, hand in hand.

The figures at each end wore long, flowing robes — one scarlet, one blue. Of the others, one was tall and dark, another a small blur of blue-gray, and the one in the middle . . .

Lief stared in disbelief. His heart gave a great thud. The next moment, he was scrambling to his feet, shouting, waving both arms wildly above his head.

Barda was roaring and waving beside him, but Lief was hardly aware of it. Dizzy with joy, he had eyes only for the black-haired girl in the center of the shimmering line, and ears only for her thin, distant cries floating to him over the sand.

A black bird became visible, soaring above the girl's head.

Kree, Lief thought dazedly. *Kree, flying . . . but — but he is only just keeping up with them! How . . . ?*

And then he realized that the robed figures were Zeean and Marilen of Tora, and understood. He himself had sped on the wings of Toran magic.

He watched, fascinated, as the five swept towards them.

❋

Long would Lief remember that reunion in the place he learned to call the Sleeping Dunes.

First there was Jasmine, scolding, laughing, and crying by turns as she embraced him. Then there was Josef's former assistant, Ranesh, beaming, with his arm around Marilen, pumping his hand. And Zeean, her wrinkled face made young by joy. And Manus of Raladin, small hands clasped and button eyes wide, as speechless as he had been when first they met him, but this time with relief.

After that came a series of shocks.

There was Lief's and Barda's shock on learning that *The Lady Luck* had been invisible to all who searched for them, and that they had been missing not for a single night, but for ten long days!

There was the shock of the newcomers when, filled with awe, they gazed upon the dragon of the amethyst imprisoned in the dune.

There was the dragon's shock when Zeean briskly insisted that it was not going to die. And its even greater shock when, not long afterwards, a hundred Torans swept into the Dunes, raised their arms, and sent the sand that imprisoned it flying, freeing it at last.

"I did not expect this," the beast told Zeean, flexing its mighty limbs and gingerly unfolding its crumpled, sand-crusted wings. "I had accepted my fate. But I thank you, woman of Tora."

Stiffly, it bowed.

Zeean bowed also. "To assist you was our privilege, dragon of the amethyst," she said. "Long may you fly Toran skies, and your descendants also."

"We will see," said the dragon. And raised its wings to the sun.

✳

There was so much to talk about, so much to explain, so many questions to be answered.

"Ten days!" muttered Barda. "How can it be?"

"Time stands still on *The Lady Luck*, it seems," Lief said.

He glanced out to sea and for a moment thought he caught a glimpse of a dark, ragged shape and the moving sticks of oars.

He stiffened, looked again, and saw only white-flecked water and the purple sheen of the dragon slowly wading in the shallows.

His heart thudding violently, he turned back to his companions. Clearly they had noticed nothing.

"I arrived in Tora to inspect the Bone Point Light," Manus was exclaiming. "Little did I know that I would be searching for lost friends instead!"

The ship was my imagination, Lief told himself. *It was a shadow — a vision born of fear. That is all.*

"It has been a dark time," Zeean sighed. "The morning after Jasmine and the Kin called for our aid, we in Tora felt a shadow pass, as though a cloud had swept over the sun. I thought this was a sign that you were no more."

"I did not believe it," Jasmine said stoutly.

"You did not," agreed Zeean, smiling. She looked apologetically at Lief and Barda. "By the end, Jasmine was the only one of us who still had hope that you would be found alive. The rest of us were certain that we were searching only for your drowned bodies — and the Belt."

Lief gripped Jasmine's hand as Zeean told the story.

Every day Jasmine had joined the search. Every night she had drunk Dreaming Water and fixed her mind on Lief. And after nine nights of emptiness, suddenly there Lief was — alive! — lying on a shore with Barda, in a place where dunes rose like waves running back from the sea.

"When Jasmine woke me and told me of the place she had seen, I knew it was the Sleeping Dunes," Zeean said. "We came at once — but I confess I had little hope. How could you be so far south, almost at the border of our territory, and yet still live? I thought Jasmine's dream was one of wishing, rather than of truth. How glad I am that I was wrong!"

✳

At sunset, Toran tents fluttered like giant silken butterflies on the dunes. A great fire burned brightly, and the smell of cooking mingled with the tang of the sea. The amethyst dragon, refreshed and fed, had removed itself to a quiet place farther down the shore.

Lief, Barda, and Jasmine, sternly bidden by Zeean to rest, sat together under a purple silk canopy a little away from the others. It was growing colder, but none of them wanted to move.

They had resisted Zeean's efforts to persuade them to return to Tora for rest. The evil chance that had delayed them had also brought them very close to their goal. They wanted to press ahead with all speed.

It had been more difficult to resist Ranesh's urgent desire to go with them.

"Whatever you are doing, wherever you are going, I can surely be of use to you!" Ranesh had argued as soon as he had been able to speak to them alone.

"You are already being of use," Barda said. "Are you not helping to rebuild Where Waters Meet, the town of your childhood?"

Ranesh's eyes darkened and he turned his head away.

"That work is complete," he muttered. "The people who have returned have safe homes — for all the good it does them, since food is scarce, the well is sour, and the waters of the Tor and the Broad are not fit to drink. I am spending most of my time in Tora now. And Tora — though it is Marilen's home — is not really to my taste."

Lief could well imagine it. Ranesh's love for Marilen had taken him to Tora, but clearly the quiet, elegant life of the magic city did not suit him.

Any more than it would suit me, Lief thought. *Ranesh must loathe the fact that none of the luxuries Tora provides can be used for the people starving outside its walls. The food of his father-in-law's table must be dust and ashes in his mouth.*

Ranesh's mouth twisted in a rueful smile.

"Also, Josef can reach me all too easily in Tora," he said. "Almost every day a messenger bird arrives with a letter from him complaining about Paff's mistakes and begging me to return to Del. But how can I return?"

He shook his head in despair. "I do not know that I even *want* to spend the rest of my life working in a library! And even if I did, I cannot leave Marilen! Yet how can I keep refusing Josef, when I owe him so much, and he is in such trouble? I feel I am in a trap!"

He frowned as if he felt he had revealed too

113

much. Then, without saying anything more, he strode away across the Dunes.

"I pity him greatly," Jasmine said. "I know what it is to feel useless — and trapped. I felt the same in Del, while I still lived in the palace, and before I began training the messenger birds. It was a kind of torture."

"Ranesh has spent too long living on his wits to settle into a life where everything is made easy by magic," Barda agreed. "But we cannot take him with us. He must solve his own problems, as best he can."

Silence fell. Jasmine began feeding Filli some nuts she had found in her pocket. Barda drew out the puzzle box he had carried with him all the way from the Os-Mine Hills.

Lief watched him idly. Two smooth rods now protruded from the carved surface of the little cube, but the box remained stubbornly locked. He wondered if Barda would ever discover its secret.

He leaned back, and paper crackled under his cloak. With a start he remembered the little wax-sealed packet Zeean had discreetly passed to him.

"Messages for you from Del, sent before knowledge of your disappearance reached anyone there," she had whispered.

Wearily, he took the packet out, and lifted the wax seal with his thumbnail.

Three small papers were inside, folded closely together. He unfolded them almost with dread. He knew that no news from Del could be good.

LIEF,

I rejoice to hear that all is well with you. Thank you for sending the curious sample of plant life, which I found most interesting.

Rumours abound in Del about your travels and whereabouts. No doubt news of your latest adventures will reach eager ears very soon, and cause even greater interest. I hope this does not inconvenience you too greatly.

I know what a bore it is to find a safe means of sending messages while you are travelling, so will not expect to hear from you for a time. I expect Sharn soon, and will tell her all your news.

My greetings to Barda and Jasmine.

DOOM

PS. I enclose a note from Josef, who for weeks has been wild to contact you. He is missing you and Ranesh greatly, and is in frail health. But I find it hard to be patient with him, I fear.

The first paper was covered in writing he knew well.

Lief shook his head ruefully. He realized that Barda and Jasmine were looking at him and passed them the note.

"Not in code?" Barda said in surprise, glancing at the letter.

"There was no time to work in code, I imagine," said Lief. "Doom expected us to stay in Tora only for a few hours, and wanted to be sure his message reached us. But the note *is* in code of a sort."

Jasmine had been reading her father's note carefully.

"So it is!" she exclaimed. "His real meaning lies under the plain words. He rejoices that the Sister of the North has been destroyed. He recognizes the piece of Boolong cone, so knows we sent our message from Dread Mountain. He warns us that the Shadow Lord will now be even more intent on stopping us — "

"As if we are not all too aware of that!" snorted Barda.

"And he tells us not to write again too soon," said Lief. "Plainly his fear that any message will fall into the wrong hands is even greater than it was before. Only the sentences about poor Josef, added at the end, are what they seem."

He turned to Josef's letter — two pages hastily torn from a little notebook.

He smiled. How Josef must have hated being forced to send such a rough message! It would have offended all his ideas of what was proper. Quickly he scanned the first page of the note.

Your Majesty,

My mind is all confusion.
I have just heard that I may at last
send a note to you if I make haste.
I wish I had been given more notice,
but I must not complain.
Since you left, I have put aside work
on my new book. Instead I have been
studying certain important maps and
writings in the Deltora Annals, *hoping*
to assist you in planning the next
stages of your journey. The results of
my study have shocked me more than
I can say.
If I am right, the danger is very great.
I fear for you, and for us all.

Lief frowned. He turned to the second page, which proved to be even more confused than the first.

I pray that I am in error, but only you can tell me if I am. Doom refuses to say where you are going. Perhaps, as he claims, he does not know. He has grown very moody of late. I fear he does not trust me. I hope he will not suppress this letter because I have spoken too plainly.

Please reply urgently. Quite apart from the perils outlined above, something about my results worries me, but as yet I have not been able to put my finger on what it is. If only I could clear my mind—

I must finish. Doom is in the hallway, calling angrily for my note.

In haste—

Josef

"What does the old windbag say?" Barda yawned.

"He says that Doom is moody, and that we are in danger," Lief said dryly.

Jasmine laughed. "Well, that is news indeed!" she said. "Does he say nothing else?"

Lief sighed again. "He thinks that by studying Doran's maps and writings he has worked out where we are going. He wants me to tell him if he is right."

Barda looked up. "You will not do so, I presume?"

"Of course not." Lief lay back, frowning, and closed his eyes. He did not like to think of Josef waiting vainly for an answer to his urgent request.

And there was something else. Lief's frown deepened. He had ignored the fussy old librarian before — and regretted it. Josef's mind was sharp, and he knew the *Deltora Annals* like no one else.

. . . something about my results worries me . . .

"Lief!"

Lief's eyes flew open. Manus was standing in front of him, his small face screwed into an apologetic smile.

"I am sorry to disturb you, Lief," Manus said softly. "But I have a promise to keep."

He held out a small package wrapped in white paper and tied with string.

"On my way to Tora from Raladin, I stopped at Tom's shop to buy a packet of No Bakes for the journey," he said. "Tom gave me this. He said it was for you."

13 - Strange Tidings

Lief stared at Manus in astonishment and growing dismay. How had Tom, the strange shopkeeper of the Plains, guessed where he was?
They had told no one but Doom that they planned to
visit Tora. Even the Kin had not known where they
were going until they were in the air.

Yet the wind came to Bone Point, Lief reminded
himself. *The wind from the Shadowlands, which swept us
out to sea and nearly killed us all. The Shadow Lord
knew where to find us. And now, it seems, Tom the shopkeeper . . .*

"Did you tell Tom you would see me in Tora,
Manus?" he asked sharply.

Manus's eyes widened. "Of course not. How
could I?" he squeaked. "I did not know it myself! I
thought you were still travelling in the north-east, and
so I told Tom. In fact, I told him he should keep the

120

package, for you would very likely visit his shop yourself, before too long."

"And what did Tom say to that?" Barda demanded.

Manus wrinkled his nose. "He just smiled, in that knowing way he has, and said I might see you when I least expected it. He said I was to give you the package with his compliments, but no one else was to know of it."

He saw the companions glance at one another and his face grew troubled.

"It seems you are not pleased," he murmured. "I hope I have not done wrong."

"No, no, Manus!" Lief said quickly. "We are only surprised, that is all."

He took the package and turned it over in his hands. There was nothing written upon it at all.

"Open it, Lief!" Jasmine urged.

Lief pulled off the string. The wrapping paper fell away to reveal a jar of fire-making beads and a bag of large, round, pink-striped sweets that smelled strongly of peppermint.

"There!" exclaimed Manus, leaning forward. "He has sent you a gift!"

"A gift from Tom?" snorted Barda. "I do not believe it. That man cares only for business. He has never given away anything in his life without being forced into it!"

"There is no note?" Jasmine asked curiously.

Lief shook his head. He smoothed out the thick, white wrapping paper and peered at it in the fading light. Both sides were smooth and unmarked.

Manus glanced over his shoulder at the fire. "The Torans think I am fetching my flute," he murmured. "They would like some music, they say."

"And so would we," said Barda heartily. "Be off, then!"

Manus grinned and scurried away.

The three companions looked at one another, and then at the bag of pink-striped sweets sitting before them on the sand.

"They look and smell very good," Lief said longingly. "But I daresay we would be foolish to eat them."

"Indeed!" Barda said. "It would be best to bury them, or throw them in the fire."

"What reason would Tom have to poison us?" Jasmine exclaimed. "He is a rascal, perhaps, but surely not a villain. He guessed where we were in Deltora, but this does not make him our enemy. After all, Josef claims to have discovered our whereabouts, too, and we do not suspect *Josef* of evil intentions."

"Josef says Doom does not trust him." Lief was frowning. It had been a great shock to discover that their movements were known to so many, despite all their care.

Jasmine snorted. "Doom does not trust anyone but himself," she said.

The sweet sound of Manus's flute drifted to their ears on the cool wind.

Jasmine picked up the jar of fire beads and rattled it thoughtfully. "We know what these are, at least," she said. "They could be very useful to us in the time to come. I will try one now, as a test."

She scraped a shallow hole in the sand before her, then broke the seal on the jar and took one bead. She placed the bead in the hole.

"Move back," she said. "Just in case . . ."

Lief and Barda edged farther under the canopy.

Sitting well back on her heels, Jasmine reached forward and hit the bead sharply with the hilt of her dagger.

The bead burst into flames. Nothing else happened. After a few moments, Jasmine added another bead and soon they were all enjoying the warmth and light of a small but cheery fire.

Barda held his hands out to the blaze and shook his head. "So it *was* just a simple gift," he muttered. "A welcome one, too. But it is very strange."

Lief bent to move the bag of sweets and the discarded wrapping paper away from the fire. As he did, he saw something that made his jaw drop.

Words were appearing in the center of the paper. Dark brown words that had not been there before.

He snatched the paper up. It was stiff and warm. "Tom sent a message after all!" he gasped. "A message written in ink that is invisible until it is warmed."

Barda stared at the paper, fascinated. "That was why he sent the fire beads, no doubt — to make sure we lit a fire at once!"

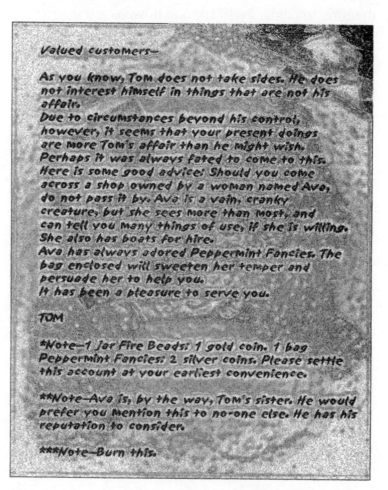

Valued customers—

As you know, Tom does not take sides. He does not interest himself in things that are not his affair.

Due to circumstances beyond his control, however, it seems that your present doings are more Tom's affair than he might wish. Perhaps it was always fated to come to this. Here is some good advice: Should you come across a shop owned by a woman named Ava, do not pass it by. Ava is a vain, cranky creature, but she sees more than most, and can tell you many things of use, if she is willing. She also has boats for hire.

Ava has always adored Peppermint Fancies. The bag enclosed will sweeten her temper and persuade her to help you.

It has been a pleasure to serve you.

TOM

*Note—1 Jar Fire Beads: 1 gold coin. 1 bag Peppermint Fancies: 2 silver coins. Please settle this account at your earliest convenience.

**Note—Ava is, by the way, Tom's sister. He would prefer you mention this to no-one else. He has his reputation to consider.

***Note—Burn this.

Lief raised his head from the message, and met his companions' astonished eyes.

Jasmine was the first to recover.

"I am astounded!" she said. "And most of all, I think, to learn that Tom has a sister! It is impossible to imagine him as a child, and part of a family."

"Plainly he *was* a child once, however," growled Barda. "And it sounds as if his sister is as strange a bird as he is."

"Even stranger, perhaps," Lief muttered. "But who is to say we will ever meet her? Her shop could be anywhere."

Still, he carefully tucked the bag of Peppermint Fancies away inside his jacket. He felt excited and uneasy, both at the same time.

Something about the note nagged at him. It was not just Tom's knowledge that they were in the west. It was something else — something he felt he should see, but which eluded him.

Slowly he crumpled the paper and tossed it into the fire. It flared up. One line showed bright in the flames.

Perhaps it was always fated to come to this . . .

Then the paper blackened and crumbled to ash.

✳

The next morning, soon after dawn, the companions left the Sleeping Dunes. They left alone, yet not alone, for the thoughts of the Torans went with them, and sped them on their way.

Barda was the only one of the three who had not experienced the rush of Toran magic before. For a long time he could only stare, wide-eyed, as first the Dunes, then the broad coast road that lay beyond them, slipped rapidly away beneath his flying feet.

At last, he managed to speak. "This is incredible!" he muttered huskily. "Why — in minutes we have gone half a day's march! If only this magic could be harnessed — used all over Deltora. Think what it would mean!"

"The Torans have tried," Jasmine said. "Or so Marilen tells me. But beyond the borders of their territory, their power weakens, then dies. Only between Del and Tora is the path strong, because it was opened by the ancients."

Filli was peeping from beneath her collar, chittering cheekily at Kree, who was flying close beside them. Kree squawked loudly.

"Do not be jealous, Kree," Jasmine grinned. "Soon you will be flying ahead of us again, as is proper."

Sure enough, it was not long before their speed slowed. They were still travelling far faster than normal walking pace, but their surroundings no longer flashed by in a blur. Now they could see pounding waves on their right, and the occasional ruined house amid the barren land to their left.

"You see? We have crossed the border," Jasmine told Barda, as Kree drew ahead of them with a triumphant screech. "The magic is fading."

And we are in the land of the diamond, Lief thought. He glanced down at the Belt of Deltora. The great diamond winked in the sunlight.

He put his hands to the gem, closed his eyes, and willed the diamond dragon to wake and come to him. But he felt no special warmth, no answering glow.

In his mind he saw Doran's Dragon Territories map, and the broad, empty spread of the land of the diamond.

By the time we reach the Isle of the Dead, the diamond dragon will have sensed the Belt, he told himself. *Wherever it lies, however far away, it will wake and come to me, as the other dragons have done.*

It will come if it can, a voice in his mind replied. And Lief's thoughts flew back to the amethyst dragon, as it had been when he bid it farewell at dawn.

"So you are taking the amethyst away, though I am still too weak to fly," the great beast had said.

Lief had swallowed. "I am sorry," he had said stiffly.

"There is no point in grieving over what cannot be helped," the dragon had replied. "Now I am a little stronger, I feel the poison in my land. Its evil source is south of here — beyond my border. The dragon of the diamond must help you defeat it. Is that not so?"

Lief still remembered the wave of relief that had flowed through him when he heard those words, spoken so calmly, and with such dignity.

"I pray that the dragon of strength and purity will

aid you as it should," the amethyst dragon had continued. "But if it should fail you, call me to your side. If it
is within my power, I will come. I will do it for love of
Dragonfriend. I know he would have wished it."

"Thank you, dragon of the amethyst," Lief had
managed to say. He had been very moved.

"And if you call me, king of Deltora," the dragon
had finished, "it would be best, to make sure I hear
you, that you call me by my true name. It is . . . Veritas."

The last words were spoken softly, so softly that
Lief had been forced to bend to hear them. He had
straightened, very aware of the honor he had received.

"I thank you, Veritas," he said humbly. "I swear
that never will I use your name unwisely, and that I
will honor it. My true name is Lief."

The dragon had nodded, but said nothing more.
And quietly, Lief had left it where it crouched, motionless on the sand.

"Look! Ahead! Lief, *look!*"

Lief's eyes flew open at the sound of Jasmine's
voice. He blinked. His heart pounded.

They had rounded a bend in the road, and suddenly the end of their journey was in sight. Suddenly,
they could see ocean not only to their right but to their
left, and far ahead as well.

Before them stretched a long, narrow point of
land. Like a thin flat finger tipped with rock and
fringed with foam it jabbed through the blue of the sea,
stretching away into the distance stretching to . . .

Lief's eyes dazzled. Something was flashing at the end of the point — flashing like the Bone Point Light in Verity's painting.

"What is it?" Barda exclaimed. "Can it be another lighthouse? I thought — "

Kree screeched wildly overhead.

"It is the island!" cried Jasmine.

And as Lief ran forward, squinting, he saw with wonder that it was so. The source of the dazzling light rose from the sea beyond the tip of the point.

High, steep, and bare, the Isle of the Dead shone like glass. Every surface glittered and flashed in the sun, as if the Isle itself was one vast diamond.

In front of the great mass of light, separated from it by a strip of boiling foam, was a small gleam of scarlet.

The first island, Lief thought. *The smaller one shown on the map. It shines like a ruby, just as the other is like a diamond.*

And then, as his eyes moved on to the mainland, he saw something else that the brilliant light of the Isle of the Dead had caused him to miss at first glance.

A gleaming shape was floating above the ground at the tip of the rocky point, burning like a silver beacon against the blueness of sea and sky:

14 - Ava

L ief squinted at the gleaming shape. Almost instantly he realized that it was not some strange
vision floating in midair, but a huge metal sign.
The sign was attached to the roof of a small building
that was so brown, low, and rounded that it looked as
if it had grown out of the rock.

Ava's shop, he thought, his hand moving to the
bag of Peppermint Fancies in his jacket pocket.

He knew he should be amazed to find Ava's
shop — any shop — here, in this wild and lonely
place.

Yet he was not amazed. And slowly he admitted
to himself what in his heart he had known all along.

Tom would not have sent that message and the
gift for Ava unless he had been sure that Lief, Barda,
and Jasmine would pass this way. He had been certain

that the companions' goal was the Isle of the Dead. He knew his sister could help them.

. . . she sees more than most, and can tell you many things of use. . . . She also has boats for hire . . .

Their eyes narrowed against the bright light of the island, the companions moved forward, barely noticing that their feet were now on the ground and that they were moving at normal walking pace.

The point narrowed more and more. At last they reached a place where the road curved to return to the main line of the coast. Ahead was a ragged arrow of rock pointing to the two islands.

Ava's dwelling, topped by its glaring sign, was perched almost at the tip of the arrow. The companions left the road and began to trudge towards the building, their heads bent against the wind.

"A very strange place for a shop," said Barda, shading his eyes as he scanned the rock and the sea beyond.

"It is likely that this place was not so deserted, once," Lief said. "The coast road is very broad — and why would anyone make such a road, if there was no one to travel on it?"

"Besides, Ava's sign is like Tom's," Jasmine pointed out. "It can be read the same way from both sides, so it can be seen from the sea as well as from the road. She may have had customers who came to her in ships."

"If she did, she has them no longer," Barda said gruffly. "There are no ships in these seas now."

Lief glanced at him. There had been an odd tone in his voice.

Barda had turned away from the ocean and was frowning down at his feet. A muscle twitched beside his mouth, and his fists were clenched.

Lief felt a sudden chill. He looked quickly out to sea. But there was nothing to be seen. The only dark spot on the white-flecked surface was a flabby mat of seaweed floating near the shining Isle.

If Barda had seen something else — a ship with a broken mast and slowly dipping oars, for example — it was no longer visible.

Or it was not there at all, Lief told himself firmly. *It is natural that memories of* The Lady Luck *should haunt us. But we must not fall into the trap of believing that the ghost ship is truly dogging our footsteps. That way lies madness.*

Sea spray was cold on his face. The waves seemed very loud. He looked ahead and with a slight start saw that they had nearly reached the end of the point.

Across the sea, the scarlet island glimmered and the high, shining peak of the Isle of the Dead flashed in the sun. And now Lief could see that the two islands were linked by a ragged bridge of rock — a natural arch spanning churning white water.

But closer, much closer, was the glaring sign. Ava's shop was directly ahead.

Brown and hunched, built of rounded stones

mottled with sea moss, the building was larger than it had appeared from a distance.

The front looked like a modest cottage, with a central door and shuttered windows. The back was higher, with bare, windowless walls.

The boat shed, Lief thought. Again his hand crept to his jacket pocket, as if the bag of Peppermint Fancies hidden there was a talisman.

If the diamond dragon answered his call, it might carry him and his companions directly to the Isle of the Dead. But they could not depend upon it. The dragon might not come at all. Or it might come, but be unwilling to carry them. They needed a boat.

Slowly the companions approached the shop. Its low roof was thatched with dried seaweed. Wind whistled about its walls, rattled the shutters that covered its windows, and tore the smoke rising from its chimney into tatters of swirling gray.

A small notice was fixed to the door.

Charms. Cures. Love Potions.
Your Fortune by the Cards.
~~Bait.~~ Fishing Supplies.
Boats for Hire.

FREE GIFT FOR EVERY CUSTOMER!

"Ava is a witch!" hissed Jasmine.

"More likely just a fraud who is as crafty in business as her brother," muttered Barda. He pointed to the last line of the notice. "As I recall, *Tom* promises a free gift for every customer also."

"He does," Lief whispered. "But he only gives it if you remember to ask. I wonder if his sister is the same?"

"Enter, friends, if you are of good will!"

They all jumped violently as the husky voice called from within the shop. With a nervous glance at his companions, Lief pushed the door open.

Inside it was warm and very dim, for the only light came from a glowing fire. The air was heavy with the scents of herbs and smoke.

Peering through the gloom, Lief noticed first that the walls of the room they had entered were lined with shelves that stretched from floor to ceiling. Every shelf was crammed with jars, bottles, tins, and boxes.

Then he saw, crouched in a sagging chair beside the fire, a figure shrouded in a hooded cloak made entirely of the black and white feathers of seabirds.

"You have found Ava," the figure whispered. "What is your wish?"

Lief took a breath, but could not speak.

"A love potion?" Ava muttered. "No. I can see there is no need for that. A cure, then? No . . . not yet a while." She tittered unpleasantly.

Barda cleared his throat. "We would like to

hire a boat, if you please, good lady," he said loudly.

Ava raised her head.

Lief's heart jolted. The face framed by the hood of the feathered cloak was powdered chalky white, even to the thin lips. Dull brown hair hung limply about the hollow cheeks. The eyes were covered by a tightly wound band of black silk.

Then, for the first time, Lief noticed the white stick leaning on one arm of the chair.

Ava, whose symbol was the eye, was blind!

. . . she sees more than most . . .

"I have no boats for hire," Ava said softly.

"The sign on your door says you do!" Jasmine exclaimed.

The woman shrugged. "I have only one boat now," she said. "I do not care to lend it to strangers."

Her thin white lips curved slightly at the corners. For a fleeting moment Lief saw an eerie resemblance to Tom.

"Your brother told us of you, Ava," he said quickly, before Barda or Jasmine could say anything more.

"Brother?" The figure in the chair grew very still.

"Your brother Tom is — a friend of ours," Lief said, feeling in his pocket for the Peppermint Fancies. "He told us that you could help us — if you were willing. He sent you a gift."

Cautiously he moved towards the chair, holding

out the bag of sweets. Ava seemed to have relaxed a little. Her nose twitched, but she did not stir.

Lief placed the gift in her lap and stepped smartly back. He held his breath as hands warm in thick black woollen gloves crept from beneath the feathered cloak and clasped the bag firmly.

"Peppermint Fancies," the woman sighed. "Ah, Tom always remembers his little sister's favorite. Clever Tom! But then, he was always the cleverest of us all, even in the old days. Or so it was said."

She tilted her head slightly.

"It is not like Tom to admit our relationship," she said. "Tom values his privacy, as do I. He must have a special reason for helping you. What might that be, I wonder?"

Again her lips curved into that slightly mocking smile. Again Lief felt a stab of recognition.

But this time . . . this time it was different. This time the smile reminded him not only of Tom the shopkeeper, but of someone else as well.

He caught his breath as memories flooded through him.

It is a matter of business . . .

Due to circumstances beyond his control . . . your present doings are more Tom's affair than he might wish. . . . Perhaps it was always fated to come to this . . .

Tom always saw himself as the cleverest of us all . . . of us all . . .

"Of course!" he exclaimed aloud.

He had seen the resemblance — the thin, wide mouth, the lean face, the long limbs, the mocking smile — seen it with his own eyes! But at the time he had not made the connection. He had not realized . . .

Barda and Jasmine were staring at him. Ava's smile was fading.

Lief wet his lips. "I think Tom felt he had no choice but to help us, Ava," he said. "He felt he owed it to us. Somehow he learned that we had fallen foul of his brother — and yours. The man we know as Laughing Jack."

Jasmine and Barda gasped. Ava's shoulders stiffened beneath the feathered cloak.

"That man is no brother of mine," she rasped.

"I think he is," Lief said. "The likeness is — "

"Jack, Tom, and I are of the same blood, that is true," Ava broke in harshly. "As children at home on the Plains we were very alike to look upon, it is said, and our minds could link as though we were three parts of a whole. But when we grew old enough, we went our separate ways to seek our fortunes. Tom went not so far. I went very far, to the sea where I had always longed to be, though I could not see it with the eyes of the body . . ."

Her voice trailed off.

"And Jack?" Lief prompted softly.

"Jack went . . . farthest of all." Ava's white lips

were trembling. She made an obvious effort to firm them, and went on rapidly.

"Long ago Jack made choices that parted him from me — and from Tom — forever. That is why I say he is no longer our brother. Now and then fragments of his thoughts still whisper like evil ghosts in the dark corners of our minds. He is still part of us. But he is our enemy."

"He is our enemy, too, Ava," Lief said softly. "And the greater Enemy he calls his master is trying to destroy our land. Please help us! Lend us your boat!"

"And if I do, where will you take it?" Ava asked. She waited for Lief's answer, her head tilted to one side, her mouth a straight, hard line.

It is a test, Lief thought. *She has seen or guessed where we want to go. She is waiting to see if we will lie to her.*

"We must go to the Isle of the Dead," he said firmly.

"So, you have decided to trust me," Ava murmured. She sank back in her chair, folding her hands beneath her cloak. The Peppermint Fancies slipped from her lap and fell to the ground, but she did not seem to care or notice.

"Very well," she said. "Then hear what I say. No boat can land on the Isle of the Dead. The sea churns around its rocks like milk boiling in a cauldron. To reach the Isle, you must go first to the scarlet island and cross by the rock bridge."

"It sounds almost too easy," Barda said.

Ava raised her head. The silk band that bound her eyes gleamed in the firelight.

"The journey to the Isle may be easy," she said slowly. "But the Isle itself is another matter. I can tell you nothing of it — except that no one who has set foot upon it has ever returned. If you value your lives you will forget it, and go on your way."

A cold knot tightened in Lief's stomach as she smiled.

15 - The Scarlet Island

An hour later, Lief and Barda were rowing Ava's tiny, battered boat across the channel that lay between the mainland and the scarlet island. The channel was rough, and wider than it had first appeared. They were still only halfway to their goal, and though the tide was with them, the work was hard.

Spray beat on them from every side, and for once they were glad of the stiff oiled coats they had taken from the fishing hut in Broome. Choppy water slapped against the blunt stern where Jasmine sat with Filli chittering unhappily beneath her collar. Kree flew overhead, the only one who was dry.

Finding that her guests were determined to make their journey, despite her warnings, Ava had shrugged and told them to take the boat if they wished. They would find it by the water, she said, tied to a post.

The hire fee, she had added coolly, was five gold coins. And for an extra gold piece she would store their packs until they returned, for the boat was too small to take extra weight. In silence she had held out her hand, her lips moving as Jasmine counted the coins into her gloved palm.

"Robbery!" Barda growled now, as he bent over the oars, water streaming from his cap, hair, and beard. "Even if I had not known the woman was Tom's sister, her outrageous prices would have made me suspect it. Five gold coins for a boat that is barely seaworthy! And one for keeping our belongings!"

"It does not matter. There is still a great deal of gold in the bag the Dread Gnomes gave us," called Jasmine, who still cared no more for money than she had when she lived in the Forests of Silence. "Besides, Ava no doubt expects us to die on the Isle. She thinks she has seen the last of her boat."

And indeed, as it turned out, Ava's boat was destined never to return to its owner. Just past the center of the channel, the companions suddenly found themselves ankle deep in water.

Ragged holes had appeared in the boat's hull, and water was pouring in. Jasmine snatched up a small bucket and began to bail frantically. Lief and Barda redoubled their efforts, gritting their teeth and pulling with all their strength.

The boat drew closer, closer to the island. But every moment the holes in the hull were opening wider, and despite all Jasmine's efforts the water was rising.

The boat began to settle. Waves lapped over the sides. Filli shrieked piercingly.

"We are in for it, I fear!" Barda said grimly. "Lief — we seem to be making a habit of this. Pull your oar free and use it to keep afloat. I will take care of Jasmine."

Lief did not argue. Barda was a far stronger swimmer than he was.

In minutes they were floundering in freezing water.

Again! Lief thought desperately. Clinging to the oar, he shook the wet hair out of his eyes and looked around for Jasmine and Barda.

He saw their heads bobbing just ahead of him. Barda was swimming strongly, pulling Jasmine with him. Filli was clinging in silent terror to Jasmine's hair. Kree was flying above them, screeching encouragement.

The tide will aid us, Lief told himself, beginning to paddle slowly forward. *And this time it is day. This time we can see the shore. And Barda and I are practiced at surviving in the sea, after all.*

The last thought made him smile, even as his teeth chattered with cold. How strange and ridiculous that his and Barda's ordeal beyond Bone Point might be the very thing that saved them now.

And just at that moment, something made him look over his shoulder.

Far away across the water, Ava's towering sign gleamed in the sunlight. But Lief could not see the cottage beneath the sign, or the waves foaming at the tip of the point.

His view was blocked — blocked by a dark ship with a broken mast and the rags of sails fluttering in the wind. Silently the ship rocked at anchor about halfway across the channel.

The Lady Luck. Waiting.

In terror, Lief turned, cast aside the oar, and struck out wildly. Fear gave strength to his arms and banished the cold that might otherwise have slowed him. His eyes fixed on the red blur ahead, he plowed through the water, using the waves as he had learned to do, thinking of nothing but flight.

And sooner than he would have believed possible he was clambering onto dry land and falling, panting, beside Barda and Jasmine into a dense, fragrant mass of scarlet lilies.

✳

Barda and Jasmine could not see *The Lady Luck* when they turned to look for it after Lief had blurted out his story. Lief could no longer see it, either. But the ruby in the Belt of Deltora was palest pink, signalling danger. Lief knew the ship was there. Visible or invisible, it was there, anchored in the channel.

Barda groaned and ran his hands through his wet hair.

"I sighted the cursed ship, too, when we had almost reached Ava's shop," he admitted reluctantly. "It was moving towards the point then. I thought my mind was playing tricks."

"As I did, when I first saw it," Lief muttered, clambering to his feet. "But it was no illusion, Barda. *The Lady Luck* has followed us. It has followed us all the way down the coast." His stomach churned at the thought.

Barda, too, looked sick.

Jasmine glanced uneasily from one to the other. "Let us move on," she said, jumping up quickly and tugging at Lief's arm. "It would be better, perhaps, to be away from the sea."

They began walking, carefully threading their way through the tall, bloodred flowers that seemed to grow thickly all over the island, clothing it in a rich mantle of scarlet.

The lilies bent and swayed around them, black-fringed petals cool and fleshy, golden stamens leaving trails of golden pollen wherever they touched. Not far ahead, rising high on the far side of the island, was the rocky outcrop that marked the beginning of the archway. Beyond that was the diamond brilliance of the Isle of the Dead.

But Lief hardly noticed his surroundings. His

mind was still on the specter of *The Lady Luck*. Nervously he glanced over his shoulder and as he turned back he saw that Jasmine was watching him in concern. He suspected that she thought he and Barda had been seeing visions.

"We are not imagining this, Jasmine!" he snapped. "The ship is real! You searched for us for over a week, and you could not find us — even in your dreams! Yet we were on the ship, within Deltoran waters, all the time."

"I know this!" Jasmine shook her head. "But how could the — the crew — have known what happened to you after you jumped overboard? How did they know where to find you?"

"Somehow they must sense us," Barda muttered. "Somehow . . ." Suddenly he stopped, his face alert.

"The gold piece!" he hissed. "Lief! You won two gold coins when you played that game, but you only returned the one you had borrowed. Perhaps . . ."

Lief dug deep into his pocket and pulled out the gold coin he had won after playing the beetle game.

"Throw it away!" Barda urged. "Throw it into the sea! Perhaps, once we are rid of it, the ship will cease haunting us."

"If you throw it into the sea, it will be lost forever," Jasmine hissed. "Who knows what will happen then?"

She held out her hand impatiently. "Give the coin to me, Lief! I am unknown to the crew of *The Lady*

Luck. I owe them nothing! I have never set foot on their accursed ship."

Lief hesitated, then handed over the coin. Nodding with satisfaction, Jasmine put it away in the Dread Gnomes' money bag.

"There," she said, returning the bag to her jacket pocket. "Now, let us concentrate on what is to come. The guardian of the Sister of the West no doubt awaits us on the Isle of the Dead. We must — "

She broke off with a startled cry as Kree suddenly swooped at her head and wheeled away, screeching. Filli, clinging to her shoulder, gave a high, despairing squeal.

A curious expression crossed Jasmine's face. She looked down and her eyes widened in horror.

Puzzled and alarmed, Lief and Barda looked down, too. But there was nothing to be seen — nothing but nodding scarlet lilies, trembling golden stamens, a few green leaves, and the deep, soft earth beneath.

"Beware!" Jasmine shrieked. She began to kick and stamp violently. Lilies toppled and fell around her, crushed beneath her feet. She bent amid the ruin of the flowers and began brushing wildly at her legs.

Lief and Barda gaped at her. What had come over her? They could see that the dull cloth of her leggings was bright with smears of golden pollen beneath a clinging mass of lily petals. But what did that matter? Where was the danger in . . . ?

And then they saw the blood — the blood dripping from Jasmine's hands, the blood soaking her leggings, running down into her boots. And they saw that the black fringes of the swollen "petals" she was clawing from her legs were wriggling. They saw feelers like golden stamens twitching angrily and razor-sharp pincers snapping as they were dragged from raw wounds.

The things clinging to her are not lily petals, Lief thought, numb with shock. *They look exactly like them, but . . .*

"Beware!" Jasmine shrieked again, still tearing the creatures from her legs. "Lief! Barda! They are on you, too! They are — eating us alive!"

16- Blood and Bone

The next moment Lief and Barda, too, were stamping, kicking, shuddering as they plucked from their bodies the hundreds of scarlet petal-shaped horrors that had cut through their clothes, then begun gnawing at their flesh.

Lief's hands were slippery with blood. His head was spinning. As fast as he tore the creatures away, others were attacking, crawling up from the trampled lilies beneath his feet, slipping silently from the stems that nodded all around him.

His blood ran in streams into the rich earth, and it seemed to Lief that the lilies around them trembled with pleasure as they drank.

He felt disgust, horror, fear. But he felt no pain. Dizzy and unbelieving, he watched as a red creature fastened itself to his wrist and bit deeply. Blood flowed over the smears of yellow pollen that marked his skin. He pulled the creature off. A scrap of his flesh tore away with it, but he felt nothing at all.

It is the pollen, he thought hazily. *The pollen numbs the skin. That is why we did not realize what was happening. The lilies shelter the creatures and prepare their victims. The creatures' leavings feed the lilies. It is a partnership. A horrible partnership . . .*

He stared, revolted, at the flowers around him, seeing them properly for the first time. He saw the scarlet petals fringed with black, the cluster of trembling stamens in the center, heavy with pollen.

Blood lilies. Blood lilies . . . and fleshbanes.

The names floated into his mind quite suddenly. And with the names came a picture — a vivid painting of scarlet flowers. For some reason the memory made him think of the library in Del. The library . . .

And suddenly his face burned as he realized that he had seen the painting in Josef's book — *The Deltora Book of Monsters*. But he had read none of the text except the title.

Leafing quickly through the book so as to be able to tell Josef that he had read it, he had not even noticed the creatures that Josef had no doubt shown camouflaged among the lily flowers.

Fool! he told himself savagely. *If you had taken the time to read the words you would have known the blood lilies were on this island. You would have known of the fleshbanes. You would have been warned —*

Why did Ava not warn us?

150

The question pierced his mind like an arrow, but before he could think too much about it he became aware that Jasmine was shrieking to Barda.

The next moment Barda charged forward and, ignoring the fleshbanes still clinging to his body, began felling lilies by the dozen with great sweeps of his sword.

That will do no good, Barda! Lief thought in desperation. *The lilies may die, but the fleshbanes will live on. They will keep attacking us from below.*

He pressed his bloodstained hands to the Belt of Deltora.

"Help us!" he whispered, concentrating with all his might. "Dragon of the diamond, hear me! Help — "

His heart leaped as suddenly Barda jumped back and with a crackling roar the heap of slashed lilies burst into flames. The next moment juicy stems were spitting and hissing as they burned. Leaves and flowers were shrivelling. Fleshbanes in their hundreds were curling and dying.

Joyfully Lief looked up, searching the sky for the dragon that must at last have answered his call.

But no vast, glittering shape hovered above them. No matter how keenly he looked, he could only see Kree, swooping and screeching amid the slowly rising smoke.

Dazed with disappointment and confusion, he looked down again. Where the fallen lilies had been there was now a smoking circle of blackened earth littered with the charred bones of birds that had fallen victim to the fleshbanes in times past. And stepping onto the blackened patch, grinning in triumph, was Jasmine, the jar of fire beads clutched in her hand.

In seconds she was wreathed in steam as her wet boots sank into the hot ground. As Lief watched, she took more beads from the jar and threw them violently into the lilies ahead of her.

Flames leaped upwards. The lilies caught fire, burning like torches, then collapsing into piles of soggy ash. The blackened patch lengthened.

Lief stumbled into the center of the burned ground with Barda close behind him. Safe from further attack at last, they tore the remaining fleshbanes from their skin and crushed them into the steaming earth.

"I think we have enough fire beads to clear a path to the other side of the island," Jasmine panted, turning back to them as Kree landed on her shoulder with a triumphant squawk. "But it will be a near thing. The lilies are damp and the fire will not spread."

"That may be just as well," Barda said. "It would be a pity for us to escape being eaten alive only to be burned to cinders."

He looked ruefully down at his blood-soaked leggings. "I think we should try to stop this bleeding before going on."

Jasmine nodded quickly, crouched on the scorched ground, and began pulling balm and bandages from one of her bulging pockets.

"I cannot believe that none of us felt those creatures attacking!" she said, passing bandages to Barda. "If it had not been for Kree seeing what was happening from above, we would have been lost — staggering from loss of blood, unable to escape."

She glanced at Lief and her face changed. "Sit down, Lief!" she said abruptly. "Put your head between your knees. You are pale as a ghost."

"I am all right," Lief muttered. "I mean — I am not faint, only worried. When we were most in danger, I called the diamond dragon. It did not come."

"It is on its way now, no doubt," Barda said. "Never fear, it will be with us by the time we reach the other side of the island."

"If we *do* reach it," Jasmine said grimly, glancing at the lilies waving softly around them. "Those flesh-eating creatures are not going to give up. As soon as the ground cools, they — "

She broke off. She was staring along the short, blackened trail left by the fire. Lief followed her eyes and saw, in the newly burned area, something stretching across the path.

The obstacle looked like part of a huge cage. It had been scorched, but had remained standing while the lilies smothering it had fallen to ashes.

"What is it?" Barda frowned. "A fence? Could it

be that these cursed plants were once kept in a field?"

They began walking quickly along the blackened path. But as they grew closer to the mysterious barrier, their footsteps slowed. There was something very familiar about the barrier's shape. All of them had begun to have grave fears about what was ahead.

"Jasmine — more fire beads," Lief said quietly.

Jasmine bit her lip. She threw fire beads to the left and right of the blackened trail. The blood lilies on both sides of the mysterious object flared up, wilted, and at last fell to ash, revealing what in life they had hidden.

Half-buried in ash and earth was the skeleton of a vast beast with enormous fangs, huge wings, and ribs so mighty that they looked like a tall, curved fence. The beast's huge skull rested peacefully on the long bones of outstretched forelegs. Its long, spiked tail curved gently around its body.

It had died in the hollow where it lay, without a fight.

His throat aching, Lief fell to his knees beside it and gently touched one bare, curved rib. He knew that he had at last found the diamond dragon.

"The fleshbanes ate it while it slept," he muttered. "They stripped it to its bones."

"But why would it have risked sleeping here?" exclaimed Barda. "This island was part of its territory. Surely it knew — "

"Perhaps there were few blood lilies on the island then," Jasmine said soberly. "Perhaps they grew only around the margins — just enough to keep intruders away. The dragon did not count on their spreading so vastly over the centuries."

"No doubt it did not think its sleep would last so long," said Lief.

He was filled with a terrible sadness. His heart ached to think of the mighty beast sinking into enchanted dreams at the bidding of the man it called Dragonfriend, not knowing that it would never wake.

But he knew that he had no time for grief. The dragon was dead. It could not help them to destroy the Sister of the West. He bowed his head and put his hands to the amethyst on the Belt of Deltora.

Veritas! he thought fiercely. *Veritas, I need you! Come to me if you hear me. Come to me if you can!*

He felt the amethyst warm feebly beneath his fingers.

"What is that sound?" Jasmine hissed suddenly.

Lief glanced over his shoulder at her, very startled. Jasmine was frowning, bending forward. Filli was clinging to her collar, his eyes wide, his gray fur standing on end. Kree was standing rigidly on her shoulder, his head on one side. Plainly whatever Jasmine could hear, they could hear, too.

"What sort of sound?" Barda put his hand on his sword.

"A ticking," Jasmine breathed. "There."

She pointed to the huge, scorched skull. Cautiously she moved closer and bent to listen again. Then she kneeled and began scraping away earth and ash from beneath the tip of the mighty lower jaw. Kree squawked uneasily.

"Jasmine, take care!" Barda exclaimed.

But Jasmine did not even look up. By the time Lief and Barda reached her she had made a sizeable hole in the soft earth.

And now all of them could hear the ticking, tapping sound.

"It is under the tip of the jaw," Jasmine breathed, as her companions peered into the hole. "Between the bones of the forelegs. Almost as if — "

And at that moment her eyes widened. Her fingers had touched something.

Lief watched, holding his breath, as slowly she brushed the remaining earth away. And there, clasped between the long white bones of the dragon's forelegs, protected beneath the jaw, was something smooth, pale, and glittering.

It was a giant egg. And within it, something was tapping.

Carefully Jasmine eased the egg out of its hiding place. Earth and ash showered from its shining surface as she lifted it into the sunlight and wordlessly held it out to Lief.

Lief took the egg in his hands. The tapping sound stopped abruptly. For a moment there was silence. Then there was a sharp crack, and the smooth surface split from end to end.

A sharp snout forced its way through the opening. Small clawed feet scrabbled violently. The eggshell separated into halves and fell to the ground. And there, squirming in Lief's hands, was a tiny, perfect, glittering dragon, blinking in the sunlight.

17 ~ The Isle of the Dead

As the companions stared at the tiny beast in awe, Filli edged down Jasmine's arm, his eyes wide with curiosity. The baby dragon snapped its jaws, and Filli hastily retreated. The dragon yawned and stretched its wings. Then it made a harsh, barking sound and snapped its jaws again.

"It wants food," said Jasmine, and began feeling in her pockets.

"I cannot believe this!" exploded Barda, finding his voice at last. "How could an egg remain fresh for centuries?"

"Why not? What do we know of dragon eggs?" Lief murmured, staring at the little creature in fascination. "Plainly the shell was too thick and hard for the fleshbanes to crack. And the Belt roused the baby to hatch, as it would have roused its mother, had she lived. It is wonderful!"

"That is all very well," Barda said. "But what are we to do with it now? We cannot stay here. The flesh-banes are driven away for now, but they will be back."

The dragon barked again, baring its tiny fangs, and hastily Lief flattened his hands a little, to keep his fingers out of harm's way.

Jasmine had found some strips of dried fish and was soaking them in water from her flask.

"Put it in the pocket of your coat, Lief," she said briskly. "It will be comfortable there, near the Belt."

She lifted the flap that covered one of Lief's deep coat pockets and tipped the mess of softened fish inside.

Cautiously Lief lowered his hands until the dragon was beside the pocket, which Jasmine was holding invitingly open. The baby dragon raised its head. Its tiny forked tongue flickered in and out. It barked excitedly, then abruptly slithered into the pocket headfirst. The next moment they heard greedy chewing sounds.

"Good," Jasmine said with satisfaction. "Now we should go."

"Indeed?" snapped Barda. "With a dragon in Lief's pocket? What do you think it will do when all the fish is gone?"

Jasmine shrugged. "I imagine it will go to sleep," she said.

They skirted the diamond dragon's sad skeleton and, with Jasmine in the lead throwing fire beads to clear the way, began to move slowly forward.

The sound of the sea grew louder. The brightness of the Isle of the Dead began to fill the horizon. And at last they stepped out from among the lilies onto the narrow band of flat rock that formed the island's rim.

The archway rose in front of them, craggy and dark. Wind whistled around it. Wild water raged beneath it, churned to thick white foam. The thought of using it as a bridge was terrifying.

"Once the two islands were one, no doubt," Barda said. "The sea divided them — wearing the softer rock away till only the archway spanned the gap. Perhaps one day it, too, will fall."

"Not today, I hope," Lief said grimly.

He was not prepared for this. In his heart, he had always believed that a dragon would carry him and his companions to the Isle of the Dead.

But the dragon of the diamond was no more. In its place was a baby far too small to carry anyone. And there was no sign of the dragon of the amethyst. Veritas was still too weak to fly, it seemed.

"Lief! We must move from here," Barda said urgently.

Lief glanced behind him. Fleshbanes had begun to creep down from the lilies on either side of the burned path. Already they were seething in a great semicircle at the edge of the rock where the companions stood.

Hastily he began to climb, with Barda and Jasmine close behind him. He heard the roar of flame as Jasmine threw more fire beads down after them.

The arch began to curve over the sea. Lief flattened himself against the rock and crawled on his belly, trying not to think of the wind tearing at him, the sea roaring below.

He did not dare look up, even when he realized that he must have reached the highest point of the arch. But still he was aware of the blinding glare of the island ahead.

And evil, he thought. *Evil and malice.*

He could feel it, burning into his skin.

He began to move downwards, picking his way along, determined not to slip. And slowly he became aware of a sound mingling with the roaring of the sea — a low ringing sound, growing louder and louder, boring into his ears and his mind.

The song of the Sister of the West.

Sweat broke out on Lief's brow. His knees felt weak. But he forced himself to move on, to move towards the glaring light, towards the terrible sound.

Abruptly the slope became steeper. And then, without warning, the rough rock beneath Lief's hands and knees changed to a surface as slippery as ice.

With a shout of warning he slithered forward. He could not stop himself, could not even slow. When at last he came to a halt, he desperately rubbed his watering eyes, trying to focus. He could hardly believe what he was seeing.

He was not far from the peak of an island that looked as if it was made of shining glass. There was not a tree or a bush or a blade of grass to be seen. Every surface was hard, smooth, and slippery. Every surface blazed in the sunlight.

And every surface seemed to vibrate with the terrible, low ringing of the Sister of the West.

Lief lifted his eyes to the island's peak. A huge cave gaped there — the only dark spot in all that world of glittering light.

There was the source of the sound. There the Sister lay hidden. He knew it without question.

Slowly and carefully he stood up. He looked down and his head swam. Far below him a great mat of seaweed drifted like a blot of ink in an ocean of brilliant blue, and creamy foam swirled among the jagged rocks of the shore.

He heard voices and turned. His companions were picking their way towards him, Kree flying slowly above their heads.

Only then did Lief remember the baby dragon. With a feeling of dread he lifted the flap of his pocket and peered inside. But the banging and jolting of his slide to the island had not disturbed the baby at all. It was curled up, breathing peacefully, fast asleep.

Barda and Jasmine reached him. Both were squinting in the glare, and both looked exhausted, as though already the place was draining their strength.

No doubt I look the same, Lief thought. *And we have only just begun.*

An overwhelming wave of despair rolled over him.

"I do not know why we are here," he muttered. "Without a dragon to aid us, we cannot win. And there is no escape for us now."

Jasmine and Barda looked at each other. Then Barda took Lief's arm, turned him around, and pointed towards the ground.

Lief shaded his eyes and looked. And there he saw, not two steps from where he was standing, a flat gray stone jutting from the glittering rock. It was a warning stone very like those they had seen in the

east and the north, though more pitted by the weather and bearing a different verse.

Lief turned away from the dread thing, gritting his teeth. "I am a fool!" he muttered. "Of course there would be a warning stone here, as there was in the east and the north! How could I have let it take me un-awares, and cast me into despair?"

"Do not blame yourself for that, Lief," Jasmine said restlessly, glancing at the standing stone, then quickly looking away. "All along, this quest has felt different from our times in the east and the north. For one thing, we have not been troubled by the guardian of the Sister of the West — if indeed there *is* a guard-ian at all."

Lief made no reply. He had his own grave ideas about the guardian of the west, but he did not wish to speak of them. He did not want to think what they might mean.

Gingerly, their boots slipping dangerously on the treacherous rocks, the three edged past the grim stone and began to climb towards the peak.

It was slow and perilous work, and every mo-ment it grew harder as the evil power streaming from the cave above grew stronger, pressing them down. Kree fluttered awkwardly ahead of them, his feathers ruffled, making no sound.

They stopped to rest on a flat rock that shone like a mirror. Her face strained and white beneath the streaks of ash and blood, Jasmine ran her hand over the glossy surface.

"It is almost as if this has been painted with something clear, like lacquer — painted many, many times," she said, plainly trying to occupy her mind with something that did not fill her with fear. "I am sure there is ordinary rock deep beneath this surface. When you look closely, you can see it."

"Why would anyone paint rock?" Barda grunted, wiping sweat from his furrowed brow. "Jasmine, I have been thinking of what you said — about there being no guardian of the west. Has it not struck you that Ava, who was to be so helpful to us, according to her brother, nearly killed us twice?"

Barda had voiced Lief's secret thoughts. Lief's heart sank. He stared down at the blue sea crawling far below. He noticed idly that the drifting mat of seaweed that had looked like an inkblot was gone, and wondered what had become of it.

"First, Ava gave us a boat that sprang mysterious leaks in the middle of the channel, so we nearly drowned," Barda went on. "Then she sent us to the scarlet island without breathing a word of the flesh-eating horrors that infest it."

Jasmine frowned.

"Indeed," Lief said reluctantly. "I fear we must accept it. Either Ava is not what Tom thinks she is, or — "

"Or Tom himself is as much a servant of the Shadow Lord as his brother and sister," Barda broke in heavily. "And to me this seems the more likely. Ava let slip that all three of them share minds. Surely, if she had joined Jack on the dark side, Tom could not help but know it."

He was right. Lief knew that he was right. But he did not want to believe it. With all his heart, he did not want to believe it!

Jasmine's eyes darkened. "If Ava is the guardian of the west, then she must sense we have reached the Isle," she said. "And that means — "

Suddenly Kree screeched — screeched wildly, rising into the air, his beak gaping wide.

The companions scrambled to their feet in alarm.

And saw, clambering up the glittering rocks towards them, a huge, gold-brown beast with flippers for forelegs and a great mane of loose, flabby strips of skin, pimpled and mottled like seaweed.

The fins of the beast's mighty tail lashed the rock. Its thick blue tongue, furred with bristles, lolled from its cavernous mouth. Where it crawled, it left a trail of silver slime, glistening in the sunlight.

Its tiny eyes looked up at the companions, burning with fury. Its terrible mouth opened wider, and it roared.

"Climb!" Barda bellowed. "Climb for your lives!"

18 ~ The Sister of the West

U p, up they climbed, hands grasping frantically, feet sliding and slipping. But the beast was close behind them, heaving its vast body effortlessly over the shining rock. Its roars were thunderous in their ears. The smell of it — the dank odor of the sea — filled their nostrils. Again and again its long, bristled tongue shot out, slapping at their heels.

"It is sorcery! Ava — in another form!" Barda shouted.

"No," Lief panted. "It was in the sea — as we approached Ava's shop. I thought — it was seaweed. Ava was inside then — sitting by her fire."

Kree was diving at the monster's head, snapping and screeching, golden eyes ablaze. But the beast was paying no attention. It did not try to snatch Kree from the air, did not falter for a moment. Its rage-filled eyes

167

were fixed on those who had dared to set foot on its territory, who had dared climb its rocks, glazed by the hardened slime of centuries.

The companions' chests were aching. Their minds were blurred by pain and fear. Above them loomed the darkness of the cave, and from it streamed the evil power that every moment weakened them.

At the cave mouth the chase would be over. At the cave mouth they would have to turn and fight.

But they could not win. They all knew it. The song of the Sister of the West would beat them to their knees. The rage of the beast would overwhelm them.

Lief hauled himself up onto the broad ledge that lay before the cave. He heard Barda and Jasmine clamber up beside him. He struggled to rise, fumbling for his sword.

His eyes dimmed. He could hardly see. Again he tried to get to his feet, but a great weight seemed to be pressing him down.

The monster was bellowing just below him. He could hear its vast body, its trailing mane, slapping on the rock. He tried to draw his feet back, imagining the long blue tongue curling around his ankle, pulling him down.

Then Jasmine screamed.

Lief thrilled with pure terror. He struggled to his knees, then to his feet, and his sword was in his hand.

Wind tore at his hair and beat on his face. Wildly he looked around for Jasmine.

And she was standing beside him. She was standing there unharmed, her dagger raised, her hair flying around her head, eyes wide with shock.

For below, a battle was raging. The mottled beast had reared up, its vast body rigid, the fleshy strips of its mane swollen and whipping around its head, its terrible teeth bared. And clawing at it from the air, great purple wings blocking out the sun, purple fire belching from snarling jaws, was Veritas, the amethyst dragon.

At first it seemed that the monster's death was certain. How could any beast of land and sea, however vast, however savage, defeat a dragon?

But Veritas was weakening. Lief could see it — see it in the dimming of the purple scales, the ragged beat of the leathery wings. The flight from the Sleeping Dunes had nearly exhausted what little strength the dragon had. And the monster was defending its territory. Its rage was terrible.

He watched in terrified suspense as Veritas lurched downward, talons spread.

The monster's tongue lashed out, curled around the dragon's leg, and jerked backward. Wings beating vainly, the dragon fell, crashing to the rock. And then the beast was upon it, teeth like knives tearing savagely at the pale, exposed underbelly.

The dragon roared. Flame gushed from its mouth and seared the monster's mottled hide. The monster lifted its head and bellowed its pain and fury, dragon's blood dripping from its jaws.

Then the dragon was twisting away from it, launching itself awkwardly into the air. Blood streaming from its terrible wound, it rose higher, higher. The beast below reared up, but could not catch it.

Lief, Barda, and Jasmine fell back, beaten by the wind of mighty wings as the massive purple shape rose, rose to hover beside them, then dropped heavily to the ground in front of the cave.

The song of the Sister of the West rang on, mingling with the bellows of the beast.

Slowly the companions crawled to their feet. "Lief, see to the dragon," Barda rasped. "It is all that can save you now. We will defend . . . for as long as . . ."

He could not finish. He was swaying. His sword hung from his hand as if it was too heavy for him to lift. But still he stood facing attack, and Jasmine stood with him, though her eyes were blank and her shoulders sagged.

Lief staggered to the dragon's head, fell to his knees beside it, and pressed his cheek to the dimming scales of the neck. With all his might he willed the strength of the amethyst to flow through his body and into the wounded beast.

He could hear the beat of the dragon's mighty

heart. His own heart leaped as he saw the faded scales brightening.

The voice of Veritas whispered in his mind.

Where is the dragon of the diamond?

"The dragon of the diamond is dead," Lief said.

Ah . . .

Lief looked back to where Barda and Jasmine stood together, bowed by the evil power of the cave.

The beast still had not reached them. It was raging just below, lunging upwards, then falling back, wallowing in a mess of dragon's blood and its own slime.

Why does it wait? Lief thought in amazement.

"The evil in the cave holds it back," hissed Veritas, as though he had spoken aloud. "It will force its way up here at last, but it will not enter the cave. There we will be safe."

The massive body quaked, and Lief realized with astonishment that the dragon had laughed.

"Safe! Ah, that is a great joke," Veritas snorted. "Dragonfriend would have liked that. Move aside!"

Lief moved hastily out of the way. As the dragon heaved itself to its feet he saw that the wound on its belly had closed. The long tear was still raw and red, but the blood had ceased to flow.

Jasmine and Barda turned. Lief beckoned urgently and they began stumbling towards him.

The mottled beast below them roared in rage. It reared, and with a mighty effort threw itself upwards.

But it was too late. By the time it reached the place where its enemies had stood only moments before, they had gone — gone where it could not follow.

The darkness of the cave had swallowed them up.

✳

At first Lief could see nothing, but gradually he realized that the cave was dark only in contrast to the blinding light outside. Slowly he began to make out the shape of the dragon, the shapes of his friends, and the walls of a huge cavern shrouded in spiderweb.

The floor beneath his feet was thick with dust, but beneath the dust it shone like the rocks outside. Once then, long ago, this cavern had been the den of the monster of the Isle — the same beast now bellowing outside, or that beast's ancestors.

Lief's ears throbbed with the sound of the Sister of the West pulsing from the back of the cave.

But he could hear the dragon, too. The dragon was close beside him. He could hear its heart beating. He could hear its hissing breath.

Behind him, his companions stumbled and groaned.

Lief wet his lips. "Jasmine. Barda. Come no farther," he said, his voice a croak he hardly recognized as his own. "The dragon and I will go on alone."

Neither Barda nor Jasmine replied. But still they followed him.

Step by painful step they struggled on. Every step was an effort. Every breath was pain.

Lief's sword was in his hand, but he doubted he could lift his arm. It was as if the Sister's song had penetrated every bone, every muscle of his body, poisoning his blood, spreading an aching weakness.

Then suddenly the end of the cave was in sight.

Lief's skin crawled. A dim shape hunched there. A dim, pale shape that was the source of the sound, the source of the evil, the source of the poison.

He forced himself forward, bracing himself against what he might see.

Then he felt the dragon shudder. He heard the dragon's heart begin to thunder in its chest.

And he saw what the pale shape was.

It was a man, sitting on a carved throne of stone — a man so ancient that he seemed almost transparent. A long white beard trailed down his chest. Long white hair fell to his waist. His rough garments were gray with age and dust. A spiderweb floated about him. It netted his gaunt face, sealed his eyelids, and covered the bone-thin hands that rested on the arms of his throne.

But he was alive. Shallow breaths stirred the white threads that spanned his withered lips.

And the Sister of the West was inside him. From the frail chest, pure evil poured.

Lief's head was roaring. He could not breathe.

He heard the sound of Barda's sword clattering to the ground behind him.

The man's eyes opened beneath the veil of web.

The hazy gray stare fixed on Lief for a moment. Then it drifted away, to rest on the dragon. Web threads broke and drifted as the pale lips parted. The voice came, like dead leaves rustling.

"Veritas."

The dragon was quivering all over.

"Doran," it hissed.

Lief's heart seemed to leap into his throat. Suddenly his mind was burning with the memory of the Shadow Lord's evil, gloating voice.

The upstart has the fate he deserves . . .

With horror such as he had never known, Lief stared at the ancient, tormented being on the throne.

So this had been the fate of the upstart, the one who had dared to try to foil the plan of the Four Sisters. This had been the punishment of Doran the Dragonlover. Enslaved by the Shadow Lord's sorcery, he had been condemned to centuries of half-life as the guardian of the very evil he had tried to destroy.

The gray eyes moved to meet Lief's. The lips opened. And again came the faint, rasping voice.

"You — wear the Belt of Deltora. You — are the king."

"Yes," Lief said. "I am Lief, son of Endon and Sharn, heir of Adin." It was hard to speak. The power of the Sister of the West was beating him down. But his heart was aching with pity and rage equally as he gazed into those suffering eyes, and he made himself go on. "And you are Doran the Dragonlover, beloved by the tribes of the underworld, savior of the dragons of Deltora. The one whose map led me here."

Doran's eyes flickered. A tiny spark seemed to leap within them.

"The Four Sisters . . ." he whispered.

"Only two remain," Lief said. "The Sisters of the West and of the South."

"The Sister of the West is within me," rasped Doran. "Kill me and destroy it, as I could not."

"No!" groaned Veritas. "No, Dragonfriend!"

The gray eyes warmed. The dry lips curved into a smile.

"This is not life, but living death, my friend," Doran said gently. "To me, true death would be the greatest gift. Would you deny me?"

The dragon bowed its head.

"I will die knowing that my life was not in vain," Doran murmured. "I will die knowing that the Enemy may be at last defeated. And I will die in happiness knowing that you live, Veritas. You and your kind . . ."

His voice trailed away. His faded eyes grew puzzled. "But . . . I was forgetting," he said. "This is the land of the diamond. Where is — ?"

"That dragon is dead," Veritas said stolidly.

Shadows of grief crossed Doran's ancient face. "And so, despite all, her tribe has ended," he said. "I would give much that it was not so."

Lief could not bear it. He forced his hand to his pocket and lifted out the baby dragon. It seemed to him larger and heavier than it had before.

The baby made a small, complaining sound, but did not wake as Lief held it where Doran could see it.

The amethyst dragon moved uneasily.

But Doran's face was transformed. Relief and love lit his eyes as he gazed at the small, glittering creature in Lief's hands.

"Make haste, Veritas, I beg you," he said suddenly. "Give me your gift . . . in this moment . . ."

The dragon of the amethyst bent forward.

"Farewell, Doran," it said softly. "I will see you again, in the place above the clouds. There we will be young, and we will fly together once more."

"Veritas, my true friend, we will," said the man.

The dragon moved closer, bending its neck till its head masked the figure on the throne. It paused for a moment, then drew a deep, shuddering breath.

And when it moved back, Doran's face was peaceful, like a face that was sleeping, and the gossamer threads around his mouth no longer stirred.

"What — ?" Lief heard Jasmine choke.

"He is gone," whispered the dragon. "I took his breath, as he wished."

Freed at last from its bondage, the ancient body

on the throne began to crumble. A few coins, a silver flask, and a strange, many-colored stone rolled to the ground as Doran's garments, hair, flesh, and bones fell to dust. But the horror that had been concealed within him remained.

There on the carved rock, revealed at last, was a rippling, jellylike thing, creamy white and veined with pink and gray.

Malice streamed from its shapeless form, and its song was poison, hatred, doom, and despair.

The Sister of the West.

19 ~ Vows

The dragon roared, and in that thunderous sound was all the rage, grief, and hatred of its aching heart. Fire gushed from its snarling jaws, and the soft thing on the rock throne writhed and shrank as violet flame engulfed it.

Pressed hard against the dragon's leg, the diamond baby sheltered in the crook of his arm, Lief gripped the amethyst. In a daze of heat and fear, he felt the ancient power of the gem flow through him, pouring strength into the beast.

Again Veritas roared, and again, till the throne was a bath of purple fire. The shapeless thing in the fire darkened and smoked. The veins netting its surface swelled. The low ringing sound faltered, then rose to an ear-splitting screech.

Lief screwed his eyes shut and pressed his burning face against the dragon's scales.

Abruptly, the screeching stopped. The dragon, too, fell silent. The cavern seemed to echo with a silence that was somehow more terrible than sound.

Lief felt the beast draw a deep breath. Then he heard a long, low hissing and felt a blast of white heat so intense that he fell to his knees.

There was a sharp crack. Lief opened his eyes as the hissing sound dwindled and died.

The throne had split in two. And where the Sister of the West had been, there was only a dull gray stain on the rock.

"So that is done," Veritas said soberly. "Lief, gather Dragonfriend's possessions. They must not remain here. And nor must we. Now that the evil has gone, the beast outside will claim its den once more."

Lief staggered up. The baby dragon in the crook of his arm stretched and yawned.

The flat, purple eyes blinked.

"You will never know Dragonfriend, small dragon of the diamond," Veritas said. "But your life made his last breath joyful, and so I will tell you, in times to come."

*

In less than a minute, the dragon was bursting from the cave with Lief, Barda, and Jasmine clinging to its neck. The baby dragon had been crammed back into Lief's pocket. Filli was invisible beneath Jasmine's collar. But Kree flew below the dragon's wings, his golden eyes fixed to the ground, ready to attack.

There was no need. The beast of the Isle had retreated from the peak during the battle with the Sister of the West and was only now sliding back onto the ledge before the cave.

It roared as they escaped, but could not reach them in time to harm them. The last they saw of it, it was disappearing into the cavern, the den of its ancestors and part of its domain again at last. It had forgotten them already.

"You were right, Lief," Jasmine shouted against the rushing of the wind as they soared over the scarlet island and on across the channel. "The beast was not Ava. Ava is there — outside her shop! But what is she doing?"

Lief looked past Jasmine's shoulder. In the distance he could see Ava's feathered cloak flapping in the wind as she hurried towards the back of the shop building. Ava was carrying a large bag over one arm, and dragging three packs behind her.

"The wretch!" roared Barda. "She has sensed we escaped the Isle! She is fleeing, and taking our packs with her! She has a good boat hidden in the shed behind the house, you may depend upon it. See? The door is standing open!"

Lief could not answer. He had just seen something that Barda had not. Directly in front of them, anchored just beyond the tip of the point, was *The Lady Luck*.

Lief felt something deep within him tremble. At

the same moment he realized with dread that the dragon was losing height. It was panting with exhaustion.

"Just a little farther, Veritas!" he urged.

"I — will — try," the dragon gasped. But even as it spoke, it sank lower.

The ragged shape of the ship grew larger. Lief shut his eyes and held his breath as they passed over it.

He felt the dragon drop farther. He felt spray on his face. Then there was a hard jolt.

Lief opened his eyes on dry land. Dizzy with relief, he slid from the dragon's neck.

His companions had scrambled down before him. Both were running towards Ava, shouting at her to stop.

Lief was seized by a terrible sense of foreboding.

"Barda! Jasmine! No!" he called. But they did not hear him. He glanced at Veritas and knew that the dragon could not help him. It lay where it had fallen, eyes tightly closed.

Lief began to run. In horror he saw Jasmine reach Ava and catch at her arm. He saw Ava swing around. He saw the glint of steel.

And in seconds Jasmine was off the ground, a bony arm around her neck, the point of a knife pressed to her throat.

The movement had been all too familiar. With sick terror Lief saw the feathered hood fall back.

The face revealed was powdered dead white to the lips. Long brown hair whipped in the wind. But the black silk band no longer covered the eyes.

And those blazing, hollow eyes were the eyes of Laughing Jack.

"Keep back, or the girl dies!" he snarled.

Lief and Barda stopped in their tracks.

Filli darted from beneath Jasmine's collar and bit the man's wrist. At the same moment the point of Kree's sharp beak struck his head.

But Laughing Jack did not flinch. Perhaps he had not even noticed the attacks. For now Lief could see the heavy sweat of panic that was dissolving the powder on his face and causing the dye to run from his hair.

The man was terrified. And this made him more dangerous than ever.

"Let her go, Jack!" Lief shouted. "Let her go, and we will let *you* go, to run and hide where you will!"

From the boathouse came the sound of horses rearing and neighing shrilly.

Jasmine cried out and began to struggle. The bony arm tightened around her throat, and blood ran from beneath the point of the knife.

"Let her go, Laughing Jack!" Lief shouted again, willing Jasmine to keep still. "You have no time to waste here with us. Your evil master ordered you here to make doubly certain we would die before we even set foot on the Isle of the Dead. You came, despite your fear of this coast, because you had failed him in the north and you had to win back his favor."

Laughing Jack's eyes burned, but he said nothing.

Lief pressed on. "But now you have failed the Shadow Lord yet again. The Sister of the West is destroyed, and soon he will know it. If he finds you, nothing can save you!"

The hollow eyes suddenly widened, and Lief's stomach turned over as he saw flickering within them a spark of hope.

"I have a bargain for you, king," Laughing Jack snarled. "The life of your little comrade for the Belt of Deltora — the one thing that may save me yet."

Lief hesitated. Then he bowed his head as if in defeat and unfastened the Belt. He placed it on the ground and stepped back.

"Very well," he muttered. "Take it. Only let Jasmine go."

His heart sank as Laughing Jack shook his head.

"Oh no," the man sneered. "Do you think I am a fool to be taken in by that trick? I know I cannot touch that cursed Belt without harm."

He took a step back, pulling Jasmine with him. With his free hand he felt behind him, into the boathouse. Finding what he was looking for, he jerked viciously.

With a clatter of hooves the four black horses came slowly into view, dragging the heavy wagon behind them. Jack cursed them and heaved again at the bridle of the one closest to him until the wagon was fully out of the shed.

Dragging Jasmine to the back of the wagon, he flung open the door. He pulled out what looked like a bundle of rags and threw it to the ground at his feet.

The bundle moaned. In horror Lief saw that it was a thin woman, cruelly bound and shivering with cold. Her face was powdered to a deathly paleness. Her tangled hair was brown. Her sightless eyes were gleaming white.

"My worthless sister, Ava," snarled Laughing Jack. "It was because of her that I was ordered to come here, and make sure my brother Tom knew of it. My master knew Tom would get word to you, and try to help you through Ava. Tom has always felt responsible for my doings, however he pretends otherwise."

He gave a sneering laugh.

"Tom played into my hands to perfection! What use was Ava's famous gift when she felt my approach? She could not protect herself from me. And so I took her place. Dressed in her loathsome garments, I waited for you to come to me. In her name I gave you the advice that should by rights have sent you to your deaths!"

"But your plan failed, Jack," whispered the woman on the ground. "I saw it would be so. I warned you — "

Laughing Jack silenced her with a vicious kick.

He had not taken his eyes from Lief, and now his mouth stretched into the familiar death's-head grin.

"I kept Ava alive in case she could be of use to me," he said. "And now, it seems, she can. Put the Belt around her waist. She will carry it — until I reach a place where I can dispose of her, and rid myself of two nuisances at one time and earn back my master's favor."

"Beware, brother," muttered Ava, her white eyes gleaming. "The path you are treading leads to ruin. I see death and decay around you."

"Indeed?" sneered Laughing Jack. "Save your party tricks for those who they impress, my dear sister."

Lief felt deathly chill. He glanced at Barda's face, set hard as iron. He looked into Jasmine's eyes, bright as green fire. Then he met Laughing Jack's hollow glare.

"You cannot win, James Gant," he said softly.

Laughing Jack flinched. "Do not call me by that name," he snarled.

"That was the name you used when you tried this trick before, long ago," Lief went on, still in that same soft, level tone. "Remember what happened then, and know this. I will no more give you the Belt of Deltora than Red Han would put out the Bone Point Light. And Jasmine will not ask me to betray my people, any more than Verity would ask her father to betray his trust."

Laughing Jack's grin had gone. Hair dye mixed with sweat ran down his face, making dark tracks through the white powder that masked his face.

"Remember the lesson you learned at Bone Point," Lief said, holding his gaze. "There are some things that people of honor will not do, no matter what you threaten." He picked up the Belt and fastened it again around his waist.

For a moment Laughing Jack simply stared. Then he spat.

"So be it," he sneered. "Then if I cannot have the Belt of Deltora, I will exchange the life of the girl for safe passage away from here. You say you are people of honor. If that is true, you will not follow me, wherever I may go."

"We will not," Lief said grimly, ignoring Jasmine's eyes, which were darting in anguish at the horses. "I swear it."

Jasmine struggled violently, ignoring the choking grip around her throat. She tore at her garments, as if trying to reach her dagger. Possessions fell from her pockets — a comb, her jar of balm, and, with a soft chinking sound, the Dread Gnomes' money bag.

"Ah," breathed Laughing Jack. He snatched up the money bag and patted it, grinning broadly.

"I think it is only fair that I am paid for my inconvenience," he announced. "So this gold is mine now. All mine."

And suddenly, everything seemed to stop.

Lief caught his breath. Jasmine's eyes burned in savage triumph.

Laughing Jack's grin grew fixed. And then his own voice came floating to him across the water, echoing through the years.

All the gold is yours, my loyal crew. . . . If I take one piece of it for my own, I myself will take to the oars. I swear it on my soul!

His face became a mask of horrified disbelief. He stared at the money bag in his hand. He screamed.

Then he was gone, and all that remained where he had stood was Ava's feathered cloak, collapsing silently onto the ground.

Shuddering, Lief swung around to look at the place where he had last seen *The Lady Luck*. The ship was still visible. It was very near. And it was no longer deserted, no longer still, no longer silent.

I hear your words, James Gant, and they will bind you . . .

The ringing voice was Verity's. The wooden figurehead was turning, turning to gaze with clear, painted eyes at the skull-faced man scrabbling on the deck in an agony of fear. And without emotion, hard as the wood of which it was made, it watched as rotting arms reached for him, and dragged him below.

20 ~ Old Friends

For a moment there was utter stillness. Then there was a creaking groan, and slowly the hulk of *The Lady Luck* tilted and sank beneath the surface of the sea. Great bubbles rose as it slipped into the depths, and as it disappeared Lief saw that the prow was empty. The figurehead had gone.

He heard a strange mixture of sounds behind him — a whispering sound like sand falling, the snorting of horses, the clattering of hoofs, and Jasmine's loud squeal of joy.

And when he turned to look, he saw that the wagon had fallen into dust, and three horses stood pawing the ground among Laughing Jack's possessions, still scarcely able to believe they were free.

Only one horse, the smallest, was still black. The second was a powerful chestnut. The last was golden, with a creamy white mane and tail. She pawed the ground and whinnied to Lief delightedly.

"Honey!" he breathed, holding out his hand to her in disbelief. "Bella! Swift! How . . . ?"

Then he shook his head. He knew that he would never find out exactly how Laughing Jack had come to own the horses the companions had last seen at the edge of the Forests of Silence. Honey, Bella, and Swift could not tell them, and the guards who had been in charge of them were all dead.

Perhaps Laughing Jack had found the horses straying. More likely a villager had caught them, and had later been forced to give them to the moneylender in payment of a debt.

It did not really matter. All that mattered was that their suffering at Laughing Jack's hands was over.

He turned to Jasmine, who was hugging Swift, her face a picture of delight. Now he knew why she had not been able to forget Laughing Jack's horses.

"You knew the horses were ours, Jasmine!" he said. "You have known ever since we saw Laughing Jack's wagon at The Funnel, on the way to Shadowgate!"

"And you did not tell us!" Barda exclaimed. He was cutting Ava's bonds and helping her to her feet, while Bella rubbed his shoulder with her velvety nose.

Jasmine shrugged. "I saw no point in making you as miserable as I was myself," she said. "We could do nothing to save the horses then."

189

She shook her head, her eyes darkening as she remembered.

"But I wanted to tell you. It would have been bad enough leaving any beast in slavery to Laughing Jack. But it was agony leaving our own three horses — "

Three horses . . .

Lief looked around, startled. "But there were *four!*" he exclaimed. "Where is the last?"

"Here," said a gruff voice from behind the horses.

And then, astounded, the companions saw, climbing unsteadily to his feet, a big man with a rough red beard and eyes as blue as the sea.

In that moment they understood how Laughing Jack had spent the largest part of the sorcerer's powers given to him by his evil master. He had chosen to use it for spite — revenging himself on the one man who had defied his will.

For they all recognized the man standing, swaying, before them. He was Red Han, the lost keeper of the Bone Point Light.

✳

Much later, when all the stories had been told, Bella, Honey, and Swift had been fed and stabled in the boat shed, and Red Han and Ava had fallen gratefully to sleep in Ava's cottage, Lief, Barda, and Jasmine sat with the amethyst dragon, looking out to sea. The baby diamond dragon was beside them, gobbling fresh fish for the first time in its life.

The sun was setting as Lief opened Doran's silver flask.

The flask was filled to the brim with sand. And hidden within the sand, as Lief had suspected, was a rolled scrap of parchment — the fourth and last part of Doran's map.

AND IF AT LAST
THEIR VOICES CEASE
THE LAND WILL FIND
A FINAL PEACE.

Lief shook his head, dumbfounded. He had been certain that the Sister of the South would be in some wild, deserted place. But it was not so. It was in the city of Del, where their quest had begun!

"No wonder poor Josef is half mad with worry," Jasmine murmured. "If he has guessed that the fourth Sister is in Del — "

"We cannot be sure that he has," Barda broke in.

"He may only have guessed that the Isle of the Dead was our third goal. According to Lief, Josef knows of the blood lilies and fleshbanes on the red island. Surely that would be worry enough."

"Josef knows where the Sister of the South is," Lief said flatly. "He has worked it out. As we could have done ourselves."

He took out the other three parts of the map and fitted them together on the rock.

"You see?" he said, pointing at each of the four Sister signs in turn. "The Sister of the East was hidden at Dragon's Nest, Deltora's most eastern point. The Sister of the North was at Shadowgate, Deltora's most northern point. The Sister of the West was on the Isle of the Dead, our most western point . . ."

"And the Sister of the South is in Del, Deltora's most southern point," Barda finished heavily. "Yes, I see. The Enemy was taking no chances. He circled the land with evil."

They sat for a moment in silence. The sky flamed as the sun slipped below the horizon.

Barda felt in his pocket and pulled out the little puzzle box. "At least I can now look at the sea without the fear of seeing *The Lady Luck* haunting us," he said.

"I do not think it ever *was* haunting us," Lief replied. "It was haunting Laughing Jack. And now it has him, forever."

He winced at the memory of those rotting hands

pulling Laughing Jack below. He took care not to look at Jasmine.

"I do not regret what I did," she said defiantly. "It was his choice to pick up the gold and claim it for himself. All I did was remember what you had told me of his oath, and make sure he saw the money bag."

"And that was very fortunate," said Barda, playing idly with the box. "If that villain had escaped, he would have taken not only our horses with him, but Red Han as well. Now the Bone Point Light can shine again. And Verity is released from the curse. She can rest in peace."

"As can Dragonfriend," the amethyst dragon murmured, rousing itself. "Yes. We have done well. It is a good ending."

"Not quite an ending for us, I fear," Lief said shortly. "We have more to do."

He glanced down at the four parts of the map lying on the rock before him. In the dimness, the Sister sign beside the city of Del seemed to writhe like a snake.

Suddenly he was tired to his bones. His exhausted brain teemed with questions for which he had no answers.

What if we fail at this, the last hurdle? he thought. *What if we have saved all the rest of the kingdom, but we cannot save our home? How could it be that the fourth Sister is in Del? Where in heaven's name can it be hidden?*

How can we even begin to find it? And why do I feel, like Josef, that there is something I am not seeing? Some further mystery . . .

Barda gave a grunt of surprise and held out the puzzle box. A third little rod was sticking out of the box's carved side.

"I have no idea what I did to make that happen!" Barda complained, tugging at the box's lid. "And look at that! Three locks undone, and *still* it will not open. Curse the thing! I should throw it into the sea!"

"If you did, you would be sorry," the dragon said shrewdly. "You would never know what was inside."

Barda snorted. But Lief noticed that he pushed the box safely back into his pocket.

Tomorrow he will try again, Lief thought. *Whatever he says, he will keep trying until all the locks are open and all the secrets are revealed. But for now he will put the problem out of his mind.*

It came to him that he should do the same. Slowly he picked up the four map fragments and put them away.

"Very good," Veritas said approvingly.

Lief looked up in surprise.

"There is a time to plan, a time to act, and a time to rest," the dragon said. "It is wise to know which is which."

Its eyes gleamed like dull purple stars in the gloom. Slowly Lief felt his tense muscles relax.

He felt the baby diamond dragon creep close to him, and curl itself to sleep as near to the Belt as it could.

Tonight is the time to rest, he thought. *Tomorrow is the time to plan. After that — we will go to Del. And there, where this all began, it will end.*

Then he thought no more, but only sat watching the empty sea, while the quiet night fell.

THE SISTER OF
THE SOUTH

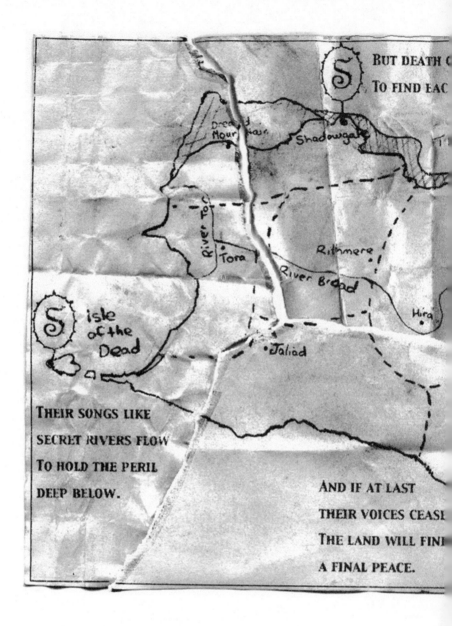

BUT DEATH (
TO FIND EAC

THEIR SONGS LIKE
SECRET RIVERS FLOW
TO HOLD THE PERIL
DEEP BELOW.

AND IF AT LAST
THEIR VOICES CEASE
THE LAND WILL FIN
A FINAL PEACE.

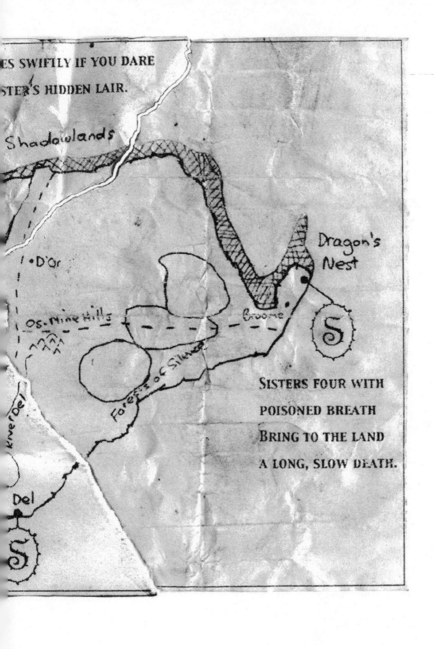

ES SWIFTLY IF YOU DARE
STER'S HIDDEN LAIR.

Shadowlands

D'Or

Os-Mine Hills

Forests of Silence

River Del

Del

Dragon's Nest

Broome

SISTERS FOUR WITH
POISONED BREATH
BRING TO THE LAND
A LONG, SLOW DEATH.

Contents

The story so far . . .

Lief, Barda, and Jasmine are on a quest to find and destroy the Four Sisters, evil Shadow Lord creations that have been poisoning Deltora for centuries. They learned of the Four Sisters plot through the Enemy's crystal, left in the palace in Del after the Belt of Deltora was restored and the Shadow Lord's tyranny over Deltora ended.

To succeed in his quest, Lief must wake Deltora's last dragons from their enchanted sleep, for only when the power of a dragon joins the power of a gem in the magic Belt of Deltora can a Sister be destroyed.

Centuries ago, Deltora's dragons, fierce protectors of their land, were hunted almost to extinction by the Enemy's seven Ak-Baba. When only one dragon from each gem territory remained, the explorer Doran the Dragonlover persuaded the beasts to sleep in safety until a king wearing the Belt of Deltora called them to wake.

Too late, Doran learned of the Shadow Lord's plan to use the Four Sisters to starve Deltora's people. Now that the dragons had gone, there was nothing to stop the Enemy from putting the Sisters into place. Doran tried to warn of the danger, but was not believed. Leaving a map showing where he thought the Sisters were, he set out to find proof. But the Enemy wreaked a hideous revenge upon him on the Isle of the Dead, and his map was torn into four parts and hidden.

Despite terrible dangers, Lief, Barda, and Jasmine

have managed to find all the fragments of Doran's map and have destroyed the Sisters of the East, North, and West. They have also found Red Han, the lost keeper of the magic Bone Point lighthouse, raising hopes that trading ships loaded with badly needed food may now sail to Deltora across the western seas.

But the companions cannot rest. To their amazement and horror, the final map fragment has shown that the last Sister, the Sister of the South, is in their home city of Del. This is very bad news. Jasmine's father, the legendary Resistance leader Doom, is already struggling to prevent Del's starving people from sinking into despair. Lief's mother, Sharn, who might bring the people comfort, is still in Tora, Del's magic sister city in the west. Messages from Josef, the old palace librarian, are inceasingly confused and frantic. And wherever they are, whatever they do, it seems that the Shadow Lord's eyes are upon them.

Now read on . . .

1 - Bad Tidings

The grave of Doran the Dragonlover contained only his silver flask and a strange, gleaming, many-colored stone. These ancient objects were all that remained of Deltora's greatest explorer.

The grave was in as wild a place as Doran could have wished — looking over the windswept rock that pointed to the Isle of the Dead, where the Sister of the West had been destroyed.

Lief, Barda, and Jasmine stood at the graveside. With them were Ava the fortune-teller and Red Han, the lost keeper of the Bone Point Light. There were also two dragons — Veritas, dragon of the amethyst, and the orphaned baby dragon of the diamond, who was as yet unnamed. And it was these two, Lief thought, whose presence would have pleased Doran the most.

After careful thought, Veritas had scratched the lettering upon the grave marker.

IN MEMORY OF DORAN,
EXPLORER AND HERO,
KEEPER OF PRECIOUS
SECRETS, FRIEND
TO THE DRAGONS OF
DELTORA.

"It is fitting that we used his true name," Veritas said quietly. "For dragons, to know a true name is to have power over that name's owner. But Dragonfriend is at peace. Nothing can harm him now."

As Lief turned away from the grave, his heart was very full. He knew that the many-colored stone was Doran's soul-stone, filled with the great explorer's memories. When Lief had placed it in its final resting place, his mind had been flooded with pictures.

Wild and beautiful places. Thousands of faces. The secret seas of the underworld. Flying with dragons . . .

And through it all ran Doran's voice, whispering in a strange language. Whispering, it seemed, of Veritas.

Veritas hopian forta fortuna fidelis honora joyeu . . .
Veritas hopian forta fortuna fidelis honora joyeu . . .

No doubt Veritas would know what the words meant, but Lief could not ask. The soul-stone had shown him the secrets of Doran's heart. He felt he had no right to speak of them.

"You were always in Doran's mind, I think," he contented himself with saying to the grieving dragon, when it, too, turned from the grave.

"As he will always be in mine," said Veritas. "That is why, though I long to return to my own territory, I will stay here for a time. The diamond infant must be taught to know her own land and the ways of dragons. Dragonfriend would have wished it."

✳

An hour later, the companions set off along the broad coast road, with Red Han striding eagerly before them, and their horses, Honey, Bella, and Swift, trotting no less eagerly behind.

Kree had left hours earlier, carrying a message for Zeean that all was well, that Red Han had been found, and that the companions and the lighthouse keeper wished to be sped to Tora.

Plainly the message had been safely delivered, for already the travelers could feel the faint tug of Toran magic. By nightfall they would be in the white city of the west.

There, Red Han would find the help he needed to return to Bone Point, where he longed to be. And there Lief, Barda, and Jasmine and the horses would find food, rest, and then safe, quick passage to Del, their final goal.

"How I long for a hot bath and a comfortable bed!" Barda exclaimed.

"It is fresh fruit I long for," sighed Jasmine, and Filli, riding on her shoulder, chattered fervent agreement.

The magic strengthened, and they began to move faster. Crisp, salty wind beat against their faces. They exclaimed and pointed at the seabirds swooping over the waves close to shore, feasting on the tiny fish that swarmed just below the sparkling surface.

Only twenty-four hours had passed since the destruction of the Sister of the West, but already the land and sea were coming to life.

So it will be in Del, Lief thought. *So it will be in the whole of the south, if we can find the last Sister.*

Plainly Jasmine's thoughts had been running along the same lines.

"I cannot think where the Sister of the South might be hidden in a bustling place like Del," she said. "Could it be buried deep on the shore, perhaps?"

"It is hard to imagine it." Barda frowned. "At the time the Sister was hidden, Del harbor was a busy port — always crowded with boats and people."

"I was thinking of the maze of drain tunnels beneath the city," Lief said.

"Of course!" Barda's face lit up. "One of those tunnels begins in the palace. Doom knows of it — has even used it. It would have been simple for the Shadow Lord servant Drumm, the king's chief advisor in those days, to creep out through that tunnel and put the Sister somewhere in the maze."

"And easy for him, and all the chief advisors who followed him, to visit it in secret and protect it," Lief added.

"But there are no longer chief advisors in the palace," Jasmine put in. "Who protects the Sister now?"

"Indeed," Barda said heavily. "Who is the new guardian? It could be anyone. Del is a large place."

"It is," Lief said. "But very few people in it have any way of finding out where we are or what we are doing. Yet time and again the Shadow Lord has known where to find us."

"That may have nothing to do with the guardian of the south," Barda said. "I have begun to wonder whether something we are carrying helps the Enemy track us. I suggest we leave our packs — even our garments — behind us when we depart for Del."

Lief nodded agreement. He was remembering Ava's voice hissing in his ear as he bid her farewell.

"Beware, Lief of Del!" the blind fortune-teller had whispered. "You might have faced the Kobb of the Isle of the Dead and survived, but I see creeping darkness in your future. The way upon which you have set your feet leads to disaster. Heed my warning, and turn aside from it!"

"I cannot do that, Ava," Lief had said gently.

And Ava had stumped away from him in anger, muttering and hunching her shoulders.

Jasmine's voice broke into Lief's thoughts. "We have almost reached the border," she cried. "Soon we will be caught in the magic of Tora, and we will fly!"

✳

In Tora, a great crowd was waiting to greet them. The horses were led away to be cared for. Red Han was escorted to the feast that had been prepared. And soon Lief, Barda, and Jasmine were alone in the great marble square with only Zeean, Marilen, Ranesh, and Manus the Ralad man.

Surprised, Lief looked around for his mother.

"Sharn returned to Del," Zeean said quietly. "It seems that the city is being besieged by a golden dragon. The people are arming themselves and demanding that the dragon be hunted down."

"No!" Lief exclaimed in horror. "The dragon of the topaz must not be harmed!"

"Sharn seemed to know that," said Manus, his black eyes grave. "She believed she could calm the people. She left for Del the moment she heard the news — the same day we heard that you were safe in the Sleeping Dunes. But — "

"But what?" Lief cried, in a fever of impatience.

"You must prepare yourself for a shock, Lief," Zeean said bluntly. "Almost as soon as she arrived at the palace, Sharn fell ill. And I fear it is no ordinary illness. It is a deadly infection, now spreading very fast through the city. Your mother still lives, but hundreds of others in Del have died."

Lief stared, aghast. Jasmine put her arm around him.

"Does not the diamond in the Belt of Deltora protect from pestilence?" she said. "And it gives strength, as well. Never fear, Lief. Sharn will recover as soon as you reach her, I am sure of it."

"What is this illness?" Barda demanded. "Does it have a name?"

Zeean's lips tightened. "It has been *given* a name," she said curtly. "Because Sharn was the first to fall ill, your people appear to believe that she was the one who carried the disease to Del. They are calling it the Toran Plague."

She thrust two notes into Lief's hands. "The bird Ebony brought the one from Doom an hour ago," she said. "The other came on the day Sharn left us."

"It is from Josef, by the hand," Ranesh muttered. "He is becoming more and more desperate. I should go to him, but — "

"But your place is with your wife, who is with child and needs you," Zeean broke in. "Josef has more than enough people to tend to him."

She turned to Lief, Barda, and Jasmine. "Manus

and I must go," she said. "Red Han wishes to go to Bone Point at once, so the Light can shine this very night. Food awaits you in the dining hall, and your chambers have been prepared. Rest well."

She swept away, her back very straight, with Manus trotting after her.

"Zeean grieves for Sharn. And it hurts her that Tora is being blamed for the plague," Marilen said in her soft voice.

"Ah yes," said Ranesh drily. "For, of course, only good can come from Tora."

Marilen glanced at him. "Let us go and fetch food from the dining hall," she murmured. "Our friends will prefer to eat in a quiet place, I am sure."

The moment Marilen and Ranesh were gone, Lief opened Doom's note.

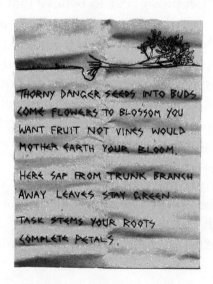

THORNY DANGER SEEDS INTO BUDS
COME FLOWERS TO BLOSSOM YOU
WANT FRUIT NOT VINES WOULD
MOTHER EARTH YOUR BLOOM.

HERE SAP FROM TRUNK BRANCH
AWAY LEAVES STAY GREEN.

TASK STEMS YOUR ROOTS
COMPLETE PETALS.

Slowly, following the code, Lief read out each sentence backwards, leaving out all words that had anything to do with plants.

" 'Your mother would not want you to come into danger. Stay away from here. Complete your task.' "

Barda gave a mirthless laugh. "To complete our task, we *must* go to Del. But, of course, Doom does not know that."

Slowly Lief opened the second, older note — the note from Josef.

Lief—I seize this chance to write again—must beg your pardon for troubling you. I long to talk to you—see you—you have much to do, however—urgent matters to attend to. Forgive me—fearful old Josef—news of you will come soon no doubt. Keep well—tell your companions the same—no one misses you all more than I do.

Josef

P.S. So many dashes! They show my state of mind. I pray you will understand. The message, after all, comes from my heart.

Frowning, Lief passed the paper to Barda and Jasmine.

"His mind is failing, I fear," Barda said, after a moment.

Lief sighed. It seemed that Barda was right. And yet . . .

"Someone has read this before us!" Jasmine exclaimed, tapping the note. "Look! There are two sets of fold lines on the paper. It has been opened, then folded again in haste."

"That is no mystery," said Barda. "I have no doubt that Doom reads every note sent from the palace, in case it might be helpful to a spy."

"Then he wasted his time with this," Jasmine said, handing the letter back to Lief. "It says nothing at all."

Lief read the note again. He could not rid himself of the feeling that there was something strange about it. The words seemed hasty and confused. Yet the old librarian's handwriting was just as usual.

He glanced at the lines below the signature.

So many dashes! . . . I pray you will understand. The message, after all, comes from my heart . . .

Lief's skin prickled.

. . . dashes . . . the message, after all . . .

Lief went back to the beginning of the note, but this time he read only those words that came after a dash.

214

— *I . . . — must . . . — see . . . — you . . . — ur-*
gent . . . — fearful . . . — news . . . — tell . . . — no
one.

I *must see you.* Urgent. *Fearful news. Tell no*
one.

2 - The Dream

Lief felt the blood rush into his face. What news was so fearful that even Jasmine and Barda were not to know of it? Or Doom? For plainly Josef had written his message in code so it would escape Doom's notice.

The news could not be about the plague, or about Sharn's illness. The letter had been written before either of those things had happened.

Possibly Josef's mind really *was* failing and his "fearful news" was just some foolish fancy. But what if it was not? What if he had discovered where the Sister of the South was hidden?

"Does any of the Kin's Dreaming Water remain, Jasmine?" Lief asked abruptly.

"A little," Jasmine said. "It should be enough for you to see Sharn." She pulled a small flask from one of her pockets and held it out.

Lief took the flask with a muttered word of thanks. He disliked allowing his friends to believe he wished to see his mother, when in fact he wanted the Dreaming Water for something else. But he had no choice. He had to keep faith with Josef — at least until he had seen how things were and had made up his mind what to do.

✳

Later, alone in his cool, white Toran bedchamber, Lief drained the flask of Dreaming Water and thought of Josef. He crawled into bed and lay still, but his mind was too active for rest. It seemed hours before exhaustion finally overcame him and he slept.

Almost at once, he began to dream.

He found himself standing just inside Josef's room at the back of the library. Josef was hunched over his desk, his back to the door, working by the light of a candle. To his left was a stack of paper neatly tied with blue ribbon. To his right lay an open volume of the *Deltora Annals* and a clutter of paint pots, brushes, pens, and empty teacups. His body hid whatever was directly in front of him.

Lief's heart began to thud as he moved farther into the room. He found himself treading softly, though he knew he could not be heard or seen. With every step, he became more shocked and grieved. Even from behind, it was easy to see that Josef was sadly changed.

The old librarian's white hair was dull, and

much of it had fallen out so that patches of pink scalp showed between the long strands. The warm rug draped around his shoulders could not disguise how frail he was.

As Lief watched, Josef pushed aside a metal ruler with which he had been working. The hand clutching the ruler was like a blue-veined claw.

But Josef was not like this when we left Del! Lief thought in dismay. *How could he have weakened so quickly?*

He jumped as Josef groaned.

"No, there is no doubt," the old man mumbled. "I have made no mistake. Oh, what wicked trickery is this? If only I had seen it before! If only I had remembered! Fool! Fool!"

Lief moved closer. He was just about to peer over Josef's shoulder when there was the sound of loud footsteps outside in the library.

Josef started violently. His bony hand shot out and grasped the open volume of the *Deltora Annals*. Paint pots and cups overturned as he dragged the book to the center of the desk, covering whatever lay there.

Doom strode into the room, dragging Josef's assistant, Paff, by the back of her collar. He was scowling ferociously. Paff's eyes were bulging with fright.

Josef turned to face them. His face was gaunt, his eyes were dark hollows. But still he straightened his shoulders and climbed to his feet, making a pathetic attempt to appear in control of the situation.

"What is the meaning of this?" he quavered.

"Lindal of Broome caught your assistant trying to creep into Sharn's room, Josef," Doom said coldly. He shook Paff like a puppy, and a choking sob burst from her lips.

Josef's hand tightened on the back of the chair. "Release her, if you please," he said in a high voice. "She was only doing my bidding."

Doom's eyes seemed to flash. "So it seems," he said. "She was carrying this."

He held a paper out in front of him. Lief read it, his heart sinking.

> My Lady Sharn,
>
> I beg that you will ask to speak to me—insist on seeing me—without telling a soul the reason. I must speak with you urgently.
>
> Forgive me for troubling you while you are ill, but I have nowhere else to turn.
>
> In faith.
>
> Your servant,
> Josef
>
> P.S. Burn this.

"Did I not tell you, Josef, that Sharn is gravely ill?" Doom said through tight lips. "And did I not tell you that the Toran Plague is highly infectious? By the heavens, can you not smell the funeral fires of those wretched souls who came in contact with her before her illness was known?"

Lief felt cold with dread.

Josef lifted his chin. "I must see the lady Sharn," he said stubbornly. "You have no right to keep me from her, Doom. If Lief were here — "

"Lief is *not* here!" snapped Doom. "*I* am. You cannot see Sharn, Josef. If you have something of importance to say, you can say it to me."

Josef pressed his lips together and did not speak.

Doom made a disgusted noise and released his grip on Paff's collar. She darted away from him and scurried to Josef's side.

Together the frail old man and the fluffy-haired girl faced Doom — strange allies in a very unequal battle.

"Keep your secrets, then, Josef!" Doom said angrily. "But I warn you, the next time you feel like sending Paff on such a mission, think again. She was panting so loudly with fear as she crept up the hallway to Sharn's bedchamber that Lindal heard her through the door!"

Josef glanced at Paff irritably. She flushed pink and her lips quivered.

220

"I am sorry, Josef," she whispered. "I waited, just as you said, until Lindal of Broome went out for more hot water. She was carrying a jug. I heard her footsteps going away. But it was all a trick! She must have crept back. I had taken but one step into the room when she was upon me!"

Her eyes filled with tears. "She twisted my arm — treated me like a criminal," she whispered. "I am so ashamed."

"Josef is the one who should be ashamed!" barked Doom. "Let him do his own dirty work in future!"

Paff looked up. Suddenly her tear-filled eyes were angry.

"Josef can hardly walk!" she cried. "He cannot go up to Sharn's bedchamber without guards to carry him — you know that! How *can* you taunt him with his weakness!"

"I did not mean — " Doom began impatiently. But now that Paff had begun speaking, it seemed she could not stop.

"And in any case, Josef did not *force* me to help him," she said. "I agreed gladly. His old assistant, Ranesh, would have done it in a moment. And I — I am sick to death of being compared to Ranesh and found wanting. I was not going to refuse my one chance to prove myself!"

"I daresay Josef knew that only too well," said Doom drily.

Lief saw a flicker of shame cross Josef's haggard face, and groaned inwardly.

"Josef, I can waste no more time with you," Doom said to the old librarian. "You must cease your troublemaking. You must accept once and for all that you cannot see Sharn."

"But why should he not see her?" shrilled Paff. "Why should Lindal of Broome, who is almost a stranger here, sit with the lady Sharn while Josef is kept away? Is it because Lindal is your ally in all things, and Josef is not?"

Doom's scarred face darkened. His eyes narrowed.

"Paff, go to your room," Josef muttered urgently.

Red-faced and silent, Paff left his side, edged past Doom, and disappeared through the open doorway into the darkness beyond.

Josef watched her go, swaying slightly where he stood.

"I have given you all the news I have, Josef," Doom hissed. "Sharn could tell you no more, even if she could speak. I showed you the message from Zeean saying that Lief, Barda, and Jasmine had succeeded in the west. Can you not be satisfied with that, and be at peace?"

Josef put a trembling hand to his brow, but said nothing.

"You are not well," Doom went on in a level voice. "Your mind is clouded. That girl Paff is too

222

weak-headed to see it, but I see it. And you yourself must know it."

He looked keenly at the swaying figure before him, and shook his head as if to clear it.

"If I have been impatient with you, Josef, I beg your pardon," he added. "But I have not slept more than an hour or two at a time in more days than I can count. And even at the best of times, soft words are not my way."

For Doom, this was a generous apology. Lief willed Josef to understand. But the old man kept stubborn silence. He stood gripping the back of the chair, his knuckles white, his gaunt face as rigid as a piece of gnarled wood.

Doom cursed under his breath and left the room.

Only when the sound of his footsteps had died away did Josef move. His face sagged with exhaustion. Trembling, he lowered himself into his chair.

"Oh, why does Lief not come?" he whispered. "Lief must speak to me — he *must* — before anyone else knows he is here — before anything else is done! Did I make that plain enough? I cannot . . . remember."

Again he put his hand to his brow. "I *did* send the message, did I not?" he mumbled. "It was not just a dream? Oh . . . why can I not *think*?"

He buried his face in his hands.

"Josef!" Lief exclaimed in frustration. "What do you want to tell me? Say it aloud!"

The old man's head jerked up. Slowly he turned in his chair. But the next moment his face had vanished, and Lief was back in bed, blinking up at a white ceiling flooded with moonlight.

He lay still for a moment, gathering his thoughts. Then he jumped out of bed and made for the door.

He regretted having to wake Barda and Jasmine from the first peaceful sleep they had enjoyed in many days. But he could not leave them behind, and they would think his feeling of urgency had been caused by a dream of his mother, and ask no questions.

He had to see Josef. And he could not wait.

※

In less than an hour, three shadows were speeding towards Del. Only the birds and beasts of the night saw them pass. A few villagers, stirring in their beds, thought they heard the beat of flying hoofs. But the sound passed so quickly that they told themselves they had been dreaming.

Following Barda's plan, Lief, Barda, and Jasmine were wearing Toran garments and carrying only their weapons. Their bright robes fluttering in the wind, they bent forward over their horses' necks, lost in a dream of speed.

Back in the white city of the west, Zeean alone was awake. But her will was enough to speed them along the well-worn path to Del.

Kree was flying far behind the horses. The old wound at the back of his neck still troubled him, but he had refused to ride tamely with Filli in the crook of Jasmine's arm. Perhaps he had once or twice allowed himself to be carried on the back of a dragon. But, sped by Toran magic or not, Honey, Bella, and Swift were ordinary horses of Del, and Kree was far too proud to ride with them.

He knew Jasmine and Filli were safe, wrapped in Toran magic. So he flew alone beneath the slowly sinking moon, enjoying the night and the silence, taking his time.

Neither he, nor the riders ahead of him, sensed the moment when an evil presence stirred and woke to knowledge of them. None of them felt the explosion of hatred that erupted at the warning of their approach.

They sped, untroubled, through the night as a liquid black shadow filled with malice slipped beneath a door and began its secret, oozing progress through the darkened palace of Del.

3 - Del

The moon had set and the sun had not yet risen when the companions reached the city gates. The four guards on watch held up their lanterns, saw the horses and the Toran robes of their riders, and drew back, quickly pulling scarfs over their mouths and noses.

"What is your business here, people of Tora?" one of the guards called. He sounded far from friendly.

"We are here to advise Doom on the matter of the Toran Plague," Jasmine called back, as planned. "Our presence was requested."

"We were told of no such request!" snapped the guard.

Jasmine pulled a paper from her pocket. "I have the message here," she said. "Do you wish to see it?"

She urged Swift forward, holding out the paper.

226

"Halt! Come no closer!" the guard bellowed, taking a hurried step back and pulling his scarf more tightly around his face. "You may pass. But be aware that if you do, you cannot leave the city again until it is declared free of plague."

"We understand," Jasmine said.

"So they will die here, trapped like rats, with the rest of us," Lief heard one of the other guards growl to his neighbor. "There is some justice in that, at least."

The gates swung open. The guards shrank back as far as they could, and waited till the visitors were well past before venturing out of the shadows to close the gates again.

"Disgraceful!" fumed Barda under his breath. "They did not even *look* at the paper!"

Jasmine shrugged. "It is fortunate they did not, since it was only a note from Marilen to Sharn, and they would certainly have recognized us if they had looked at us closely."

Barda scowled. He knew that what she said was true, but his pride in his well-trained guards had been sorely shaken.

"Do not be too hard on them," said Lief in a low voice. "They would have faced an enemy without flinching, but disease is fearful to them. It troubles me more that they greeted us with such suspicion — even anger."

And as he spoke, Jasmine drew breath sharply.

227

She had pulled Swift to a halt, and was staring at a yellow notice stuck to a wall beside her.

"Look at this!" she breathed.

THE TRUTH OF THE TORAN PLAGUE
PEOPLE OF DEL, AWAKE! DO NOT BE DECEIVED!
THE PLAGUE IS NOT A THING OF NATURE. IT HAS BEEN SENT BY TORA TO DESTROY US!
FOR PROOF, READ ON & FACE THE TRUTH.

#TRUTH! The sorcerers of Tora feast & take their ease while all around them work & starve. Yet they demand our goodwill.

#TRUTH! Torans envy Del, because Del is home to Deltora's ruling family. This forced our beloved Lady Sharn to leave us & dwell for months in Tora as hostage to Toran pride.

#TRUTH! Tora's treachery is proved by history. When the Shadow Lord invaded, Tora broke its oath of loyalty and allowed the Enemy to enslave us.

#TRUTH! King Lief, in the innocence & generosity of his youth, forgave the Torans for their treachery & allowed them to return to their enchanted city.

#TRUTH! Tora has repaid the king's trust by plotting to destroy Del by stealth. The Toran plague proves it!

"All its 'truths' are lies!" Jasmine exclaimed.

"There is enough truth in most of them to deceive frightened people," Barda answered grimly.

"There *is* food in Tora. Sharn *did* go there partly to assure the Torans that their friendship was valued. The Torans *did* once break their oath of loyalty, and Lief *did* forgive them — "

" 'In the innocence and generosity of his youth,' " Lief quoted bitterly. "The writer might as well have said 'his ignorance and foolishness,' for that is what is meant."

He shook his head. "This notice is so *stupid*! It says it is going to prove that the Torans sent the plague to destroy Del. Then it says that the plague *itself* proves that the Torans are plotting to destroy Del. Where is the logic in that?"

"There is none," said Barda, ripping the notice from the wall. "But those looking for someone to blame for their misfortune will not see that, I fear. We had better move on. The sun will soon be rising. If we are seen in the streets wearing Toran garments we could be attacked before we are recognized."

They rode on, growing more and more uneasy. The air was hazy with the smoke of funeral fires. Fear and strangeness haunted the familiar streets. Now and again they came upon another copy of the hateful yellow notice, stuck to a fence or pole. Plainly the city was full of them.

As they drew nearer to the palace, many of the doors they passed were hung with charms that the owners hoped would protect their homes from illness. An increasing number were nailed shut and marked

229

with a red X to show that the people who had lived there had died of the plague.

At last they reached the bottom of the palace hill. The palace loomed above them. Lief could not see the guards standing by the entrance doors, but he knew they must be there, as they were every night.

It is almost time to make my move, he thought. But before he could speak, Jasmine pulled Swift to a halt once more.

"I will wait here for Kree," she announced. "He must not enter the palace alone. The last time he was there, he was poisoned."

"He slept through a night and a day, and believed he had been drugged," said Barda. "But he may have been merely exhausted. Who can say?"

"I will wait," Jasmine said firmly. "You and Lief go on."

"No," Lief said, swinging down to the ground and thrusting Honey's reins into Jasmine's hands. "You two wait here for Kree. I will meet you inside."

And ignoring his companions' startled, furious whispers, he darted off the road and almost at once was swallowed by the darkness.

✳

Toran robes were more suited to strolling along marble pathways than to toiling up a rough hill in the dark. But at last Lief reached his goal — the huge rock in the shape of a sleeping bear that marked the secret way into the palace.

Memories flashed into his mind as he pulled away the grass that masked the tunnel entrance.

The last time he had done this, desperate fear had been driving him. The last time he had done this, the Shadow Lord ruled in Deltora, and Doom, Jasmine, and Barda were prisoners, about to be condemned to death.

That time is long gone, he told himself, as he wormed his way into the narrow stone passage. *It is foolish, no doubt, for me to be creeping into the palace like a thief. I have been infected by Josef's fancies.*

But fear grew in him as he crawled through the black silence of the tunnel. And he did not know if the fear was remembered or real.

By the time he emerged in the palace chapel, his teeth were chattering. He replaced the floor tile that had sealed the tunnel, wincing at the small, grating sound it made as it slid into place.

Close beside him was the high marble platform that dominated the small room. Lief brushed against it as he stood up, and twitched aside instinctively.

For centuries, the honored dead of the palace had lain in state on that platform. Lief's own father had rested there for a full day after he died, and Lief had kneeled with his mother in the chill silence of the chapel for a long, sad hour or two. The ritual had brought him no comfort, and he had never visited the chapel since.

Trying to shrug off the feeling of dread that

231

seemed to hang upon him like a heavy cloak, Lief felt his way to the door. Opening it cautiously, he climbed the steps that led up to the huge, echoing space of the entrance hall.

All was silent, but he knew it would not be silent for long. Kree must have joined Jasmine and Barda by now. Soon his companions would reach the palace. There was no time to waste.

He ran lightly past the stairs and on to the library. He let himself in, and moved quietly through the dimness. Dark shelves towered around him. The familiar smell of old books filled his nose. At the end of the long room, feeble light glimmered through Josef's half-open door.

Lief moved quickly towards the light. When he had almost reached it, he saw another splinter of light to his right, at floor level.

He remembered that Paff also slept in the library, her bedchamber separated from Josef's by a storeroom and the tiny kitchen where she and Josef could heat soup and make tea. Paff's door was closed, but it seemed that she, too, was awake.

Silently, Lief slipped into Josef's room. Josef was slumped over his desk, his head pillowed on his arms. In front of him the candle flickered in a pool of melted wax.

He has fallen asleep over his work, Lief thought. He approached the desk and put a hand on the old man's shoulder.

"Josef," he whispered. "It is I, Lief."

"Lief . . ." The voice was slurred, and very faint. Josef's eyelids fluttered open, but he did not move.

Lief's heart gave a great thud. His grip on Josef's shoulder tightened.

"Lief?" the old man murmured. "Or . . . another vision?"

"No!" Lief whispered, falling to his knees by the chair. "No, Josef, this time I am truly here!"

The old librarian blinked. "Keep away," he slurred. "Lief . . . keep away!"

With an enormous effort, he raised his head. Lief caught his breath as he saw the familiar, wrinkled face gleaming with sweat and hideously disfigured with swollen scarlet blotches.

"The Toran Plague," Josef murmured. "Ah, I . . . did not dream there was real danger. Never . . . would I have sent the girl to Sharn if I had known."

His glazed eyes focused on Lief and flamed with sudden panic.

"Cover your face!" he groaned. "Get out of this room! Ah, Lief, I beg you! Do not make me a murderer twice over!"

Lief scrambled up and backed away, aghast. "I — I will fetch help!" he stammered.

"No time," Josef mumbled. "I must warn you. The Four Sisters. You . . . the sorcerer . . . you must stop . . ."

"I will, Josef!" Lief said, tears burning at the back

233

of his eyes. "Three of the four are destroyed already. Do you know where the last is? Is that why you summoned me?"

"Plot," the old man breathed. "Treachery. North . . . to south, east . . . to west . . . lines . . . map . . ."

His head drooped as though his neck was too weak to support it. "Danger," he whispered. "Fearful . . . must warn — Lief."

"I am here, Josef," Lief cried. "I know that the Sister of the South is in Del. But *where* in Del? Where — ?"

Josef's dry lips writhed as he struggled to speak. Lief strained to hear. His ears caught a single word. His eyes widened in disbelief. Could Josef possibly have said "Here"?

" 'Here,' Josef?" he gasped. "In the *palace*?"

The crease between Josef's brows deepened. "Beware, Lief . . . evil . . . the center . . . the heart . . . the city . . . of . . ."

The sighing voice trailed away.

Lief turned and ran to Paff's room. He knocked frantically, calling Paff's name, but there was no answer. With a feeling of dread, he tried the door. As he had expected, it was locked.

Lief drew back and kicked. The door shuddered, but held. He gripped the diamond in the Belt and kicked again. The lock burst, and the door swung open.

Paff sat in her bed, propped up on two pillows.

She was wearing a long-sleeved pink nightgown. Her yellow hair was neatly braided into two skimpy tails. A book lay open on her lap and the stub of a candle burned low on the bedside table beside a half-drunk cup of tea.

At first glance it looked as if she had simply fallen asleep while reading. But Lief knew this was not so. Paff's head lolled backwards. Her face was shining with sweat. Her limbs were as rigid as if they had been carved out of stone. Saliva dribbled from one corner of her open mouth. Beneath her fluttering eyelids, the whites of her eyes gleamed.

Lief backed away from the doorway, his heart thudding violently.

Then suddenly, shockingly, the silence of the palace was shattered by a hideous chorus of sounds — the high-pitched squeals of terrified horses, Jasmine's scream and Barda's roar, the wild screeching of Kree, and, rising over all, a ferocious, ear-splitting wail that chilled the blood.

4 - Attack

D rawing his sword, Lief plunged through the darkness of the library, out into the hallway and on into the entrance hall. As he threw himself against the tall front doors and heaved at the iron bar that sealed them, he heard shouts from deep within the palace.

Help was on its way, but he could not wait. He sprang heedlessly outside, almost tripping over the bodies of the night guards sprawled lifeless at the top of the stairs.

The sun was rising, casting a weird red glow over the palace lawn where Honey, Bella, and Swift reared, squealing, their eyes rolling in terror. All three horses were lame, and covered in wounds that streamed with blood.

And shoulder to shoulder, stumbling backwards

up the stairs, Barda and Jasmine were fighting for their lives.

A vast, hideous beast was lunging at them from below, driving them upward step by step. Its face was the face of a huge, snarling dog, but hideously smooth and glistening. The shapeless black mass of its body rippled like water, and from it writhed hundreds of long, razor-edged stingers that whistled like whips as they slashed at their prey.

Barda and Jasmine were defending themselves as best they could. Stingers cut through by sword and dagger pattered like ghastly rain on the stairs at their feet. But as the wriggling fragments fell they melted into puddles of oily black liquid that joined together, then rapidly returned to the beast, becoming part of its body once more. And every moment more and more stingers budded from the heaving flesh.

Screeching wildly, Kree was diving at the thing's head, driving his sharp beak into the glossy black surface again and again. Plainly he was annoying it, but still it surged forward.

As the beast turned its neck to growl at the attacking bird, Lief's stomach turned over. For at the back of its head was another face, narrow and ridged, with a cruel hooked beak and burning red eyes.

Pointless, then, to try to attack it from behind — or, indeed, to do anything but try to escape. For even as Lief leaped down the stairs, raising his sword, he knew that ordinary weapons could not defeat this horror.

It was a thing of sorcery, like the false dragon at Dragon's Nest, like the phantom that had hunted them on the way to Shadowgate.

The guardian of the south had been expecting them. Again, their movements had been known. Again, they had been betrayed.

"Barda! Jasmine!" he roared. "The doors are open! Get up to the doors!"

But as the words left his lips, he saw Jasmine fall, blood welling from a wound in her side. The stinger that had struck her held her fast, while a dozen more whipped forward to finish her. The dog face howled and snapped in triumph, flecks of foam spraying from its jaws. The beaked face behind it gave a wailing, unearthly cry.

With a roar, Barda slashed savagely at the attacking stingers. Their tips dropped and melted into puddles of oily liquid where they fell. Lief bounded recklessly down the last few steps, cut Jasmine free, and began to lift her.

"Get her inside, Lief!" Barda panted. "I will try to hold — "

He grunted in agony as three stingers whipped around his neck. Blood began to flow freely from the wounds. The stingers tightened and pulled. As Barda staggered, choking, the beast lunged at him, its two faces howling, stingers hissing through the air like striking snakes.

Leaving Jasmine where she lay, Lief sprang forward, his sword sweeping in great arcs before him. Fragments of stingers fell, squirming, beneath his blade. The severed tips of the stingers that had been throttling Barda dissolved into trails of black slime. As Barda bent double, clutching his throat and drawing in great, rasping gulps of air, the trails joined into one and slid rapidly to the ground.

The beast shuddered and drew back. The blazing eyes of the dog face met Lief's eyes, then dropped to the Belt at his waist.

"Yes!" Lief shouted, wild with rage and loathing. "I am the one you were told to destroy! But it is not so easy, is it? It is not so easy to face the Belt of Deltora. Get back — back to whatever foul place you came from!"

The foam-flecked lips of the dog face writhed back from its teeth in a snarling grin. And Lief's heart seemed to leap into his throat as the hideous mound of flesh before him swelled to twice its size, and hundreds more stingers erupted from its rippling black surface.

And the next moment, it was upon him.

He was engulfed in oily, quivering darkness. He could not breathe. He could not see. Pain racked his body as stingers whipped around him, binding his arms and legs, squeezing him in a death grip.

But worse, far worse, was the sickening sound, the ghastly rippling, sucking sound that filled his ears as he was pulled farther and farther into the cold, jelly-like mass of the beast. His stomach heaved at the vileness of it. He wanted to scream, but his mouth was sealed.

He could feel the beast's flesh twitching and quivering. The Belt of Deltora was burning it. But it did not release him. The blood was roaring in his ears. His chest ached with the need to breathe. His mind was growing hazy. Pictures of the past drifted in a sea of red behind his sealed eyes.

So this was what Ava meant, he thought dimly. *This was the fate awaiting me. Death . . .*

Not yet, king of Deltora. I am with you . . .

The voice of the topaz dragon whispered in his mind, echoing like a voice in a dream. At the same moment, he felt a jolt, as if the beast enfolding him had shuddered all over. And then he heard a roar like distant thunder and knew —

Again the beast shuddered. There was a spitting, sizzling sound, like fat falling into a fire. And then Lief felt himself falling onto the hard stairs. He felt the cold, clinging flesh slipping away from him, sliding from his nose and mouth, from his arms and legs.

Air rushed into his aching lungs as he took great, sobbing breaths. The air was hot, and smelled of burning. It hurt him. But it was glorious, glorious!

240

He opened his eyes. He was lying on his side. The air was dark with smoke. A mighty wind beat on him, pinning him down. There was a blaze of golden light, a thunderous roar, and a wave of heat.

He could do nothing. He could only lie gasping like a stranded fish, staring wildly at the trail of oily black liquid snaking into the shadows at the side of the stairs and slipping out of sight.

Painfully, fighting the buffeting wind, he turned on his back and looked up. The topaz dragon hovered above him, wreathed in smoke, its vast wings glittering in the rising sun. Again he heard its voice in his mind.

What was that foul two-faced thing? In all my long life, I have never seen its like.

Lief tried to speak, but could not. So he thought his answer — the answer he knew to be true.

It is the guardian of the evil presence called the Sister of the South.

The dragon's golden eyes narrowed. And this time it spoke aloud. Its voice was very cold.

"When you awoke me, king, I felt evil in my land. But you told me that the center of the evil was in the land of the ruby where I could not go."

Lief wet his cracked lips. "I did not mean to deceive you," he managed to croak. "I told you there were four Sisters in all, and that we only knew the whereabouts of one — the Sister of the East, in Dragon's Nest. Since then we have circled the land,

241

and three Sisters have been destroyed. But one remains, and we have just learned that it is in Del."

"I knew it was so," hissed the dragon, dropping a little lower. "Its song has been tormenting me. I hear it now. It is here, hidden deep in the city's heart."

. . . the center . . . the heart . . .

Josef's voice echoed in Lief's mind.

"You feel the evil in the palace, dragon?" Lief rasped urgently.

"I do," growled the dragon. "Why else have I haunted this place, braving the weapons of your guards? I do not care for cities, where the air is foul, and humans run about shrieking at the sight of me, like granous in a trap."

And as it spoke, there were frenzied shouts from the top of the stairs. The next instant, an arrow had flown through the air and buried itself in the dragon's soft underbelly.

The dragon bellowed and rose into the dawn sky. Its dark red blood splashed to the stairs, spattering Lief's face and hands.

Lief cried out in horror, struggling to rise, to shout to the guards to stop, stop! But the pounding wind of mighty wingbeats pinned him down, and his croaking voice could not be heard above the dragon's roars.

The dragon flew clumsily away, slowly gaining height. Spears sped after it, but could not reach it, falling uselessly to the ground. Blood dripped from its wound as it flew. Lief watched helplessly, racked with pain, filled with dismay.

He heard the sound of feet clattering down the stairs. Then someone was crouching beside him. Through the haze of smoke still drifting in the air Lief saw a square, sharp-eyed face surrounded by a frizz of brown hair. He saw the well-worn bow slung over one sturdy shoulder, and knew whose arrow had pierced the dragon's hide.

"Gla-Thon," he croaked, trying to sit up. "How — ?"

"Be still," the gnome said gruffly. "You have lost much blood. Jasmine and Barda, too. That vicious yellow beast nearly made an end of you."

"No," Lief mumbled. His head was swimming. Shadows were flickering at the edges of his vision.

Desperately he tried to hold the shadows back. He needed to explain. He needed to tell Gla-Thon, tell them all, of the two-faced beast, of the dragon's rescue. But there was something even more urgent.

"Josef. Paff," he whispered. "The Toran Plague . . ."

He saw Gla-Thon's small eyes widen. He saw her lips move, as though she was speaking.

But the shadows were closing in. Lief could not stop them. They moved faster, faster . . . and at last all was darkness.

✳

When Lief woke, he was lying in his old palace bedchamber. A feather quilt covered him. There was a soft pillow beneath his head. The faint scents of soap, clean linen, and healing herbs drifted in the air. Sunlight was streaming through the barred window, turning the swirling dust motes into flecks of gold.

For a moment he was still, his mind lost in a pleasant haze. Then memory came flooding back and instantly every nerve in his body was jangling.

He sat up abruptly, drawing a sharp breath as pain shot through him. He looked down and saw that the torn, blood-soaked Toran robe was gone, and he was wearing a crisp white nightshirt. At the same moment he realized that while he had been unconscious someone had bathed his wounds, bandaged the worst of them, and smeared the rest with healing balm.

With a jolt of panic he felt for the Belt of Deltora. But it was there, around his waist, gleaming against the white of the nightshirt.

He looked around the familiar room. His sword lay in a corner near the bed. Beside the sword was the pack he had left in Tora.

Who had brought it from Tora? How long had he been lying here unconscious? Half a day? More?

Suddenly the silence in the room was no longer peaceful, but ominous.

Lief thought of his mother. He thought of Jasmine and Barda, bleeding on the palace steps. He thought of Josef, his face disfigured by scarlet weals, and Paff, her eyes rolled back in her head . . .

In terror he glanced down at his hands and in

shamed relief saw that no red lumps marked the skin.

The Toran Plague had not touched him. Or —
not yet.

Painfully he swung his legs over the side of the
bed and stood up. The room seemed to spin around
him, and he grasped the edge of the bedside cabinet
for support. He fumbled his way to his pack, found
his clothes, and began to pull them on.

His heart lurched as he heard the click of a lock
and saw the door handle turn. Without quite knowing
why, he seized his sword and stood with his back to
the wall, waiting.

5 - A Sad Reunion

The door opened and Doom came silently into the room. He froze when he saw that the bed was empty. Slowly he turned his head till he saw Lief standing in the corner, sword in hand. The corner of his mouth tightened.

"So you have become cautious at last, Lief," he said. "Better late than never."

Lief grinned shakily and threw down his sword.

"Doom," he said, holding out his hand. "I am very glad to see you."

Doom stood where he was. "I am sure you will understand if I say that I am *not* glad to see you," he answered coldly. "Did I not tell you to stay away from here?"

Lief fought down a flare of anger. "You also told me to continue my quest," he snapped, letting his rejected hand fall. "Whether you wished me to see my dying mother or not, I had to come to Del. The Sister of the South is here."

With bitter satisfaction he watched Doom's face change. Then he saw his old friend's shoulders slump, and felt ashamed.

"Forgive me," Lief said quickly, holding out his hand again. "You could not have known. And no doubt I would have come even if the Sister were not in Del."

This time Doom moved forward and took the outstretched hand in both of his.

"No doubt you would, Lief," he said. "Your heart has often ruled your head. It is one of the many things that make you a better king than I could ever be, for all your youth."

As if fearing he had shown his feelings too plainly, he cleared his throat and abruptly released Lief's hand.

"Barda and Jasmine are still sleeping," he said, in something far more like his normal tone. "According to Gla-Thon it is a miracle that you are all still alive. Dragons can be deadly allies, it seems."

Without waiting for an answer, he held out a piece of red cloth like the one loosely knotted around his own neck.

"I know there is no hope of persuading you to keep away from Sharn, however much I might wish to," he said. "Tie this mask around your face. It will give you some protection from the infection."

"Before I see Mother, I must go to Josef," Lief said hurriedly.

Doom stared at him in angry astonishment. "You must do as you please, Lief," he said curtly. "But if you wish to see Sharn alive, there is no time to waste."

Fear swept through Lief like a cold wind, driving everything else from his mind, chilling him to the bone.

❋

Minutes later, Lief was standing by his mother's bed, his breath coming hard and fast beneath the stifling cloth mask that covered his mouth and nose.

"Do not venture too close," warned Doom, who had remained by the door. "And do not touch her."

Angry-looking scarlet lumps covered Sharn's face and neck. Her brow was beaded with sweat. Her lips were dry and cracked. Dark gray shadows smudged the skin beneath her eyes. Her breathing was very faint.

Lief's throat tightened. "How long has she been like this?" he managed to say.

"This is the fourth day," Doom answered. "She reached Del at sunset three nights ago, bearing the glad tidings that you had been found safe and well, and were traveling on to find the Sister of the South. A troop of guards escorted her to the palace. She spoke to every one of them . . . as is her way."

He paused, then continued in the same level tone.

"Her belongings were brought here, but she remained below, though she was tired and windswept from her journey. She greeted the crowds of the hungry gathered in the entrance hall and with her own hands served the soup that had been prepared for them. Afterwards she went to visit the stables, then she and I ate in the kitchen with the cooks. At last she admitted to weariness and went directly to bed."

Again he paused. Lief waited, his eyes fixed on his mother's face.

"By morning she was burning with fever and the red weals were already showing on her face," Doom went on after a moment. "The guards who had escorted her to the palace, many of the people she had served, the horse-master who greeted her in the stables, and the cooks who sat with us at table were in the same state. Most of them died the same day. Then those close to them began to fall ill. And so it went on."

"How many are dead?" Lief forced himself to ask.

Wearily, Doom rubbed his brow with the back of his hand. "Many hundreds," he said. "I have lost count over the past days. I have given orders that the dead are to be burned. The citizens have all been told to cover their faces in the streets, and while nursing the sick. But still the deaths continue."

He sighed. "The only thing I seem to have achieved is to stop the plague spreading beyond Del. No one is permitted to leave the city. That is why Gla-Thon is with us. A Kin carried her from Dread Mountain, to bring me news of you. The Kin returned at once, but Gla-Thon remained, and she was still here when the plague broke out. Gers the Jalis and Steven were trapped in the same way."

"Gers and Steven?" Lief repeated stupidly.

"Gers came asking for food for his people," Doom said. "Steven arrived a week ago, with the boy Zerry. They told me of your journey to Shadowgate and your encounters with the Masked Ones and Laughing Jack."

Lief nodded, his mouth suddenly dry.

"To me the Masked Ones were just one of Deltora's many curiosities," Doom went on somberly. "I have never known their history, or cared to find it out. I was astonished when Steven told me that the troop was founded by Ballum, the younger brother of King Elstred."

He saw Lief's eyes widen, and nodded.

"Did Steven not tell you?" he said. "You share a bloodline with the traditional leaders of the Masked Ones, Lief. No doubt that is why Bess saw a resemblance between you and her son. Steven told me that

Ballum was a magician and juggler — much loved by the people, and by his brother, the king. Then a trick went wrong and Ballum's face was badly marked by fire."

"So he began wearing a mask to hide his injuries," Lief said slowly.

"He did," said Doom. "But not long afterwards he was accused of attempting to kill Elstred out of bitterness and jealousy, and was forced to flee."

He shrugged at Lief's muffled gasp. "Yes, it is likely that Elstred's chief advisor planned it all, to ensure that Elstred listened to her alone. Your father and I were separated by the same trick, centuries later. The Enemy forgets nothing, it seems."

"Ballum was hunted, no doubt, supposedly on the king's orders," Lief said, remembering how bitterly the Masked Ones had spoken of the king in Del.

"Of course," Doom said. "But he kept to the wilder parts of Deltora, earning his bread as a traveling entertainer, and was never caught. Gradually a loyal troop gathered around him. They moved around constantly and they all wore masks, so that if ever they were attacked, the guards would not know at once which one of them was Ballum." He raised a tired hand, and dropped it again. "Whether Ballum had discovered the secret of making the masks permanent by that time, or found it out later, no one can know," he added.

Lief shuddered and turned his head away.

"Forgive me," Doom said awkwardly. "This is not the time to be speaking of such things."

He cleared his throat. "Steven's story of what nearly befell you filled me with horror, but I was glad to see him — more glad than I can say. Now I wish with all my heart that he had stayed away. If he and Nevets fall victim to this accursed plague — "

"They will not," said a quiet voice. "Did you not tell me that Steven and the boy had taken the horse-master's place? They will be safe in the stables, surely."

Lief looked up and with dull surprise saw Zeean of Tora standing by a second bed on the other side of the room. Like him, and like Doom, Zeean was wearing a mask of red over her mouth and nose. Her hands were covered by close-fitting scarlet gloves of some shining Toran cloth.

She saw him staring at her, and her eyes warmed in a sad smile of greeting. Lief saw with a shock that there was a large, darkening bruise on her cheekbone, just beneath her eye.

"As you see, I decided that I had to come after you, to bring Sharn what comfort I could," she said. "Marilen dearly wanted to come also, but her father persuaded her to remain in safety, and I am very glad of that. Del is no place for Marilen now — and not just because the risk of infection is so great, either."

She moved away towards the washstand, revealing the person lying motionless in the bed. Lief stared in horror at the strong, handsome face branded by the terrible marks of the Toran Plague.

"Lindal!" he whispered. "But only last night she was — "

"The plague works quickly once it strikes," Doom said grimly. "Consider the guards on the door last night — healthy when they went on duty, dead before dawn. I found Lindal like this when I came to tell her that you were here, and injured, and that Josef and Paff had been struck down."

He grimaced. "And now Zeean has come to take her turn in this chamber of death," he added. "She insists upon it, though neither Sharn nor Lindal would want her to risk — "

"They cannot be left alone to suffer, Doom," said Zeean calmly, dipping a cloth into a bowl of water and wringing it out. "And you cannot be here night and day. Who is seeing to Josef and Paff?"

"Gla-Thon was willing," said Doom briefly.

Zeean nodded and crossed the room to Sharn's bed with the wet cloth in her hands.

"There is little enough that can be done," she murmured, beginning to sponge Sharn's hot face. "Cool the face and hands. Be there to comfort and give water. Hope and pray that the body will have the strength to throw off the pestilence."

Lief wet his lips. "I had hopes that the diamond

in the Belt might help Mother," he said huskily. "Now I fear the help may have come too late."

Zeean hesitated. "You may be right," she said gently, at last. "Sharn has clung to life far longer than anyone else, but it is a cruel illness, this thing they call the Toran Plague."

Lief saw her mouth tighten beneath the mask.

"Doom himself came to the city gates to escort me through the city," she said. "I think that if he had not, harm would have come to me. The very sight of me — of my Toran robe — seemed to inflame the people in the streets. They called and jeered. Some threw stones."

Thoughtfully she lifted a gloved hand to the bruise on her cheek.

"Oh, Zeean!" Lief muttered in dismay. "I am so — "

"I do not mind for myself," Zeean broke in, moving back to the washstand, putting aside the cloth and picking up Sharn's silver-topped jar of soothing cream. "I mind only that your people believe that this evil has come to them from Tora, when I know it cannot be so."

"It *must* be so, Zeean," Doom said firmly. "Sharn came here directly from Tora, and there is no doubt that the plague came with her. Perhaps she was protected from its effects while she stayed within the magic city's walls, but once she left — "

Zeean shook her head, her eyes fixed determinedly on the lid she was removing from the jar. "If
the seeds of such an evil had been within Sharn in
Tora, we would have known," she said.

"I beg you not to say that outside this room,"
Doom answered gravely. "From what I hear, it is exactly what the people of Del suspect."

"What *can* you mean?" Zeean demanded, looking at him at last.

In dismay Lief saw Doom draw a yellow notice
from his pocket and hold it out to her.

Zeean was certain to find out at last, in any case, Lief
told himself as with sinking heart he watched Zeean
take the yellow paper and begin to read. *I can only
hope that she can be persuaded not to tell her people. If food
ships do begin arriving on the west coast now the Bone
Point Light is restored, Del will desperately need Tora's
goodwill.*

Gritting his teeth, he turned his back on his companions and shut their voices from his mind. Slowly
he unclasped the Belt of Deltora.

Zeean was frowning over the yellow paper.
Doom was watching her. Neither of them saw Lief
take the Belt from his waist and place it on his
mother's chest, with the great diamond over her
heart.

And neither of them saw him stare, astounded,
at what happened then.

It was as if a thunderbolt had struck him. He stopped breathing. The blood rushed to his face. For a moment he stood motionless, unable to believe what he was seeing. Then, slowly, he lifted his arms.

"Lief!" bellowed Doom, suddenly looking around. "Lief, no! What are you doing?"

For Lief was pulling the red mask from his face.

6 ~ Life and Death

Lief glanced at Zeean and Doom, who were both rigid with shock. Then he turned back to his mother and put his fingers to her wrist. Already the faint pulse was strengthening.

"Do not fear," he said. "There is no infection here."

"Are you mad, Lief?" exploded Doom. "Replace your mask! Make haste!"

Lief did not move. Doom ran his fingers through his hair in despair.

"What have you done?" he groaned. "Paff was in this room without a mask for only a moment, but still she caught the plague — and passed it on to Josef!"

Lief shook his head. "I saw Josef," he said softly. "I knelt by his chair and spoke to him. Yet I have not fallen ill with the thing you call the Toran Plague."

"But when did you see Josef?" cried Doom, astounded.

"Before the beast on the stairs attacked," Lief said. "No one knew of it, Doom. And that is why I have not fallen ill."

"What do you mean?" Zeean asked sharply.

"I mean that there is no such thing as the Toran Plague," Lief said. "All the illness, all the deaths, have been caused by poison."

Zeean gasped. Doom snorted in disbelief. But Lief knew he was right. The evidence was before his eyes.

"You know that the amethyst in the Belt pales in the presence of poison," he said quietly. "Look here!"

He pointed to the great gem, which was pale as lavender water, and saw Doom go white to the lips.

Zeean hurried to the bed and bent over Sharn. "The red marks are fading!" she exclaimed.

"They always fade as death approaches," Doom said tightly. "An hour or two after death, there are no marks at all."

Zeean shook her head. "Sharn is not dying. She is recovering! The fever is cooling. How . . . ?"

Her eyes turned to the Belt. "The emerald," she breathed. "Antidote to poison."

Lief nodded. "It saved Barda once. Now it will save Mother. Lindal, too. And Josef. And all those others who suffer, if I can reach them in time."

Slowly Zeean straightened. Then, very deliberately, she set down the jar of cream, pulled the red mask from her face, and stripped the gloves from her hands.

"This is much better," she murmured. Briskly she picked up the jar again and began smoothing cream on Sharn's lips.

"You are both making a terrible mistake," Doom said harshly. "Sharn cannot have been poisoned! She ate and drank nothing I did not share. She did not touch her water jug in the night — that was the first thing I looked at when I could not wake her in the morning. And everyone close to her has fallen ill!"

"Except you, Doom," Lief said in a level voice. "Why are you still standing?"

He would not have thought it possible for Doom to become paler, but it happened before his eyes.

"What are you suggesting?" Doom whispered.

Lief smiled ruefully. "Only that you are so wary, sleep so little, and are so careful of your food and drink, that it would be almost impossible to poison you. Others who spent time with Mother are a different story."

He shrugged. "A troop of guards shares the same water vat. Families eat together. Groups of the hungry are served from the same pot. Such people were easy victims for a killer who wanted to mimic the effects of a plague. As were Josef and Paff, who both use the same tin of tea in the library kitchen."

Doom was shaking his head. "How could a poisoner enter so many homes and move around the palace — even into this room — without being seen?"

But Lief was remembering a trail of liquid evil sliding into the shadows of the palace stairs. He was imagining it oozing beneath doors, slipping through keyholes, pooling like a living shadow in dark corners unnoticed, unsuspected.

"Something evil is living in the palace," he said in a low voice. "A thing of sorcery. I have seen it."

Doom and Zeean stared at him, then looked at one another uncertainly. Perhaps they wondered if he had taken leave of his senses.

And, indeed, Lief's head was spinning. The urgent thoughts that were flashing into his mind one after the other were threatening to overwhelm him.

Drawing fresh power from the Sister of the South, the guardian would recover and try to kill him again, that was certain. And the killing of others would continue at the same time. The false plague had begun for one simple reason, Lief was sure of that. But the guardian had quickly seen that it served other purposes as well.

There was no doubt: While the fearful, secret song of the Sister of the South rang on unchecked, its guardian would remain a threat to every living being in Del.

I must get the Belt to Josef so that he can tell me what he knows, Lief thought. *Then I must call the topaz dragon back, so we can face the Sister together. I must act quickly, before the guardian regains strength. But what of Lindal, Paff, and all the others who need the emerald's power? Must I leave them suffering and dying?*

He grew ever more panic-stricken as his thoughts ran on and on.

He had to warn the people of Del to beware of poison. Food would have to be thrown away — precious food, while people were starving! He had to make the palace guards understand that the topaz dragon was not a threat . . .

So many things to be done at once! And there was no time to waste — no time!

He looked down at his mother. The red marks on her face had still not faded completely, but she was breathing evenly. The power of the emerald had been working upon her for many minutes. He was sure that Barda had recovered in less time. Was it safe to remove the Belt now?

It will have to be, Lief thought grimly. Smothering his doubts, he snatched up the Belt of Deltora and hurried across the room to Lindal's bed.

As he bent to put the Belt down, however, he became aware that something within him had changed. His racing heart had slowed. The feeling of panic was ebbing away.

He glanced at the Belt, heavy in his hands, and saw that his fingers were gripping the golden topaz, the water-pale amethyst.

He had not thought he needed their help. He had thought he was simply facing the truth. Now he saw that the most important truth of all had been driven from his mind by fear.

This is a puzzle like any other, he thought in dull surprise, as he spread the Belt over Lindal. *I almost failed to solve it. Panic almost conquered me. But now I know what must be done — or at least how to begin.*

"Not *I*, but *we*," he said aloud. "I am not alone."

"Of course you are not!" exclaimed Zeean. "What — ?"

She broke off with a startled cry as the door crashed open. Barda strode into the room, his throat bandaged and his eyes wild. Jasmine was behind him, vainly trying to hold him back.

"Lindal!" Barda said huskily. "Is it true — ?" He caught his breath as he saw Lindal lying unconscious in the bed.

"She will survive, Barda," Lief said quickly. "Josef, too. The Belt — "

"Josef is dead," Barda said, his lips barely moving.

A chill settled on Lief's heart. Zeean gave a low cry. Doom's face darkened.

"Dead?" Lief whispered. He could not believe it. Somehow he could not imagine a world without Josef in it.

"Steven told us of it, just now," Jasmine said,

262

tears shining in her eyes. "Josef died peacefully, not long ago, with Ranesh by his side."

"Ranesh is here?" Zeean murmured.

Jasmine nodded. "Manus came with him. They had no trouble in the streets, for no one could tell by their looks that they came from Tora."

"But I warned them to stay away!" exploded Doom, clenching his fists. "Are they mad?"

"Only if love and loyalty can be considered madness!" Jasmine said sharply. "If you did not want Ranesh to come to Del, why did you tell him that Josef was ill?"

"I did not tell him!" Doom answered, just as sharply. "I, at least, have not lost my senses!"

"I fear the fault is mine," Zeean said.

Doom swung around to her. She met his furious eyes calmly.

"My heart was heavy after my arrival," she said. "Torans share their thoughts, but the distance between us now is too great for that to be possible. So I wrote to Marilen telling her of Josef's illness, the attack on Lief, Barda, and Jasmine, and . . . everything else."

Doom scowled, and Lief could well understand why. He knew that his own face must show his dismay.

Plainly, all in Tora now knew that the people of Del blamed them for the so-called plague, and that Zeean had been attacked in the streets.

263

"And how did you send your letter, may I ask?" Doom asked coldly. "The messenger birds are kept under guard."

The corners of Zeean's mouth tilted in a thin smile. "You have forgotten, I think, that the bird Ebony came with me from Tora. *She* carried my message."

Doom cursed under his breath.

Zeean lifted her chin. "It seems you would rather my people were kept ignorant of things they have every right to know," she said icily.

"Stop this, I beg you!" Lief exclaimed, unable to keep silent any longer. "Do you not see? This is what the guardian of the south *wants*! The guardian *wants* distrust between Del and Tora — perhaps only to create fear and confusion, perhaps to stop supplies coming from the west, should food ships ever arrive."

Neither Doom nor Zeean answered.

Lief flung out his hands desperately. "While we fight we can do nothing," he said. "And we must act quickly, before the guardian regains strength enough to stop us. We know that the Sister of the South is somewhere in the palace — "

Jasmine drew a quick breath, Zeean's eyes widened, and even Barda looked up, suddenly alert.

"The Sister is in the palace," Lief repeated. "Josef knew where, I think, but he is beyond telling us now. He may have left us a clue, and the topaz dragon will aid us also. I will summon it as soon as — "

"Summon that menace?" Doom growled. "You cannot — "

"Listen to me!" Lief begged. "There is much you do not understand. We must meet with Gla-Thon, Steven, Ranesh, Gers, and Manus at once. When they are with us, I will explain everything."

He saw Doom's face harden into the familiar, stubborn lines of suspicion and leaned forward urgently.

"Once, Doom, when we knew each other far less well than we do now, we stood together in the Valley of the Lost and heard Zeean say, 'the time for secrecy between friends is past.' Those words are as true now as they were then, I know it!"

The scarred man's eyes met his own. Memories flashed between them. Memories of distrust and heroism, pain and triumph. Memories of plans, of daring, of hope — and even of laughter.

"Secrecy is pointless now," Lief said quietly. "The attack this morning proves that the Shadow Lord knows full well where we are. How, I cannot imagine, but clearly it is so. Fate has decreed that the friends we trust the most are here. We must ask them to help us."

Doom bowed his head. He did not look up as Zeean stepped forward and placed her hand on his arm. But, slowly, he nodded.

"I will gather the others," said Barda gruffly. "Where is the meeting to be?"

265

"Here, old bear, or it will be the worse for you," said a slurred voice from across the room.

They whirled around. Barda gave a choked cry.

Lindal's eyes were open. She turned her head on the pillow and looked at them.

"The gathering must be here," she repeated. "For you leave me out of it at your peril and I fear that — just at the moment — walking is quite beyond me."

7 - Old Friends

Not long afterwards, a strange meeting was held in the lady Sharn's bedchamber. As Sharn herself lay lost in sleep, the Dread Gnome Gla-Thon, Steven of the Plains, Zeean of Tora, Manus of Raladin, Gers of the Jalis, Doom, Barda, and Jasmine gathered around the bed of Lindal of Broome and listened as Lief told them everything.

Only Ranesh had failed to join them. He had flatly refused to leave Josef's side. No entreaties could move him, and at last Barda had been forced to leave him where he was.

When Lief had finished speaking, there was a long silence. Everyone had believed in the Toran Plague so completely that it was hard for them to accept the truth. And all except Barda, Jasmine, and Zeean found it even more difficult to accept that an evil presence prowled the palace.

At last Steven cleared his throat. "Are you saying that this guardian of the south is an Ol?" he growled, his golden eyes flickering dangerously brown. "I thought the Belt had rid Deltora of those slimy, shape-changing creations of — "

"The guardian is no Ol," Lief cut in quickly. "The guardian is a human with powerful gifts of sorcery. The two-faced beast and the black slime I saw sliding away into the palace are merely forms the guardian finds . . . convenient."

There was another moment's silence as his audience took this in.

"If what you say is true, Lief," Gla-Thon murmured, "no food or drink in Del is safe."

"The guardian has been leaving the palace under cover of darkness, but I do not believe the Sister would be left unprotected for long," Lief said. "I think the homes closest to the palace are in the greatest danger."

"Certainly most of the deaths have occurred either in the palace itself or nearby," Doom said, frowning thoughtfully. "It seemed only natural, when we thought of this curse as a plague brought to Del by Sharn. Palace workers who go to their homes each night usually live quite near."

"Then a circle must be drawn around the affected area, with the palace as its center," said Lindal, pulling herself up on her pillows. "All food within the circle must be taken away. The people there must eat only food given back to them after it has been tested."

"Folk will not give up their private food stocks without a fight," muttered Gers.

"I think I could persuade them," Steven said cheerfully. "They have grown to know me and my caravan over the past days. The children like my horse and Zerry entertains them with magic tricks."

He grinned. "If I load the caravan with food that has already been tested, and offer to exchange it for their private stores, the people will agree in good spirits, I am sure."

Lief felt a warm wave of relief that was almost joy. Now ten minds instead of one were working on the problems Del faced. And each one of the ten had something useful to offer.

"I do not understand why, after months or years of remaining hidden, this enemy — this guardian of the south — would suddenly begin poisoning innocent people," Manus said suddenly.

"It did not poison just anyone," Lief pointed out, taking care not to look at Doom. "It poisoned Mother, immediately on her arrival in Del. And then it poisoned all those who had come in contact with her, so that it seemed she was carrying a plague. Plague victims are always isolated from others. People who wish to talk to them are kept away."

269

"Are you saying that all this began to prevent Josef from seeing Sharn?" Doom demanded.

Lief nodded uncomfortably. "I fear so. Josef had discovered something of great importance. He would have passed it on to Mother if he could. He trusted her completely."

"While I was not worthy of trust," Doom said sourly.

"Josef was addle-headed," said Gla-Thon. "I have seen it often in Dread Mountain. Some old ones remain sharp as Boolong thorns till death. Others become filled with fancies. Josef was such a one. He took against you, Doom, because you were firm with him."

Barda shrugged. "Addle-headed or not, Josef plainly had important knowledge in his keeping. And now he is dead, and his assistant, in whom he might have confided, is gravely ill."

"I doubt Josef would have told Paff anything," Doom muttered. "He disliked her."

"If Paff survives, she can tell us one way or the other," Gla-Thon said. "And she may well survive, in fact. She drank only half of the brew that Lief says poisoned her, and she has the strength of youth. If she has the aid of the great emerald as well . . ."

"She will, as soon as we have finished here," Lief said. "And until she can speak, she must be closely guarded. No harm must befall her."

Gla-Thon nodded. "I will see to it," she said, turning quickly to leave as if pleased to have something practical to do.

"Wait, Gla-Thon!" Lief called. "There is something else I must ask of you — and of your people."

"Name it," Gla-Thon said, her hand on the doorknob.

Lief looked at her steadily. "I need every large emerald from the Dread Gnomes' treasure cave. Every emerald, and every amethyst, too."

Gla-Thon's small eyes widened, and for a moment everyone in the room could see, flaring in those eyes, the Dread Gnomes' natural suspicion, and love of treasure.

Then Gla-Thon blinked, and the greedy, suspicious light disappeared.

"Certainly," she said calmly. "The emeralds to help those who have been poisoned. And the amethysts to test food."

"Indeed," said Lief, very grateful for her quick understanding. "There are some jewels here in the palace, but not enough. Naturally the Dread Mountain gems will be returned as soon as the crisis has passed."

"Naturally." Gla-Thon bowed slightly. From one of her pockets she pulled a small bag. She tipped the bag's contents into the palm of her hand and held out a small pile of emeralds, gleaming like green fire.

"I had hoped to purchase food to take home at the end of my stay," she said. "Things on Dread Mountain are improving, but the crops are still young. I soon realized my hope was foolish, but now I am glad I brought the gems with me. They will help us make a start."

"But surely only the gems in the Belt can — " Lindal began.

"Lesser gems are only shadows of the seven in the Belt of Deltora, but still they have some power, especially in large numbers," said Gla-Thon. "The Dread Gnomes have always known this. It is one of the reasons we value gems so highly."

"My plan is to gather all the sick into one place, and the emeralds with them," Lief said. "But the place cannot be the palace, which must be cleared of as many people as possible. I am not sure where else — " He glanced at Doom uncertainly.

"The great food storehouse near the square is almost empty," Doom said. "There is space there for hundreds of beds. Gers, perhaps, can begin the work while I fetch the palace jewels. I will join him as soon as I can."

Gers grunted agreement.

"Very well," said Gla-Thon. "I will see to the gems. I need only a bird to send the message, and the thing will be done."

"I will fetch a bird," Jasmine said, moving eagerly to join Gla-Thon at the door.

"Fetch two," Lief called after her. "Zeean must write again to Marilen."

"Must I indeed?" murmured Zeean. "And what am I to say?"

Lief glanced at her. She had lowered herself into a chair. Her hand was raised to the darkening bruise beneath her eye as if it pained her.

"Your people must be told that the Toran Plague is a lie, and that soon everyone in Del will know it," he said.

Zeean nodded slowly. "And what else?"

Lief hesitated. He had planned to speak further to Zeean in private. Plainly, however, she had already guessed the second part of the message and was not going to permit him to keep any secrets.

Perhaps she is right, he thought. *Everyone should understand what may be ahead.*

"Marilen must come to Del without delay," he said reluctantly. "She is the heir to the Belt of Deltora. When I face the Sister of the South, Marilen must be here, standing in readiness to put on the Belt should I not survive."

He paused. The room was utterly still. Zeean had closed her eyes. Everyone else was staring at him in shock.

"Barda and Jasmine will be with me," Lief went on, without looking at either of his companions. "It will be their task to take the Belt from me and deliver it safely to Marilen, if they feel the time is right."

"You have faced three Sisters before this, and three guardians, too, Lief," Barda said, almost angrily. "Why do you now — ?"

"This is the last Sister, and I fear it will be the most terrible, for all the rage of the Shadow Lord will be focused upon it," Lief broke in. "And — "

He looked down at his hands. *And I have felt disaster ahead ever since I set foot in the palace,* he thought. *The feeling grows stronger with every step I take towards my goal.*

"And the topaz dragon is not merely exhausted, as the dragon of the amethyst was, but injured," he said aloud. "It will try with all its might to rid its land of the Shadow Lord's evil. But the effort may destroy it, and without it I, too, am lost."

Gla-Thon gave an agonized groan. "Then if you die, the fault will be mine, for it was I who shot the beast!"

"No blame can be attached to you, gnome," growled Gers. "You thought you were saving Lief's life. I would have done the same in your place."

"And I," Lindal put in. "No one from Broome, which is built on the ruins of Capra, could doubt the treachery of dragons. And so I have been telling all who ask me, ever since I came here."

Lief did not argue. There was no time for a long discussion about the faith of dragons now.

"All the more reason, then, for Barda to warn the

guards that the topaz dragon is to be protected, not at-tacked," he said instead.

"They will not like that," growled Gers. "They think they saw the dragon savaging their king. It will be hard to persuade them differently."

"They will believe what they are told, and do as they are ordered!" snapped Barda. "If they had re-sponded to our calls for help in proper time, they would have seen the real attacker for themselves."

He shook his head, scowling. "I thought I had left them in good hands with Corris, but it seems that discipline has grown very slack."

"Corris died on the first day of the plague," Doom said. "Dunn, his second in command, is in charge now."

Barda grimaced, but whether this was in regret for Corris or disdain for Dunn, Lief could not tell.

"I suggest we end this meeting now," Doom said abruptly. "There is much to be done, and little time to waste."

There were murmurs of agreement, and soon only Lief, Zeean, Lindal, and Manus remained in the room with the sleeping Sharn.

"There are tasks for all but me, it seems," said Manus softly. "Is there nothing I can do?"

Lief put his arm around the Ralad man's shoul-ders. His heart was heavy, but he kept his voice steady as he spoke.

"You, Manus, have the most important task of all," he said. "You are a builder of Raladin. Your ancestors built this palace, stone by stone. If anyone can help me find where the Sister of the South is hidden, it will be you."

8 - Fearful Discoveries

Leaving Zeean to write her letter to Marilen, Lindal to fume at the weakness that forced her to remain in bed, and Sharn still sleeping, Lief and Manus hurried downstairs to the library.

Lief went to the storeroom and quickly found the large, flat wooden box that held the original plans of the palace drawn by the builders of Raladin for King Brandon long ago. As he lifted the box from its high shelf and took it to a work table, he felt a pang.

Josef had often pointed out this box to him, plainly hoping that he would ask to see the plans. But Lief had never asked. He was bored by the whole idea. Josef had only managed to capture his interest once, when he told Lief that the palace had taken forty years to build.

"Forty years!" Lief had exclaimed.

"Indeed!" Josef had said, beaming. "Brandon

moved in as soon as the ground floor was completed, but he did not live to see the work finished. His son, Lucan, had that honor. Now if you would just lift the box down for me, I will show you . . ."

But Lief had hurriedly made excuses and left the library, promising to examine the plans another day.

Now, it seemed, that day had come. But Josef had not lived to see it.

Manus began taking out the ancient parchments one by one, exclaiming over them in awed fascination.

"Look for secret spaces, especially in central rooms, Manus," said Lief. "Josef said the Sister was in 'the center,' 'the heart.' He may just have meant the palace itself, in the center of Del. But he could have meant that the Sister is hidden somewhere in the center of the palace."

Manus nodded vaguely, his eyes fixed on the plans.

Lief left him and went quickly to Josef's room. He tapped the door lightly, looked in, and was startled to find the room empty.

For a moment he simply stared in astonishment. Then he realized that Ranesh had almost certainly carried Josef to the chapel, where he could lie in state as befitted a Deltoran hero.

Fighting down the lump in his throat, Lief hurried to the desk. As he reached for the open *Deltora Annals* volume that Josef had pulled over his secret work, his eye was caught by the stack of paper tied with blue ribbon lying on the left of the desk.

He glanced at the top page.

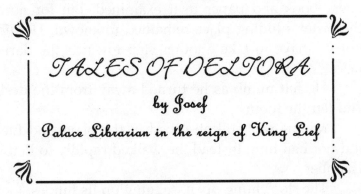

TALES OF DELTORA

by Josef

Palace Librarian in the reign of King Lief

So Josef had finished his book at last. Again the lump rose in Lief's throat. He took a breath and looked back at the heavy open volume in front of him.

It was Volume 1 of the *Annals*, where all the old folk tales were recorded. Lief's heart lurched as he noted that it was open at the tale of the Four Sisters.

Sickened afresh at the thought of the gloating pleasure the Shadow Lord must have taken in naming his own vile creations after the sisters in the old Jalis tale, Lief lifted the book aside.

And there was nothing beneath it at all. Josef, or someone else, had moved or destroyed whatever had been there.

The disappointment was like a blow. But Lief

was ashamed to find that deep within him, below the disappointment and frustration, there was a tiny glow of relief. The room would have to be searched — every book and paper in it examined. But for now, the Sister's hiding place remained unknown. He did not yet have to take another step towards the darkness.

He felt numb as he turned away from the desk and left the room.

Manus was still absorbed in the plans and Lief did not hail him. Instead, he walked rapidly to Paff's chamber.

The door hung open, sagging on its hinges. Lief called softly and went in. Gla-Thon was standing at the end of Paff's bed, bow drawn.

"Ah, Lief, it is you," Gla-Thon said, lowering her bow and moving aside.

Lief could see at once that Paff was much better. Her body had relaxed. Her eyes were closed in what seemed a natural sleep.

"All the emeralds I had are beneath the covers, close to her heart," Gla-Thon whispered. "I put them there the moment I returned. And here is the message to be sent to Fa-Glin."

She held out the note. Taking it with a nod of thanks, Lief approached the bed. It seemed to him that as he drew closer Paff stirred a little. He felt for the clasp of the Belt.

"If we leave her to recover with the aid of my emeralds alone, we will learn much that will help in the treatment of others," Gla-Thon murmured. "It would be a very useful experiment."

Lief hesitated, then shook his head. "Josef may have told her something," he said. "It is a small chance, perhaps, but the sooner she can speak, the sooner — "

He broke off and swung around as he heard the sound of running footsteps and voices outside in the library. He saw from the corner of his eye that Gla-Thon had raised her bow again.

Jasmine appeared at the door. Her face was deathly pale. Kree was fluttering on her arm, and Filli was whimpering piteously on her shoulder. Behind her Manus hovered, his small, blue-gray face creased in distress.

Lief's heart began to pound. He strode to Jasmine and she reached out for him blindly, clutching the front of his jacket.

"I went to the bird room," she said in a small, tight voice. "The guards were gone. And the birds . . . all the birds — "

"Dead?" Lief exclaimed.

"Dead or — or dying," Jasmine whispered. "Lief, you must come. You must help me. If they cannot be cured, they must be put out of their misery. They — they are suffering."

"Stay with Paff!" Lief called over his shoulder to Gla-Thon. And putting his arm around Jasmine, he hurried with her out of the room.

✳

In the center of the bird room was a living tree, its branches stretching almost to the high, netted roof. Bright sunlight filtered through the tree's leaves, mercilessly lighting the scene below.

All the perches were empty. The straw that covered the floor was littered with black, feathered bodies, some fluttering and twitching horribly, some deathly still.

Kree hunched silently on Jasmine's arm. His golden eyes looked glazed.

"We will help them, Kree," Jasmine said. But her face was haunted as she gazed at the birds, many of which she had raised from chicks, and all of which she had trained.

"Poison," Lief muttered, overturning the water trough by the door with his foot. "The guardian must have crept in here last night, as we approached Del and while the birds were still sleeping. No doubt the plan was to stop any messages being sent from Del."

"Where is the keeper of the birds?" Jasmine hissed. "Where are the guards? Doom promised me the birds would be safe. He swore it!"

"Doom cannot be everywhere," Lief said in a

low voice, unclasping the Belt of Deltora. "And he has to sleep, like any mortal."

He knelt by the nearest living bird, and gently pressed the emerald to its breast. Instantly the bird's piteous struggles ceased. It opened its eyes and clucked feebly.

Jasmine made a small, choked sound. She fell to her knees and touched the bird's head.

"There, Blackwing," she crooned. "There . . ."

Quietly Lief moved on to the next fluttering body. Briefly he remembered Paff, then pushed the thought from his mind. Paff was recovering without his aid. If she had anything to tell, it would have to wait.

✳

Half an hour later, the sun shone down on twelve occupied perches in the bird room. The dozen birds Lief had saved were ruffled and quiet, very aware of the empty spaces all around them.

"Not one of them is strong enough to fly to Dread Mountain," Jasmine said in a low voice, as she and Lief stood watching the survivors.

Kree squawked and flapped his wings.

"No, Kree!" she exclaimed. "You have just flown from Tora. You must — "

Kree screeched and snapped his beak. Clearly he was determined to go to Dread Mountain, whether Jasmine approved or not.

Lief held out the folded paper. Kree plucked it neatly from his hand and held it fast.

"Go and bid him farewell, Jasmine," Lief said gently. "I will not leave the birds until you return."

Jasmine took a deep breath, then nodded and left the room with Kree riding serenely on her arm.

Lief pushed his hands deep into his pockets and began slowly pacing the room, kicking at the straw with the toes of his boots. Around him, the recovering birds crooned and clucked.

He jumped violently as there was a noise behind him. He swung around, reaching for his sword, as the door of the room opened.

Barda walked in, grim-faced. Close behind him was a stocky guard with a balding head and an anxious expression that sat oddly on his red, good-natured face. Lief recognized him as Dunn, Barda's new deputy. A red mask hung around Dunn's neck, as though he had only recently pulled it down.

"Manus told us what had happened," Barda said grimly. "We have discovered Jarvis, the keeper of the birds, dead in his bed. The bird room guards have been found farther down the hallway here. They have not a mark on them, but they, too, are dead."

"Zon and Delta crawled away seeking help, no doubt, sir, and died where they fell," Dunn mumbled.

Barda's lips tightened. "No doubt," he said curtly. "But that must have been well before dawn, for their bodies are already cold and stiffening. Why did you not discover before this that the bird room was unguarded?"

Dunn's red face deepened to dull scarlet. "I have been forced to abandon inspections in this area, sir," he said. "We are shorthanded, sir, because of the Toran Plague. And the bird room is very out of the way."

"That," said Barda through gritted teeth, "is exactly why inspections are needed here, Dunn. And how many times do I have to tell you? There *is* no plague! Stop using the cursed word!"

Dunn wiped his mouth with the back of his hand. "Indeed, you said there was no plague, only poison, sir," he muttered. "The guards on the city gates have been told, as you ordered, and all of us have removed our masks."

Unhappily he fingered the red cloth around his neck. "But Zon and Delta are dead, sir, just like Airlie and Wax, the men who were at the entrance door last night. And none of them were poisoned, I will take my oath on it."

He met Barda's furious eyes, and glanced away quickly.

"You left the strictest orders, sir, that no guard was to accept food or drink while on duty, for in the past, guards have been given sleeping potions by enemies," he mumbled. "Zon and Delta were not the sort to disobey, and neither were Airlie and Wax."

"Nevertheless, somehow they all took poison,"

Barda said firmly. "Get that into your head, and make certain that the other men do the same."

Dunn's ears were very red. Plainly he thought Barda was wrong. He blinked rapidly, but said nothing.

Barda hesitated, then turned to Lief. "It is true, however," he said, looking directly into Lief's eyes, "that those men were good soldiers. They would not have disobeyed my instruction unless . . . they had very good reason."

Lief understood what Barda was telling him. He understood only too well. But the thought was hateful to him. His mind did not want to accept it.

Dunn was shifting from foot to foot.

"Can I go now, sir?" he asked nervously. "The men watching over Zon and Delta will be growing impatient, waiting for me."

"Be off, then," Barda sighed. "But Dunn, try to remember that you are my deputy now. Be considerate by all means, but do not fear the men's displeasure or they will not respect you."

Dunn ducked his head and hurried towards the door, pulling out a large white handkerchief to mop his brow.

"He will have to be replaced," Barda muttered under his breath. "He is far too anxious to be liked to make a good leader of the guards."

But Lief was not listening. He had darted forward and picked up something that had fallen from Dunn's pocket when the man pulled out his handkerchief.

It was a folded yellow paper. Lief unfolded it and his stomach turned over.

"Dunn!" he shouted. "Where did you get this?"

9 - The Yellow Notice

Dunn stiffened and turned reluctantly. When he saw the yellow paper in Lief's hand, his own hand flew guiltily to his pocket and his blue eyes widened.

"Th — There was a whole pile of them on the table in our eating quarters this morning," he stammered. "I did not think there was any harm in taking one."

"There was no harm in taking one," Lief said, making a tremendous effort to keep his voice level. "No harm in reading it, either. There would only be harm in believing what it says. It is all lies, Dunn."

"If you say so, your majesty," said Dunn. But he did not meet Lief's eyes.

"Is that the Toran Plague rubbish we saw pinned all about the city when we arrived?" Barda exclaimed, glaring at Dunn.

"No, this is something new," Lief said. "Very well, Dunn. You may go."

Gratefully, Dunn escaped from the room, and they heard him almost running down the hallway.

Lief held the yellow paper out to Barda. "You had better read this," he said grimly.

THE TORAN PLOT
THE SORCERERS OF TORA HAVE ALWAYS ENVIED DEL, HOME TO THE ROYAL FAMILY & CHIEF CITY IN THE LAND. NOW THEY ARE PLOTTING TO SNATCH POWER FOR THEMSELVES!

#TRUTH! While our beloved king remains childless, the heir to the Belt of Deltora is the Toran girl Marilen, the puppet of powerful Toran protectors.

#TRUTH! If King Lief dies of the Toran Plague, or is assassinated by Toran spies, Marilen will become queen.

#TRUTH! The new queen will not live in the palace of Del. Her protectors will claim she cannot do so, while Del is racked by famine, dragon attack & pestilence. She will remain in Tora.

#TRUTH! The puppet Marilen is already with child, though she is little more than a child herself. If she becomes queen, her brat will be the new heir to the Belt. It will be born in Tora, & there it will stay. Tora will become the chief city in the land, while Del dwindles.

PEOPLE OF DEL, LET YOUR VOICES BE HEARD!

Let the sorcerers of Tora know that their plot is discovered!

Make them understand that if our king is harmed, we will know who to blame!

Make them see that we will never accept the puppet Marilen as our queen!

Barda whistled. "This is indeed something new," he muttered. "It does not just encourage hatred of Tora. It . . ."

"It threatens Deltora's safety," Lief finished for him. "If Marilen does not have the trust of the people, the Belt cannot be strong. Cracks will open in the armor that protects us from invasion by the Enemy. Everything we have worked for will be in danger."

"Only if you die, Lief," Barda said bluntly.

Lief nodded. The bright room seemed to have darkened.

Indeed, he thought. *And if I face the Sister of the South, I will die. This feeling of foreboding cannot mean anything else.*

For a moment he stood motionless, his head bowed. He heard Jasmine come back into the room, and the rustle of paper as Barda passed her the yellow notice, but he did not move or speak.

Concentrate on the matter at hand for now, he was telling himself. *There is still time to decide whether to face the Sister or not. When you know where it is. When . . .*

"These notices are not being written by a citizen of Del," he said in a low voice. "They are the work of the guardian of the south."

He looked up. Jasmine had lifted her eyes from the notice and was staring at him in amazement. Barda, however, was slowly nodding.

"Do you not see, Jasmine?" Lief went on. "Raising hatred of my heir is the perfect way to make me fear risking my life by attacking the Sister of the South. The guardian is a dangerous enemy — subtle, quick-thinking, and very clever."

"It is someone we all know and trust," Barda muttered. "It is someone from whom a guard would take food or drink without suspicion, despite his orders."

Jasmine's eyes had darkened until they were almost black.

"Why do you say the guardian is quick-thinking?" she asked slowly.

Lief shrugged. "To stop Josef from telling what he knew, Mother was poisoned, and false fears of a plague were created. This led to the idea of raising hatred of Tora. Then the guardian remembered that my heir was Toran, and this in turn led to an even better idea."

He flicked the yellow paper in Jasmine's hand.

"There is such a thing as being too clever," Barda said. "These notices will be our hidden enemy's undoing. Sorcery may have been used to copy them in large numbers, but the yellow paper is real enough. I will order a search, and if we find a stock of it hidden in someone's chamber, we will know . . ."

Lief nodded. He took the notice from Jasmine, feeling as if his arm and hand were weighed down by stones.

"I must show this to Zeean," he said. "I cannot risk her seeing it by accident, as we did. And I must tell her that there is no bird fit to carry a message to Tora."

"It is fortunate that there is not," Barda said, with a grim smile. "It would be folly for Marilen to show her face in Del now — even if her father would allow her to come."

"Marilen can surely do as she likes!" Jasmine exclaimed. "She is a married woman now. And her husband, the father of her child, is here."

"Perhaps he is," Barda said, with a shrug. "But Marilen is a Toran, Jasmine. Her father has great influence over her. And if the Torans felt coldness towards Del before, it is nothing to what they will feel if they suspect that people believe this latest notice."

He grimaced. "The strange thing is," he said, "what the notice says makes good sense. Tora *has* always envied Del its favored place in the land. Marilen *is* heir to the Belt. She *does* have powerful protectors. She *is* with child — "

"But — but you almost sound as if you *believe* that Tora is plotting against us, Barda!" Jasmine cried passionately.

Barda's face grew stern. "I am saying only that we should keep our minds open," he said. "And from this moment, we should trust no one but ourselves."

❋

Hurrying up the stairs soon afterwards, Lief heard the sound of stumbling feet and labored breaths from above. He looked up and saw a hand grasping the curving railing of the staircase, high above his head.

His heart in his mouth, he pounded upward till at last he came upon Lindal, huddled on the stairs.

"Thank the heavens!" she gasped. "I could go no farther. Lief — I fear you have made a terrible mistake. Zeean is deathly ill. And Sharn . . . is sinking. But it was not poison. They ate nothing, drank nothing . . ."

Lief ran. He ran with no thought in his mind at all.

The door to his mother's bedchamber was wide open. As he rushed into the room he saw at a glance the red marks again bright on Sharn's face. He saw Zeean lying back in her chair, sweat gleaming on her brow, her cheeks, chin, neck, and arms covered with the same scarlet swellings.

Panic-stricken, he lifted Zeean and carried her to his mother's bed. He put her down beside Sharn, then tore the Belt of Deltora from his waist and stretched the Belt's gleaming length over the two of them.

The amethyst gleamed pale pinkish-mauve, tormenting him.

The amethyst calms and soothes, Lief thought wildly. *And it loses color near poisoned food or drink. What mistake could I have made?*

"The amethyst calms and soothes . . ." he repeated aloud.

293

And, abruptly, the rest of the words came to him, just as he had first seen them in *The Belt of Deltora*.

† **The amethyst calms and soothes. It changes color in the presence of illness, loses color near poisoned food or drink . . .**

The words Lief had forgotten flamed in his mind.

It changes color in the presence of illness . . .

His heart gave a sickening thud. Wildly he looked again at the amethyst. But surely it had paled, not merely changed color! Surely . . .

They ate nothing, drank nothing . . .

His mind was roaring, struggling in the grip of a nightmare more terrifying than any he had ever faced.

He had been wrong. The birds had been poisoned, certainly, but the people had not. All along, the amethyst had been reacting to illness, not to poison. The Toran Plague was real.

In horror he thought of Kree, flying to Dread Mountain. There was no other bird to send after him. And the emeralds the gnomes sent would be useless. It was not the emerald, the antidote to poison, that had revived Lindal and aided Sharn. It had been the strength of the diamond beside it that had helped them — for a time.

Every plan he had made was pointless. Everything he had said at the meeting had been based on a terrible mistake.

The meeting . . .

Lief buried his face in his hands.

Zeean had removed her mask because she had believed in him. Jasmine, Barda, Doom, Manus, Steven, Gers, and Gla-Thon had all gathered in this room unprotected — because they had believed in him.

And what of the guards even now carrying Zon and Delta away? What of all their comrades, forced by Barda to remove their masks?

I have killed them all, Lief thought despairingly. *And I have killed myself. The diamond would have protected me from the pestilence, no doubt, if I had taken ordinary care. But . . .*

But he had taken no care. He had exposed himself recklessly to infection. The plague was surely within him, and sooner or later it would show itself.

The plague works quickly once it strikes.

Not so quickly for him, perhaps. The diamond's power would keep him alive for a time. He would live to see the deaths of his mother, of Zeean, of Jasmine, Barda, Doom . . . all those he loved and had betrayed.

But he would never now face the Sister of the South. He would not die fighting, but sweating in the grip of pestilence. Then Marilen would have to claim the Belt.

Shakily, Lief pulled out the yellow notice and read the final lines.

Make them understand that if our king is harmed, we will know who to blame!
Make them see that we will never accept the puppet Marilen as our queen!

As he read, as he faced what already he knew, cold dread pierced his heart.

This was the disaster Ava had predicted. *This* was the doom he had felt looming ahead from the moment he entered the palace.

He had thought he could decide whether to take the final step or not. But the final step had been taken long ago, without his knowing it. It had been taken the moment he pulled the red mask from his face and announced that the Toran Plague was a lie.

He had delivered Deltora into the Shadow Lord's hands. He alone.

"Lief . . ."

Lief's head jerked up. Zeean's eyes were open. She was looking at him.

"We were wrong, it seems," she said softly, trying to smile.

Lief's heart felt as if it was being squeezed by a giant hand.

"Zeean, I am sorry," he choked. "I truly believed — "

"Lief, listen to me," Zeean whispered. "I am old. I have seen much, and I know. One mistake cannot ruin a life or a kingdom. It is what is done *after* that mistake, that decides. Remember the lessons of history. Despair is the enemy. Do not let it defeat you . . ."

Her voice trailed away. Her eyes closed.

Lief stared down at her. The red marks were fading from her face. Either the diamond was strengthening her a little, or she was dying.

Despair is the enemy. Do not let it defeat you . . .

"I am already defeated," Lief murmured. "Everyone is dying, Zeean. Everyone who trusted me. There is no one . . ."

Then he remembered. There was one person left — the very person who might . . .

Slowly he picked up the Belt of Deltora, and clasped it once again around his waist. He touched Zeean's cheek. He bent and kissed his mother's brow.

Then he left the room, without looking back.

10 ~ Voices of the Dead

Lindal was still crouched on the stairs where Lief had left her. She raised her head as he passed, but she did not speak and Lief did not stop. He reached the bottom of the stairs without meeting another soul. The entrance hall was also deserted. It was as if the palace was empty of life.

People could not have fallen ill so soon, Lief told himself. *They are all somewhere else, carrying out our plans, that is all.* But at the same moment, horrible pictures flashed into his mind.

He imagined Gla-Thon crumpled beside Paff's bed, Doom groaning amid a tangle of useless jewels, and Manus slumped over the palace plans. He imagined Steven writhing on the seat of his caravan, while his savage brother Nevets raged within him and Zerry cried out in terror. He imagined terrified guards backing away from Barda's plague-marked body, pulling masks back over their faces, too late. And Jasmine, lying helpless among her beloved birds.

A hollow ache began deep within him.

Despair is the enemy. Do not let it defeat you . . .

He made his way to the flight of steps that led down to the chapel. He stumbled down the steps and pushed the chapel door open.

Josef's body lay on the marble platform, dressed in the traditional velvet tunic and white gloves of a palace librarian. Candles burned around him.

Ranesh was kneeling beside the platform. He turned quickly as the door opened. His mouth and nose were covered by a red mask, and he was also wearing white gloves.

Lief let out his breath in a shuddering sigh of relief.

It was as he had hoped. Alone and grieving here, forgotten by all, Ranesh had not heard the tale that the plague was a lie. He was almost certainly the only person in the palace who had not removed his mask. By a strange accident of fate, he alone had some chance of safety.

Lief stepped into the ring of candlelight and looked down at Josef.

The old man's face was peaceful. The furrows of suffering had been smoothed away. The scarlet marks of the Toran Plague were gone.

Ranesh climbed stiffly to his feet.

"Josef deserves this honor," he said, with a touch of defiance. "He deserves it as much as any king."

"He does, indeed," Lief said in a low voice.

Ranesh stared at him. "You are not wearing a mask," he said dully. "Does the Belt protect you from the plague?"

Without waiting for an answer, he turned back to look at Josef.

"I failed him, but he said not one word of reproach," he muttered. "When I asked his forgiveness, he said there was nothing to forgive."

Lief's heart gave a wild leap. He had not realized that Josef had spoken again before he died.

Perhaps even now it is not too late for me to make some use of the last hours of my life, he thought, hope rising within him. *I have not yet fallen ill. There is still time to destroy the Sister. If Josef told Ranesh where . . .*

"Ranesh, what else did Josef say?" he asked urgently. "Did he say anything about a paper on his desk?"

Ranesh shook his head. "Every word was an effort. We had but a few moments, and he spoke only of private matters."

"Tell me!" Lief insisted. "Ranesh, I beg you."

Ranesh set his lean jaw. "He said he wanted to be laid to rest in the tunic of his office. He told me that all his personal possessions were to be mine except for the manuscript of his new book, which was to be presented to you. And . . . that was all."

The tiny pause before the last words rang alarm bells in Lief's mind.

"No!" he burst out. "There was something else, I know it. You *must* tell me — "

Ranesh swung around to face him, hazel eyes blazing with anger. "Josef said I was his son, in all but blood," he hissed. "He said he loved me, and was proud of me. And then he died."

He clenched his fists. "Now are you satisfied, Lief? Now that you have heard everything, even something that only *I* had the right to hear, will you leave me alone with my grief?"

Lief bit his lip. "I am sorry," he said softly. "But I cannot leave you alone. There is something you must do."

"I can do nothing," Ranesh muttered. "I must watch over Josef till dawn tomorrow, as is the palace way. You must ask someone else to run your errands."

Lief clenched his own fists. "By dawn tomorrow, every person in the palace will be dead, Ranesh," he said in a level voice. "The plague will have finished them. I may still be alive, but I will be so feeble that I will be useless. You are the only one who can do what must be done."

As Ranesh gaped at him in horror, he pulled the yellow notice from his pocket and held it out.

"You must take a horse and ride like the wind to Tora," he said. "Show this notice to Marilen, and tell her that it is the work of one who would hand Deltora to the Shadow Lord. Tell her that our land's fate is in her hands."

Ranesh's face darkened as he read the notice.

"Marilen must come here, despite the plague, and take possession of the Belt," Lief said. "She must convince the people that she is not just a Toran puppet, but the true queen of the whole of Deltora. And you must stand beside her, Ranesh. You are of the people, and they know you. Ranesh — "

"There is no need to say more," Ranesh murmured, tucking the yellow notice into the pocket of his coat.

Gently he touched Josef's shoulder. Then he walked to the chapel door. Standing there, he seemed taller than he had before.

"Never have I been asked to take responsibility for anything," he said. "I have been a thieving boy of the streets. I have been the student and helper of Josef. I have been the husband of Marilen. But you have put your trust in me, Lief, and I will not fail you."

"The guards will let you pass," Lief said soberly. "They will tell you that you do not need your mask, but they are wrong. Do not uncover your face until Del is well behind you."

Ranesh nodded briefly, and was gone.

302

Left alone, suddenly drained of all energy, Lief sank to his knees beside the platform.

Now he had to spread the word that he had been wrong, that the plague was real after all. Every moment he delayed, more and more people were taking off their masks, exposing themselves to infection.

But he stayed where he was. He pressed his burning brow against the platform's cold marble. The heavy silence of the small, chilly room was so intense that it seemed to make its own sound.

It came to him that his family was cursed — cursed by the wonder that was the Belt of Deltora. The Belt had weighed down generation after generation of kings and queens unworthy of its power.

And suddenly Lief was almost glad that now he would never marry Jasmine, that they would never have a child to wear the Belt in his place.

Any child of mine would come into the world only to suffer struggle, sorrow, fear, and failure, he thought. *Like me. Like my father. Better — far better — never to have been born.*

The Belt hung heavy at his waist. Suddenly he loathed it.

Let it lie here for Marilen, he thought. *I have had enough of it.*

He seized the Belt and tried to take it off. The clasp resisted his trembling fingers. Almost sobbing with frustration he struggled to loosen it. His fingers slid over the great diamond, the emerald, the lapis-lazuli, the topaz . . . and there they froze. For the next gem in line was the opal, and that he would not touch.

The rainbow stone could give glimpses of the future. And he did not want to see the future. He could not bear it.

He remembered that only one of Deltora's last seven dragons remained locked in enchanted sleep — the dragon of the opal, the dragon of hope. *It is an omen,* he thought. *Now the opal dragon may never again fly Deltora's skies. Just as hope may be lost to us forever.*

The topaz warmed beneath his fingertips. And suddenly the chapel was filled with shadows, drifting around him like smoke.

✝ **The topaz is a powerful gem, and its strength increases as the moon grows full. . . . It has the power to open doors into the spirit world . . .**

Lief began to shiver. *Tonight it will be a full moon, as it was the night we burned the Enemy's crystal, the night this all began,* he thought. *The spirits of my ancestors came to me then, to aid me. Now they come to me again, but this time . . .*

Spirit voices began echoing from the marble walls, crying out wildly. Lief could not make out what they were saying. But the misty faces were angry and fearful. No doubt they were accusing him of cowardice and faithlessness. He did not care.

"I *will* take it off!" he roared, tearing at the clasp of the Belt. "I will *die* free of it, at least!"

And then, among all the shadowy forms, he saw Josef. Josef was holding out his arms beseechingly. His lips were moving, but Lief could not hear a single word.

"Josef, I cannot hear you!" Lief shouted. "Josef — "

He swung around as the chapel door opened.

A small blue-gray figure stood in the doorway, a large piece of parchment clutched in his hand.

"Manus!" gasped Lief. Quickly he glanced back to where he had last seen the shade of Josef. There was nothing there. All the shadows had gone.

"I am sorry to disturb you, Lief," Manus said, a little nervously. "I did not know you were here. I came to see — "

He broke off, staring at Josef's body lying on the candle-ringed platform.

"Ah, how could anyone do such a terrible thing?" he exclaimed, in a completely different tone. "It is — abominable!"

"I am not sure now that Josef's death was planned," Lief managed to say, clambering to his feet. "Manus — "

"No, no!" Manus broke in, hurrying forward. "I was not referring to Josef's death. I meant this — this great ugly monument here. Abominable!"

He kicked the side of the marble platform violently.

Lief stared, trying to gather his wits. He had never seen the Ralad man so angry. Even the tuft of red hair on Manus's head seemed to be quivering with rage.

"This chapel was one of the first rooms to be completed when the palace was built," Manus panted. "It was to be a place of peace — a refuge from the bustle of palace life. And so it was, by the drawings. It was exquisite!"

Again he kicked the side of the platform. "And then, this monstrous *thing* was built right in the center of the floor, completely ruining the space! Look at it! High as your shoulder, and half again as long! Ah, that man! King or no king, he was a buffoon!"

Lief's heart had begun pounding painfully. "King Brandon?" he asked huskily.

"Not *Brandon*," snorted Manus. "Brandon had an eye for beauty. This — this *crime* was committed by his son, King Lucan."

He scowled ferociously. "The Ralad builders played no part in it, I assure you. They were working on the upper floors of the palace by then. The first they knew of it was when Rufus, their chief, visited the chapel and saw what had been done."

He flapped the parchment angrily. "Rufus was horrified, of course. He found the original plan of the chapel — I have it here — and wrote a note upon it to the king, begging that the room be restored to its original state. But King Lucan refused absolutely. Or so

306

his chief advisor said, in the insulting note he wrote back."

"What was this chief advisor's name, Manus?" Lief asked in a low voice.

Manus thrust the parchment forward. "See for yourself!" he exclaimed bitterly, stabbing a finger at the words penned beneath the Ralad builder's note.

The King wishes the chapel to remain exactly as it is. Do not raise the matter again.

DRUMM

11 - The Dare

Lief turned away from the parchment and looked down at Josef's peaceful face. *So this is what you were trying to tell me, Josef,* he thought. *The evil is here, in the palace's dead heart, the center of centuries of grief and pain.*

Gently he gathered the old man's body in his arms and lifted it from the platform.

"Lief, what are you doing?" Manus cried, very shocked. "The platform is vile, yes! But I did not mean — "

But cradling Josef's frail body, Lief was already walking to the chapel door.

"Drumm was chief advisor in the time of Doran the Dragonlover, when the Four Sisters were put in place," he called back over his shoulder. "He caused the platform to be built. The Sister of the South is here, I know it."

"But this is not the center of the palace, Lief!" Manus exclaimed, trotting anxiously after him. "It could not be farther to the side!"

He gestured behind him at the far wall of the chapel. "That is the palace's east wall. The Place of Punishment once stood just outside. The Great Hall is above — "

"I know, Manus," Lief said quietly. "But still this is the place."

He carried Josef's body up the steps and placed it gently on the floor of the entrance hall.

"But — but you cannot leave him here!" Manus cried in horror.

"Better here than where he was," Lief said. He turned to go back into the chapel.

"Lief, wait a little," said Manus nervously, plucking at his sleeve. "You are pale as a ghost! Your hands are trembling. You — you are not well."

"I fear I am not," Lief murmured. "I do not know how much time I have left. And that is why I must hurry."

His shadowed eyes focused at last on the Ralad man's worried face, and he blinked, as if waking from a dream.

"I am sorry, Manus," he said softly. "There is no easy way to tell you what I must. I have made a fearful mistake, and all of us will pay for it. There is no poison. The Toran Plague is real."

Manus took a sharp, hissing breath and clasped

his hands over his heart. Lief braced himself for the cries of shock, fear, and blame that he knew must come. But the Ralad man bent his head, and when he looked up again, his black eyes were clear and calm.

"What must I do to help?" he asked simply.

For a moment Lief could not speak. Then he put his hand on Manus's arm — so small and thin, and yet so full of strength.

"What is below the chapel?" he asked.

"Why — nothing," Manus said. "The outside wall runs down beneath the earth, to meet the palace foundations. The inner wall beside us here continues down to form the first wall of the dungeons below the entrance hall. By the plan, there is only empty space in between — a cavern too small and low to be used for anything."

"The Enemy found a use for it, it seems," Lief said grimly. "Now listen carefully, Manus. Everyone, except those too ill to walk, must leave the palace at once. Tell them it is by order of the king. Tell them to put their masks back on, go down to the city, and spread the word that the plague is real. Then go yourself, Manus. Find Doom, Gers, and Steven, if you can, and tell them I . . ."

His throat closed. He struggled to go on, but this time he could not.

"You have not mentioned Barda and Jasmine," Manus said quietly. "They are here, in the palace. Do you really think that they will leave 'by order of the king'?"

Lief gave a twisted smile. "No," he admitted. "If they are still able to come to me they will, whatever I say. We will stand together against the Enemy, one last time."

Manus nodded, his eyes very bright, and darted away without another word.

Lief put his fingers on the topaz once more and silently, insistently, called to the golden dragon.

✻

The top of the platform was a smooth slab of marble bordered by a raised band carved in swirling patterns. Lief wondered if it could be removed. He put his shoulder to the slab and pushed. The slab did not budge.

"You will not shift it that way," boomed a familiar voice. Lief looked around to see Barda striding towards him, with Jasmine by his side. Over his shoulder the big man carried the vast iron bar from the entrance doors, as easily as he might carry a log of wood for the fire.

"Jasmine and I met at the bottom of the stairs," Barda said, lifting the bar from his shoulder with a grunt and moving to the side of the platform. "She had just been talking to Manus and was coming here, so I thought I would join her."

Jasmine took Lief's arm. "The birds are all well,"

she said. "They, at least, *were* poisoned, and the emerald worked to a marvel. Oh, Lief, it gives me such joy to know that they will live to fly again."

Very moved, Lief looked down at her. She was smiling.

Barda eyed the platform and nodded. "It seems to me that brute force would best serve our purpose here," he said. "It is not an elegant way to solve a problem, but sometimes it is better to cut through a knot than to waste time trying to untie it. More satisfying, too, on occasion."

He tapped the side of the platform with the end of the bar. "It sounds hollow," he said with satisfaction. "Move the candles aside, my friends. We need room to move."

"Barda — " Lief choked, as Jasmine began pushing the nearest candleholders away.

But Barda shook his head. "What Lindal did not tell me when I met her upstairs, Jasmine told me just now," he said over his shoulder. "We both know all there is to know, Lief, and there is no more to be said. Let us do what we are here to do, while we are able."

He stood back a little and aimed the bar so that it pointed directly at the center of the platform's side.

"Stand behind me, Lief, and take hold of the bar. We are going to use it as a battering ram."

Speechless, Lief did as he was told.

"When I give the signal, thrust the bar forward

with all your strength," Barda instructed. "Jasmine, keep your head down and Filli out of sight. Splinters of marble may fly."

He drew the bar back. "Ready . . . NOW!"

Lief lunged forward. The end of the bar smashed into the side of the platform with a clanging jolt. The shock of the impact jarred Lief's arms and ran all the way to his jaw.

"Again," roared Barda, pulling the bar back. "Put some muscle into it! Ready . . . NOW!"

Again the bar hurtled forward, striking the marble with a fearful crash. There was the sound of falling stone and Jasmine gave a shout of triumph.

Eagerly, Lief craned his neck to see.

The platform's side was cracked, and a chunk of marble had fallen away near the center, leaving a small, jagged black hole.

"That is what we want!" growled Barda. He settled his mighty hands on the bar once more. "Ready, Lief . . . NOW!"

The end of the bar battered straight into the weakened spot. A huge piece of marble broke away and fell, smashing on the ground.

"And again!" Barda roared.

Again they lunged forward. And this time, when they drew back, the ground at their feet was heaped with smashed marble, the air was full of dust, and most of the platform's side was nothing but a gaping black hole.

They let the bar fall. It crashed to the ground with a dull, ringing sound. Barda bent forward, his hands on his knees, panting.

Lief's hands were slippery with sweat. Sweat was dripping into his eyes and soaking his hair. He wiped his brow dazedly with the sleeve of his jacket, and realized that his hands were trembling.

The black hole loomed before him, dark as pitch, gaping like the entrance of a tomb. He could see nothing inside it. Fear twisted in his stomach.

Jasmine pushed a candle into his hand. The flame wavered dangerously as he bent in front of the hole. Holding his breath, he thrust the candle forward . . .

Except for a scattering of broken marble, the cavity was completely empty.

"There is nothing here," Lief called, his voice echoing eerily against the marble walls. "There is nothing — "

The candle fell from his shaking hand. It rolled twice and then lay still on the base of the cavity. Its struggling flame flickered on the flat, gray stone that lay beneath the rubble of broken marble.

Lief's mouth went dry. He crouched, grasped the dying candle, and swept it from side to side, clearing the chips of marble away.

"On the floor," he said in a low voice.

Barda and Jasmine knelt beside him, each holding a fresh candle. By the flickering light they all read

314

the words on the stone — words still as sharp and clear as the day they were carved:

LOSE AND WIN? OR WIN AND LOSE?
ROYAL COWARD, YOU MUST CHOOSE.
BOW YOUR HEAD AND CREEP AWAY,
OR YOU AND YOURS WILL CURSE THIS DAY.

Lief felt his face grow hot with fury. A wave of trembling sickness swept through him and he closed his eyes, waiting for it to pass. He did not know if the sickness was caused by the evil of the stone or by the Toran Plague. It did not matter. All that mattered were the sneering words on the stone — the words of the Shadow Lord, meant for him, only for him.

"This verse is not like the verses on the stones in the east, north, and west," Jasmine muttered, putting Lief's raging thoughts into words. "Those others were true warnings, intended for the eyes of any passing stranger. This is — personal."

"Indeed," Lief said thickly. "It is a dare. The Enemy is daring me to look beneath the stone. As once he dared me to look for the first part of the map."

He remembered the voice of the Shadow Lord, hissing through the crystal.

. . . this king will never find it. I dare him to try, and go more quickly to his death . . .

But I did find the first part of the map, and I did not die, Lief thought. *Then I found the second part, and the third, and the last. And I am still here.*

But he knew that the Enemy had planned for this, too. The message on the stone proved it.

Plans within plans . . .

"Smash the evil, sneering thing," Jasmine muttered. "Smash it to pieces!"

"Stand aside," Barda said grimly, getting to his feet and reaching for the iron bar.

Lief and Jasmine scrambled out of his way.

And Barda, teeth bared in a snarl of hatred, smashed the end of the iron bar down on the warning stone. He struck once, twice . . . and on the third stroke there was a sharp crack and a brilliant flash of white light.

Barda staggered back, his hands pressed to his eyes. The heavy bar fell, clanging, to the ground. Cracks ran crazily over the stone till the whole flat, carved surface was a maze of black lines. Then, suddenly, the shattered stone fell away, fell with a sound like thundering hail. And all that was left in its place was a yawning pit from which evil poured like a thick, vile smell.

Jasmine cried out and covered her face. Lief fell to his knees and stared. His eyes were watering, but he could not look away.

For down in the center of the darkness something gleamed — something as beautiful and beckoning as one of the gems on the Belt of Deltora.

The Sister of the South.

12 ~ Creeping Darkness

Shouts of terror and warning were echoing in the entrance hall. The sounds floated into the chapel, but Lief did not hear them. He was staring down into the pit, staring at the shining thing that lay there.

He could see it clearly now. It was a great gem, gray as the evening sky, but swirling with lines of scarlet light. It was singing to him, singing the song of his land, the song that was part of him, the song he had first heard in the cradle, without knowing it.

It was beautiful, alive, filled with terrible power.

He knew that if only he could touch it, hold it, have it for his own, he could do anything — anything in the world.

I did not understand, he thought, awestruck. *I did not dream . . .*

He slid his hands over the marble floor tiles that

318

edged the pit. With his fingers he felt the rough, sawn edges of the wood beneath.

In his mind he saw dark figures cutting through the chapel floor. He saw the shining gem lowered into place, and the stone placed over the gap in the floor to seal it. He saw the marble platform being constructed, to conceal what lay beneath.

Long ago, so long ago . . . and ever since, the wonder had lain in the darkness, singing the song of its power, and waiting, waiting for *him*.

"LIEF!" The bellow penetrated his consciousness. He stirred irritably, turned to see who had interrupted him.

A frizzy-haired gnome stood at the door of the room, waving her arms at him. Lief frowned. Perhaps he knew her face. He could not remember. But did the fool not realize that he had no time for her ravings now? Could she not feel the power — ?

"Lief, you must come!" the gnome gabbled. "The golden dragon — the dragon I injured — it is flying over the city! It is roaring, breathing fire. Lief — "

Her voice, harsh as the screeching of a raven, broke off. Her face paled. Her foolish eyes widened. She fell to her knees, wrapping her arms about her head.

Lief smiled. *Now she feels it,* he thought. He began to turn back to the pit.

"Gla-Thon — get away from here!" a shaking voice called behind him.

319

Jasmine's voice.

Jasmine . . .

Lief paused, a shadow of doubt flitting across his mind. For a moment he had forgotten Jasmine existed. How could that be?

"Paff is dying," the gnome whimpered. "The plague is eating her alive. Her eyes have rolled back in her head. Her limbs have become rigid as stone. I could not lift her. I had to leave her. Then — I saw — the dragon. The people in the city — screaming, running . . ."

Lief swayed. The power in the pit was calling him. He longed to turn to it once more, feast his eyes on its beauty, lose himself in its wonder, and at last slip silently into the soft, thick darkness to take it for his own.

Then there would be no more pain, no more fear. There would be nothing he could not do, nothing he could not have.

But he did not turn. Something deep within him was resisting, holding him back.

What was it? Numbly his mind groped for the answer, and caught hold of that frail, fluttering shadow of doubt.

Jasmine . . .

If he had forgotten Jasmine, what else had he forgotten? What else . . . ?

There was a roar like a clap of thunder, and

a shuddering thud. The outside wall of the chapel shook.

Gla-Thon cried out in terror.

A soft voice whispered in Lief's mind, hissing through the song of the Sister of the South.

I am with you, king of Deltora. We are separated only by a little earth and stone, and that will soon be gone.

The dragon of the topaz, Lief thought, almost in surprise. *It is there, in the palace garden, on the other side of the wall.*

He looked down at the Belt around his waist. He saw the topaz shining like a great, golden star. It was as if he was seeing it with new eyes, as he had seen for the first time, in the Forests of Silence.

At the beginning. At the very beginning. When he thought he knew exactly who he was. When Jasmine and Barda were still almost strangers. When he had no idea what fate held in store for him, for all of them.

He laid his fingers on the topaz, felt its golden warmth.

This was what he had forgotten . . . this. The dangerous, beautiful thing in the pit had almost snared him. It had almost drawn him in, with its dizzying promises of power, glory, and freedom from the pain of loss.

And for the first time he saw fully the dark power that had enthralled his enemies, those others who had embraced the cause of the Shadow Lord. He almost understood them . . . Rolf the Capricon. Kirsten of Shadowgate. Laughing Jack. And the unknown enemy here, in Del.

I feel the evil presence, very near, king. It is time to put an end to it.

Lief turned his head towards the wall through which the voice had come. He felt he could almost see through the stone — could almost see the great, golden beast crouching there.

The dragon of Del. The dragon of faith.

Yes, he answered silently. *It is time.*

And his heart leaped as he heard the sound of massive talons raking the earth, as he heard the roar of flame searing stone walls exposed to the air for the first time in centuries.

The mortar between the stones at the base of the chapel wall began to crack. Then there was a scrabbling sound, and the stones themselves began to move.

And at that moment Lief heard a muffled shout beyond the wall. He held his breath, straining to hear.

"It is attacking the palace!" the voice roared. "It is clawing at the very foundations! Did I not tell you, Manus? This is what the dragons did to Capra! Ah — you foul, deceiving beast!"

"Lindal, no!" wailed Manus faintly. "Come away! Do not — "

There was a mighty roar of rage and pain, quickly followed by a high scream.

Lief was frozen to the spot, his mind flooded with the dragon's agony, the dragon's anger. He could not move. He could not speak. He could only imagine the blood flowing beneath the point of Lindal's spear, the golden eyes flashing with fury, the huge, spiked tail lashing, crushing, and maiming . . .

"Lindal!"

The shout was Barda's. Barda had staggered to his feet and stumbled to the far wall of the chapel. Now he was leaning against it, leaning against the shifting stones, one hand still pressed to his eyes.

"Lindal!" he bellowed. "Lindal, answer me!"

"Barda, get back!" Jasmine cried sharply.

There was the sound of grating stone. Barda jumped back just as a great gap suddenly appeared in the wall at his feet. Light poured through the gap, blocked instantly by blazing fire, and then by vast talons raking away more stones, and more.

Lief heard Filli squeal in terror. He did not turn. His eyes were fixed on the fiery wall.

The dragon's voice hissed in his mind, cold with anger.

The giant woman speared me. I have dealt with her.

Lief's breath caught in his throat. Instinctively he glanced at Barda, who had backed against the end of the marble platform and was now turning slowly, hands fumbling for the platform's edge.

323

In anguish, Lief realized that Barda was blind. In anguish he remembered the searing flash of light that had burst from the warning stone as Barda struck it for the third time.

The dragon's voice came again.

Hundreds of people and soldiers are running up the hill — enemies with clubs and swords. I will kill them all.

No! Lief thought back frantically. *They are not enemies. Our enemy is within. Dig deeper. I am here, but the evil is below.*

Through the charred gap in the wall he saw the flashing golden scales of the dragon, saw earth flying as the vast beast began to dig.

Lief tried to rise, but could not. It was as if his knees were fixed to the ground, as if the thing in the pit had thrown an invisible web around him and was holding him fast.

"Jasmine! Gla-Thon!" he shouted desperately. "People are coming to defend the palace. You must go out and stop them from attacking the dragon!"

There was no reply. And suddenly Lief remembered Filli's scream.

The hair rose on the back of his neck. Slowly he turned his head.

Gla-Thon was crumpled just inside the doorway. Her limbs were twitching horribly.

Plague . . .

But the word had scarcely shaped itself in Lief's mind when Gla-Thon stiffened and jerked onto her back. Then he saw that it was not plague that ailed her.

There was something horribly wrong with her face. Her eyes were bulging. Her mouth was a gaping, bubbling black hole. Her nose was running with what looked like black blood. Thick, black blood was streaming onto the white marble floor.

Lief thrilled with horror. Frozen to the spot, he followed the stream of blood with his eyes. And then he saw, like a vision in a nightmare, someone twisting and thrashing in a pool of surging darkness.

It was Jasmine. A lighted candle still clutched in her hand, Jasmine was drowning in the black blood that seemed to have a life of its own, that seemed—

Lief moaned aloud as he saw the thick, black liquid for what it was. In the same split second he realized that this was how the guards at the entrance door had died. How Zon and Delta had died.

They had not disobeyed orders. They had not died of the plague, or accepted poisoned food or drink from anyone. Taken by surprise, mouths and noses filled with clogging blackness, they had fallen and suffocated, unable to make a sound. And then the black slime had slipped away from them and gone on its way, leaving no trace.

"Let them go, guardian!" he screamed. "It is me you want! Let them go!"

"Lief, what is it?" shouted Barda, his shoulders

tensing, his eyes staring sightlessly around him. "What is happening? Lief—I cannot see . . ."

Black slime reared over Jasmine's struggling body, surging towards Lief like a wave. But Jasmine's face was still covered, and Gla-Thon's mouth and nose were still plugged. Lief knew that part of the slime could overwhelm him while the rest remained with its present victims until all breath had gone, all life had ceased.

There was only one thing that would make it leave them, gather itself together in one place. There was only one threat it could not ignore.

He turned back to the pit. He let himself be drawn closer and closer to the edge.

He looked down to where the Sister of the South glowed in darkness. He felt attraction and repulsion, both at the same time.

"I will destroy you!" he whispered.

And, clutching the Belt of Deltora in both hands, he slid his legs over the edge and jumped.

13 - The Sister of the South

Lief hit powdery earth and rolled. The song of the Sister was like a knife cutting into his brain. He groaned in agony and curled himself into a ball, his eyes screwed shut. But still he gripped the Belt of Deltora, gripped it so tightly that his hands ached, and slowly, slowly the soothing power of the amethyst, the strength of the diamond, gave him the will to open his eyes.

He was lying beside a stone wall. *The outside wall of the palace,* he thought dimly, for through it he could hear the roars of the dragon, and the sound of digging. Painfully he turned his head.

There, not far away, lay the Sister of the South.

It was exactly the size and shape of the seven great talismans in the Belt of Deltora, but he could see it now for what it was — a false gem, a jeering copy.

Beneath its perfect, polished surface, beneath the veins of angry red that twisted and flashed in imitation of life, it was cold, dead gray to its core.

Lief stared at it in fascinated repulsion. Now, with the real gems of the Belt warm beneath his fingers, he could not imagine how he had ever desired it. Yet still he found it hard to tear his eyes away and look above it, to the square hole in the cavern roof.

Dim light shone through from the chapel above, but only a little, for the space was almost filled with bulging, oozing blackness.

Lief's heart thudded. As he had planned, the guardian was coming after him, and coming in haste. He could only hope that the threat he posed to the Sister of the South had been enough to make it gather all its forces together, to leave Jasmine and Gla-Thon before it was too late.

He crawled to his knees and then, painfully, to his feet. Above his head ran the huge lengths of wood that supported the chapel floor. There was just enough height for him to stand upright.

He watched the hole in the roof intently, waiting for a black stream to begin pouring to the ground. Behind him, through the agonizing ringing in his ears, he could hear the dragon's roars, very near. And he could feel — he was sure he could feel — heat radiating from the stones at his back.

The dragon has uncovered the wall, he thought. *It is breathing fire onto the stones. Soon the mortar between the stones will crumble, as it did in the chapel. The stones will loosen and the dragon will be able to rake them away. If only it can reach me before the guardian does! If only . . .*

Make haste! he urged silently. *You are nearly there.*

The only answer was a gust of pain.

And now Lief realized that other sounds were mingling with the dragon's roars. Through the cracks in the wall he could hear roaring voices and the clash of metal.

The guards! he thought in horror. *The guards are attacking the dragon.*

He wanted to turn, press himself against the wall, and scream to the guards to stop. But he knew it would be useless. The men would not hear him. And he did not dare to take his eyes from the hole in the roof, from the crawling blackness that hung there.

He licked his lips nervously. The black slime was moving, rippling downward, he could see it. Why was it not falling?

Then he glanced beyond the hole, at the great beams of wood that made the roof of his prison. And with a thrill of terror, he understood.

The timbers were black with slime. The slime was surging towards him across the roof. It had almost reached him.

With a cry he threw himself to one side. At the same moment, with a harsh, grating sound, a block of stone was ripped from the wall.

Light poured through the gap. Smoky air came

with it, and a tumult of sound — shouting, screaming, the furious roars of the dragon.

And then one voice rose above all the rest, bellowing angrily. Lief thrilled as he heard it.

"Stop, you blundering oafs! Throw down your arms! Get back!"

Barda! Somehow Barda had found his way out of the chapel. He was there, on the other side of the wall.

The shouting died away abruptly. Metal clanged on metal as the guards obeyed their chief's order and cast their weapons aside.

Another block of stone fell away, and another, and another. The golden scales of the dragon, its mighty, clawing talons, almost filled the gap. But still flashes of daylight pierced the dimness of the cavern, dancing on the false gem lying there.

The Sister's glassy surface shone in the light, and its scarlet veins seemed to swell and brighten. Its high, ringing song rose to an ear-splitting wail. Evil belched from it like freezing wind.

Eyes streaming, Lief fell to his knees. He felt the dragon falter. And then, in terror, through the tears that blurred his sight, he saw blackness pouring from the roof of the cavern and forming itself into a bulbous mass, stingers sprouting from it like vines . . .

He knew he was screaming. But his voice was drowned by the wailing howl of the two-faced beast as it lunged towards him, stingers whistling through the air, glistening dog face snarling.

He could not move. He could not lift a hand to his sword. There was only one thing left in his power. He forced his fingers along the Belt till they found the topaz. He focused his mind on the great gem.

Have strength. Make haste. The beast is upon me . . .

The topaz burned beneath his hand. He felt a great surge of power, and with a thunderous crash the last of the wall burst inward.

The two-faced beast howled and screeched as great stones smashed its shapeless body down. And then, before Lief could gather his wits, there was a blur of gold and the flash of mighty talons, and he was raked, tumbling and gasping, out of the cavern and into the open air.

He lay choking, shuddering, half-buried in the dusty soil that the dragon's talons had clawed out with him. He was lying facedown, pressed against one of the dragon's forelegs. Its scales felt slippery wet, and he could smell fresh blood. The song of the Sister filled his ears and his brain. It was louder — louder than ever.

And yet — yet surely he was farther away from the Sister now. He was out of the cavern beneath the chapel. It was still within. Why . . . ?

He forced his eyes open and his stomach turned over. The Sister was no longer underground. It was lying just outside the ruined palace wall, its red veins blazing through a fine coating of dust.

Intentionally or by accident, the dragon had pulled it out of the cavern with him. It was very near. Its evil was battering him into the earth.

And not only him. For now Lief became aware of sobbing and crying, groans of terror and despair. The sounds seemed to be coming from above. Making an enormous effort, he rolled on his side and looked up.

He and the dragon were at the bottom of the great pit the dragon had dug to expose the underground wall of the cavern. Above them, crowded around the edges of the pit were hundreds of people in red masks.

Many were palace guards, but many were not. People had come running from the city, full of courage, determined to defend the palace against the dragon. But now they were on their knees, moaning and sobbing, their hands pressed to their ears. The evil power of the Sister had beaten them down.

Only three people were still standing, huddled together on the side of the hole that was nearest to the back of the palace. They were right at the edge, but, squinting into the sun, Lief could not make out who one of them was. It was someone tall, in any case, standing a little behind the others. Doom, he guessed uncertainly.

But there was no mistaking the two at the front.

The two at the front were Barda and Jasmine. Jasmine was holding Barda's arm. Her hair was whipping in the wind. She was swaying where she stood, and her face glimmered pale as moonlight. But she was alive. Alive!

Alive, only to die of the plague, a cold voice in his mind reminded him. *Like Barda. Like you.*

He shook the thought away. Whatever was to come, he was fiercely glad that his companions were with him now. He was glad that the enemy who had tried to destroy them was lying crushed and dead beneath the stones of the fallen wall.

If I survive this, I will know at last who our hidden enemy was, he thought. *The guardian's true form will be revealed in death. I will know . . .*

Now, king of Deltora, while I still have the strength.

The dragon's voice was faint, but still Lief heard it. He knew what was going to happen next. The dragon was going to use the last of its strength to destroy the Sister. It was going to rid its land of the menace that had invaded it, burn the evil thing to ashes.

He pressed his left hand to the dragon's leg, and his right to the topaz. He stared with loathing at the Sister of the South, lying exposed in the dust.

For centuries it had poured misery into mourners in the chapel above its hiding place, and infected with despair the prisoners in the dungeons beside it. For centuries its poison had seeped through the earth into Del, into the Forests of Silence, into the Os-Mine hills, the farms, the shore, the sea, weakening what was good, strengthening what was bad.

Now its time was over.

He felt the dragon gathering its strength. He held his breath, bracing himself for the first blazing rush of heat.

Then he blinked. His mouth fell open and he moaned in disbelieving horror.

The gap in the palace wall behind the Sister was filling with oily blackness. He could actually see more of the liquid evil oozing from between the fallen stones inside the cavity, and joining the black mass in the gap. The two-faced beast had not been destroyed! It was forming again as he watched.

The black mass bulged outward, spilled onto the earth. The beast rose, vast and glistening in the sunlight, stingers budding in their hundreds from its shapeless body. Horribly, its two faces began to form — the dog face snapping and foaming, the red eyes of the bird face burning with hatred.

But even as the faces were still writhing into being, the beast was charging, stingers whipping the air.

Lief rolled desperately aside as, with a roar, the dragon half-spread its wings and rose on its hind legs to meet its foe. Flames gushed from the dragon's jaws and the rippling flesh of the two-faced beast sizzled, quivered, and shrank beneath the searing blast.

The beast howled, but this time it did not retreat.

It lunged forward again, stingers slashing at the soft, pale underside of the dragon's neck till the scales were crisscrossed with streaming lines of blood.

The dragon bared its shining, needle-sharp fangs, preparing to strike.

No! Do not bite! Lief thought frantically, struggling to reach his sword. *That is what it wants you to do. It will fill your throat, stop your breath. Do not —*

The dragon faltered, its spiked tail lashing uselessly against the earth walls of the pit. Then it drew back and again it roared, breathing a jet of fire. Again there was a hideous sizzling sound. The dog face howled ferociously as dozens of stingers withered and fell to dust, the flesh beneath them stiffening and burning.

Then, without warning, the beast sprang. It surged forward like a great black wave, wrapping itself around the dragon's neck. The dragon tried to free itself, clawing at its clinging attacker, cutting through stingers by the dozen. But the deep channels its talons carved in the oily, rippling flesh closed instantly, and for every stinger that fell, another grew to join the others coiled around the dragon's neck, cutting and tightening.

The dragon bellowed in agony. Its forelegs crashed to the ground. Still struggling, it rolled heavily onto its side.

"No!" Lief shrieked. At last he managed to grasp his sword, pull it free. Sweat pouring from his brow, he staggered to his feet and threw himself at the beast, slashing at it wildly.

The beast's neck swivelled. The mad eyes of the dog face blazed at Lief. Foam sprayed from its snarling, snapping jaws. And at the same moment, the bird face gave a bloodcurdling screech of triumph and its cruel, hooked beak began to tear at the dragon's throat.

14 - The Battle of the Pit

There was a bellowing roar from above, and the pit was suddenly flooded with blazing yellow light. The head of the beast jerked upward, the beak of the bird face dripping with blood.

Lief heard Jasmine's scream of warning, heard something huge crashing down into the pit behind him. Before he could think, before he could move, a giant, clawed hand had sent him flying.

He landed heavily halfway up the sloping wall of the pit. Dazed, he looked down.

A golden giant with a wild mane of dark brown hair was attacking the beast, slashing its stingers with claws as sharp as knives, tearing its quivering flesh apart.

"Nevets!" Lief gasped.

Through a haze he saw Steven stumbling down

the hill of earth, following the deep track carved by his savage brother.

Perhaps Nevets was not affected by the Sister of the South, but Steven clearly was. Yet, sword in his hand, he staggered on, his eyes fixed on his brother.

Nevets and I cannot be long apart. We fight together or not at all.

Weak tears sprang into Lief's eyes. So Steven and Nevets of the Plains would die fighting. Well, better that than . . .

He felt a hand on his arm and looked up to see Jasmine crouched beside him.

"You must get away — to the top," she gasped. "Make haste — "

He could see in her haggard face what it had cost her to reach him, but he shook his head.

"I must stay with the dragon," he muttered. "For as long as I can, until the plague — "

Jasmine's fingers tightened on his arm. "There *is* no plague," she said. "Lief, you were right all along. It was poison."

Lief gaped at her. "But — but Zeean! My mother — " he began.

"There was poison in Sharn's lip cream," Jasmine whispered. "Poison taken in through the skin. It was discovered only moments ago."

Lief's head was spinning. He could not quite take in what he had heard. It was amazing. It was wonderful. It changed everything.

But in one way, it changed nothing.

"Nevets cannot defeat the beast," he said thickly. "Whatever he does to it, it will grow again. It will kill him, it will kill Steven, and then it will turn to the dragon. If the dragon has me — has the topaz — there is still a chance it can survive to destroy the Sister."

Jasmine held his gaze for a moment. Then she nodded and took his hand. "Filli is with Barda," she said.

And Lief understood that this meant she intended to stay with him — indeed, that she had always thought it would come to this.

We fight together or not at all.

He did not argue. He simply gripped her hand, and together they slid back into the pit.

The dragon was still lying on its side, its eyes closed. Its golden scales had faded to a dull, sick yellow. With Jasmine's hand in his, Lief struggled to the massive head and kneeled beside it.

The dragon's eyes opened at his touch. Lief felt himself lost, drowning in deep, golden wastes of time and space. He heard the dragon's voice, whispering in his mind.

You have returned to me, king of Deltora.

Yes, Lief answered.

You have brought the female with you, the one with the beautiful hair that is the color of the night.

"Yes," Lief said aloud. His hand tightened on Jasmine's.

Almost, the dragon seemed to smile.

Do not fear. I am no threat to her in my present state. Nest-making is far from my mind. Who is the golden giant who fights with dragon claws?

"He and his brother come from the Plains, in the territory of the Opal," Lief said, using words he felt would be understood.

The dragon sighed.

Ah, yes. The territory of the Opal breeds strange beings, so it is said.

The golden eyes closed again.

Strange beings . . .

And suddenly Lief remembered Ava, the blind teller of fortunes, speaking of her brothers, Laughing Jack and Tom the shopkeeper.

As children at home on the Plains we were very alike to look upon, it is said, and our minds could link as though we were three parts of a whole . . .

Another strange family of the Plains. Was this simply chance? Or — ?

"Lief!" Jasmine whispered urgently. "Lief — look!"

Lief turned his head and his heart leaped.

Nevets was still ripping and tearing at the two-faced beast. The golden fur covering his massive body was matted with foam, black streaks, and blood. The ground at his feet was littered with twitching stingers and chunks of oily flesh.

Steven was fighting on the other side of the beast, slashing stingers where he could, warding off the screeching bird face as it struck at him again and again.

But something had changed. The stingers on the ground were shrivelling. The lumps of torn flesh were no longer dissolving into black slime and running back to the beast's body, but were drying and hardening where they lay.

"What is happening?" Jasmine breathed. "It looks as if the beast can no longer renew itself. It is as if . . ."

"As if the sorcery is failing," Lief said slowly.

His eyes moved to the Sister of the South. Through the veil of dust that masked it, he could see that its red veins had dimmed. And — and surely its song was lower, less piercing than it had been before.

"The evil is less," the dragon murmured. "Ah . . . that is better. That is much better."

Lief glanced at it. Its golden eyes were open once more. Its scales were gaining color by the moment. The blood had ceased flowing from its terrible wounds. The muscles of its jaw rippled beneath his hand as it relished its returning strength.

"The Sister is dying," Jasmine whispered. "But why? Is it the Belt? Steven and Nevets? The sunlight?"

Bewildered, Lief looked back at the fading false gem lying in the dust, and then at the fighting beast.

It was a miracle. Just at the moment when it had seemed that all was lost, the power of the Sister had begun to fail.

And the beast knew it. Confusion and panic mingled with the savagery in the dog face's eyes. The beak of the bird face gaped wide, striking wildly at Steven as if it could not even see his slashing sword.

Steven cried out with pain as the cruel beak of the bird face struck his sword arm, tearing downward. He staggered, clutching the terrible wound. The sword fell from his hand. The bird face screeched in triumph. The dog face slavered and snapped.

And with a thunderous roar of rage Nevets plunged forward, mighty arms outstretched, terrible claws extended, and ripped the beast's head from its body.

For a long moment, the scene seemed frozen. Nevets stood snarling, holding up the glistening, two-faced head to the sun as if offering it to the heavens. The headless mass of the beast shuddered in front of him.

Then abruptly Nevets threw his hideous prize to the ground and stamped on it, stamped it to jelly. And the headless body collapsed like an empty black sack, crumpling into the dust.

Nevets threw up his head and roared, beating his chest. Then, as if suddenly remembering their existence, he swung around to face Lief, Jasmine, and the

342

dragon. His dark eyes were empty of thought, burning with the desire to go on killing and killing . . .

"No!" gasped Steven. "They are friends!"

But Nevets seemed not to hear him. He bared his teeth savagely and gathered himself, ready to spring.

The dragon growled, deep in its throat. Lief reached for his sword and Jasmine raised her dagger.

"Nevets!" Steven shouted desperately. "I am injured. I need your strength. Return to me, my brother!"

Nevets hesitated. His brutish face twisted as two powerful emotions struggled within him.

"Nevets!" Steven pleaded.

It was enough. Nevets turned on his heel and in two strides was at his brother's side. He took Steven's injured arm tenderly in both his enormous hands. And the next moment, he was no longer a solid figure, but a pillar of blinding yellow light.

Lief could not look at it. He had to turn away. And when he looked back, the savage golden giant with the mane of dark brown hair was gone, and only the golden-haired, brown-skinned Steven remained.

"Now!" Steven rasped, stumbling aside.

The dragon roared, and a plume of golden fire engulfed the dimming Sister of the South. The false gem shone dully in the blaze, then glowed red as a hot coal. Its song became a whine. The red deepened to scarlet and then to a dull brown.

The dragon hissed. And this time the narrow jet of flame that shot from its mouth was white hot. The Sister began to shrivel.

The heat was so intense that again Lief had to turn away. But always he kept his left hand on the dragon's scales, and his right hand on the topaz.

He heard the Sister's whining song rise, rise, and then — stop.

The silence was dizzying.

Slowly, Lief opened his eyes. Where the Sister of the South had been, there was just a tiny heap of white ash, already scattering in the breeze.

"So that is that," growled the dragon with great satisfaction. "It is over."

The silence was abruptly broken by noise from above. Lief looked up. The masked people lining the edge of the pit were on their feet, cheering, shouting, and stamping.

Towering among them was Barda, his arms raised in triumph, Filli squeaking on his shoulder. Beside Barda was the small blue figure of Manus, jumping up and down as if his feet were springs. Gla-Thon was there, too, bow and arrows still clutched in her hand.

And on Barda's other side was the tall straight figure of Lindal of Broome. Lief stared, overjoyed. Lindal had survived! One of her arms was strapped in a rough sling. She was cheering with all the rest. But her eyes were fixed on the dragon, and in her good hand she held a spear.

344

As Lief and Jasmine staggered upright, Steven approached them, grinning shakily.

It is over.

Lief knew that this was a moment for relief and celebration. The people above him were delirious with joy. Yet he felt nothing.

"This seems like a dream," Jasmine murmured, echoing his thoughts. "At the end, it all happened so fast. It does not seem real."

"It is real enough. And it was a near thing, too," Steven said.

"You and your brother did well, man of the Plains," the dragon said, eyeing him with interest. "But do not be proud. By the time your battle ended, the enemy had lost much of its power."

"Indeed?" Steven said politely. "Then my brother and I were fortunate."

Lief was barely listening. He was looking at the drying black scraps that were all that remained of the two-faced beast.

"The beast did not transform," he said slowly.

"Perhaps it was too badly damaged," Jasmine said. "Or it may not have had a human form after all."

"Perhaps," Lief murmured. "But the guardian of the north conjured up a phantom to hunt us on the way to Shadowgate. What if the guardian of the south had the same power, but even greater? What if the black slime was — sent?"

"But surely the guardian would have to go into

345

some sort of trance to accomplish such a feat!" Jasmine exclaimed. "And the palace is full of people. The danger of discovery would have been — "

"There would have been little danger of discovery if the dread work was done in the dead of night," Lief broke in. "And that was when it *was* done — until yesterday, just before dawn, and today, when — "

And at that moment a memory flashed into his mind. A memory. A face. A name.

He shook his head. Surely it was not true. He could not bear for it to be true. Yet as he thought frantically, searching for another answer, many things that had puzzled him fell horribly into place.

"You had better return to your people, king of Deltora," the dragon said sharply. "At present they seem happy, but I do not trust them. At any moment they may take it into their heads to attack me again, and I am not yet ready to fight or to fly."

Lief did not waste words in argument. The dragon had good reason to distrust the people of Del. And he, too, felt that his place was above.

There was someone there he had to meet.

15 - The Hidden Enemy

By the time Lief, Jasmine, and Steven had climbed out of the pit, word had spread in the crowd that the plague was, after all, no threat. All but a few cautious souls had once again discarded their masks. Guards and townspeople alike were rejoicing.

Steven mumbled something about finding Zerry, and slipped away. Lief guessed that the thought of facing the curious glances of the crowd made him uneasy.

Few, in fact, had seen Steven and Nevets fighting the beast — the dreadful power of the Sister of the South had seen to that. Only a few more had seen the dragon destroy the Sister of the South.

But all of them knew that a great battle had been fought and won, and that something wondrous had occurred. They all felt a lightness of spirit, a flooding joy.

Many kept tapping their ears, or shaking their heads as if to clear their ears of water. A sound they had always known had gone. For the first time in hundreds of years, the dull, despairing song of the Sister of the South no longer hummed through the air and earth of Del.

Why can I not rejoice? Lief thought for the hundredth time. He gripped Jasmine's hand more tightly. That small, rough hand had become a lifeline for him, a link to what was real, what was true.

He saw that Lindal, Manus, and Gla-Thon had disappeared, and that Barda was now speaking to the guard called Dunn. As Lief watched, Dunn saluted and left Barda at a run, shouting to his men.

The next moment, the guards began urging people away from the pit, and back towards the palace gates.

"That will please the dragon," Lief said. His own voice sounded strange to him — as if it was coming from far away.

Barda was standing alone now — a tall, proud figure silhouetted against the sky. Jasmine hailed him, and he beckoned.

The moment they reached him, Filli leaped from his shoulder into Jasmine's arms, chittering frenzied welcome. Lief took one look at Barda's dulled, vacant eyes, started forward, and embraced his old friend.

For a moment Barda returned the embrace. Then, embarrassed as always by shows of emotion, he pushed Lief away.

"Pah! You smell of dragon, Lief," he said, grinning. "Keep your distance!"

Then the grin faded from his face. He blinked. A furrow deepened between his brows. He stretched out his arm.

"Take my hand," he said abruptly.

Wondering, Lief clasped the outstretched hand. Barda blinked again. And then Lief saw that the blankness of his eyes had lessened.

"It is the Belt," Barda said, his voice trembling slightly. "One of the gems is aiding my sight. I can feel it!"

And Lief remembered.

✝   **The opal . . . has the power to give glimpses of the future, and to aid those with weak sight . . .**

He did not hesitate. He moved his free hand to the opal. He gripped it tightly.

Instantly his mind was filled with pictures. Gray, barren land. The skeletons of trees. A gray river, sluggish water thick as mud, with huge gray fish lying dead on the wrinkled surface. Monstrous creatures shrieking in the sky. And he felt . . .

Horrified, he tore his hand from the Belt. Panting, he looked up at Barda — at Barda's dark, clear eyes regarding him curiously.

"Was it — enough?" Lief stammered.

"Enough for now," Barda said. He waited. But Lief's throat was dry. He could not speak.

"What did you see, Lief?" Jasmine asked quietly.

Lief swallowed. "I think I was in the Shadowlands," he said. "I saw the seven Ak-Baba. I felt . . . a terrible, helpless rage. Burning — " His throat closed, and he shuddered.

"That is what the Enemy will feel when he learns what has happened here today," said a quiet voice beside him. "Perhaps it is *his* future you have seen."

Very startled, Lief spun around and saw Zeean, wrapped in a shawl and leaning on Lindal's good arm. So absorbed had he been in his vision that he had not heard the two women approaching.

"Zeean! How — why — are you here?" he stuttered, as Lindal moved joyfully to Barda's side, exclaiming over his cure.

Zeean held out her hand to show a huge emerald ring that Lief recognized as one of the royal jewels.

"This finished what the emerald in the Belt began," she said calmly. "I was able to walk from the palace with Lindal's help. Sharn is still very weak, so Gers carried her. Doom and Gla-Thon brought Paff, and Josef's body, I think."

She put her head on one side and regarded Lief and Jasmine's puzzled expressions in surprise.

"Do you not know?" she asked. "It seems there is a danger the palace will fall."

"What?" Jasmine cried in horror.

"Manus says that the hole in that foundation wall means that the palace is no longer properly supported," Barda said. "All or part of it will collapse if something is not done quickly."

He pointed into the pit, and Lief saw the small figure of Manus directing a dozen guards. The guards were laboring to raise a vast pole — a tall tree trunk — in the center of the hole in the palace wall. They kept glancing nervously over their shoulders at the topaz dragon, who was watching them narrowly, the spines on its neck raised.

And now Lief could see the ugly cracks running up the wall, running all the way up to the long windows of the great hall on the first floor.

"Why *you* are all still standing here, I do not know," said Lindal. "Manus told you to clear the area! When I saw you, I could not believe my eyes! Come away!"

But as she spoke, a chorus of triumph rose from the pit. The guards had succeeded in wedging the tree trunk into place. Manus looked up and saw the group watching him.

"It will hold!" he roared, punching the air. He turned back to his men, pointed to a second pole lying on the ground, and began giving orders.

"Excellent!" said Lindal with satisfaction. "Shall we go and tell the others, old bear?"

They strode away, laughing and talking.

"Shall we go also?" Zeean murmured. "I would be grateful for a chair."

Jasmine took her arm. "We will go in the back way," she said. "It is far quicker from here — and there are no stairs."

In silence they began to make their way to the back of the palace. They walked very slowly for Zeean's sake, and Lief was glad of it. He was not looking forward to what was ahead.

They reached the kitchen door and helped Zeean inside. A chorus of cheers rang out. Startled, Lief and Jasmine saw that the great table was crowded with people, all turned to them, smiling.

"Why, even Marilen is here!" Jasmine cried. "And Ebony!"

Lief gazed around at the familiar faces.

Marilen, glowing with happiness, Ebony perched on her shoulder. Ranesh, smiling. Gla-Thon, raising a goblet. Gers shouting. Steven, grinning broadly. The boy Zerry, taller than Lief remembered, his sharp eyes sparkling. Lindal, laughing and banging the table. Barda, beaming, pulling out chairs for Jasmine and Zeean. Sharn, very pale, royal emeralds gleaming at her throat, holding out her arms to him.

Only one was missing.

352

Lief went to his mother and embraced her. "Where is Doom?" he asked quietly.

"He carried Paff back to her bed," called Gla-Thon, overhearing. "She has recovered a little, but she is still unconscious. He will be with us shortly."

"If he has not fallen asleep on his feet," Gers growled. "He looks like death walking. I offered to take Paff myself, but he would not have it."

"No doubt he thought the poor girl was sick enough, without being scared to death by your ugly face, Jalis," grinned Gla-Thon.

With a roar, Gers swung around, reaching for Gla-Thon but succeeding only in upsetting one of the jugs with his elbow. Wine flooded the table. Everyone jumped up, shouting or laughing. At the same moment, a black bird soared through the door, heading straight for Jasmine.

"Kree!" Jasmine shouted, overjoyed.

Lief took advantage of the confusion to slip away. Only Sharn saw him go.

❋

Lief let himself into the library and walked silently through the maze of shelves. His hand was on his sword. His mind was blank.

A dim light glowed in Josef's room. Lief paused and looked in. For a moment he thought he saw a hunched figure, ruler in hand, bent over something on the desk — something that Lief now knew must have been the plan of the chapel.

353

No . . . I have made no mistake. Oh, what wicked trickery is this? . . . If only I had remembered! Fool! Fool!

Then Lief blinked, and the vision was gone. The desk was empty, and Josef's body was lying on the bed. Tomorrow Josef would be laid to rest with all the ceremony befitting a Deltoran hero, but he would spend this night in his own, humble room.

"You will be avenged, Josef," Lief said softly. "Rest well."

He glanced at the desk a second time as he turned to go. He had a nagging feeling that something about his fleeting vision had been wrong, but could not think what it could be.

He moved on to Paff's room. Here the curtains were open, and the room's air was golden with late afternoon light.

Paff lay propped up on pillows, exactly as Lief had seen her when he had first entered this room before sunrise. But she was no longer stiff and sweating. Her eyes were peacefully closed.

Beside her, in a chair dragged from behind the desk, sat Doom. A gleaming hunting knife lay across his knees. He raised his head as Lief entered the room. His shadowed face showed no surprise.

"Stay back, Lief," he said softly.

"You know I cannot," Lief said, moving forward.

Doom stared at him for a moment, then turned back to the sleeping girl. Her eyelids had begun to flutter.

354

"Soon she will wake," he said. "I should have cut her throat before this. I do not know why I hesitated."

"Perhaps because you knew I would come," Lief said. "In your heart you know I must hear what she has to say."

Doom shook his head restlessly. His long, brown fingers caressed the gleaming blade of the knife.

"You do not know what it is to be utterly alone, Lief," he said. "You do not know the agony of having all you love torn from you. You have never felt the rage, the pain, the white-hot desire for revenge that burns from within until all that remains is dark despair, a yawning emptiness craving to be filled."

"I have not felt it as you have," Lief answered. "But I have felt the evil force that promises to fill the emptiness with riches and power in return for service to its will. And I know that other choices can be made. You know it, too, Doom."

Doom shrugged and half-smiled. The knife fell clattering to the floor.

Paff's eyes opened. She stared dreamily at the ceiling, then turned her head to look at Lief and Doom.

"Josef?" she murmured.

"Josef is dead," Doom said in a level voice.

"So . . . he is silenced," said the girl, her voice soft as a sigh. "How he hated and feared you by the end, Doom. He feared you almost as much as I did.

But — but it does not matter now, does it? Nothing matters now."

Tears welled in her eyes. Slowly she relaxed her fingers, and the emeralds spilled onto the white bed cover.

"I tried so hard," she whispered, her voice so faint that Lief had to bend to hear her. "When I began, I had — such hopes! I thought of nothing but pleasing him. I did more — even more than he asked. And yet . . ."

"And yet at the last he turned his back on you," Lief said. "He abandoned you. Why, Paff? Why?"

The girl stared at him through her tears. "Perhaps I tried too hard," she whispered. "Perhaps I did too much. My Master has many plans."

And with the desperation of a trapped creature snatching at its only chance of escape, she threw herself forward and clutched the Belt of Deltora.

Lief tried to jump back, but Paff's grip was as strong as iron. He watched in horror as her face twisted, her back arched. There was a ghastly smell of burning. And with a cry that was more relief than pain, the failed, abandoned guardian of the south fell back on her pillows, released from her torment at last.

16 – Shocks

When Lief and Doom returned to the kitchen, they found it in uproar. Manus had joined the party at the table, but he was not the cause of the excitement and distress. The cause was Kree.

After hearing the news that four Kin were on their way bearing the gems Lief had asked for, Jasmine had discovered that the old injury on Kree's neck had reopened. Trying to clean away the freshly flowing blood, she had found something lodged inside the wound.

"It must have been buried deep, and gradually worked its way upward," she said. "No wonder the wound would not heal properly."

She held the object out in the palm of her hand. It was a small gray glass bead. Red lines swirled within it.

Shuddering, Lief picked up the bead and threw it into the stove. It hissed, glowed briefly, then cracked and melted away.

"So now it is clear how our enemies always knew where we were," Barda said heavily. "We were only safe when Kree was not with us. He was carrying the Shadow Lord's eye all along."

Kree squawked loudly and indignantly.

"Of course you did not know, Kree," Jasmine soothed. "The device must have been put into your neck when you were drugged that first time you came back to Del. Someone in the palace did it — someone . . ."

"It was Paff," Lief said quietly.

"*Paff?*" exploded Barda.

"Paff was the guardian of the south," Lief said. "But she will trouble us no more. The beast she sent to destroy us could withstand the power of the Belt, but she could not."

The startled faces around the kitchen table grew somber as the story of Paff's death was told. Lief and Doom did not relish the telling. Both felt they had failed.

"I wanted to spare her the horror of awakening," Doom said. "She had become a monster of wickedness, yet still I — I felt I understood how she had come to take the wrong path. She had lost everything. She was loved by no one. Her misery had made her easy prey for the Shadow Lord."

The corner of his mouth twisted in the familiar, mocking smile. "But Lief wanted her alive, to tell what she knew," he added. "For once, Lief was the ruthless one. But Paff outwitted him."

"Not for the first time," Lief said grimly. "She deceived me completely. The black slime attacked us in the chapel just after Gla-Thon came running to tell us that Paff had taken a turn for the worse. But still I did not understand. It was only when Jasmine spoke of trances, and I remembered how Paff had looked in her room just before the dawn attack, that I realized what she was."

"It was when I carried her out of the palace that I guessed it," said Doom. "She was as rigid as a stone statue. None of the other plague victims had been so."

"I confess, I tried desperately to believe it was not true," Lief muttered. "I could not bear the thought that I had left Josef helpless in Paff's hands, to be kept drugged and confused, pumped for information and finally poisoned when she had no further use for him."

"You are not the only one who will carry that burden till death," muttered Ranesh.

"I am most at fault," Doom said. "Plainly Paff was poisoning Josef's mind against me for months. My impatience only made him fear and distrust me the more."

"And you were reading his letters before they were sent," Barda put in. "No doubt he suspected you were changing them, or not sending them at all."

"I think they *were* changed — at least one of them," Lief said quietly.

He pulled out the letter he had received from Josef on their way to the Isle of the Dead.

"See here?" he said, tapping the two small pages. "Josef says he knows where we are going, but he fails to warn us of the danger lurking on Blood Lily Island. I could not understand that, but now I think I do."

He held the pages out to Doom. "Am I right in thinking that *Paff* delivered this to you for sending?" he asked.

"Indeed she did." Doom frowned. "Josef took an age to write his note, and I was impatient. I shouted from the entrance hall, and a few moments later Paff came running like a scared rabbit. I scanned the note on my way to the bird room. It was confused and scrappy enough, but I certainly did not change it."

"No, but Paff did, on her way to you, I am sure of it," Lief said. "I think Josef scribbled on *three* pages of his little notebook. The second page contained the warnings that might have spared us much grief. Paff destroyed it, and tore off the right-hand corners of the remaining pages, removing the page numbers, so we would not suspect."

"Ah, she was cunning," muttered Doom.

"Why, you almost sound as if you admire her!" growled Barda.

Doom grimaced. "If she had chosen to use her talents for good, she might have been a great asset to us," he said. "Lief and I found supplies of that yellow paper beneath her mattress, you know. She never stopped thinking and planning. I am sure that by the end she had convinced Josef that I was working secretly for the Enemy."

"I considered that myself, Doom," Jasmine said calmly.

"Indeed?" Doom said, raising an eyebrow. "And why was that?"

"Lief said the guardian of the south was subtle, quick-thinking, and very clever," Jasmine answered, shrugging. "That sounded more like you than anyone else in the palace."

"Why, thank you," Doom said drily.

"Also . . ." Jasmine checked the points off on her fingers. "You have been in the Shadowlands. You are proud and ruthless. You mix with strange people. You are awake all hours of the night. You were one of the few to see Sharn the night she fell ill — "

"Why, plainly Paff went to my room that first night and put poison in my lip balm while I was still downstairs!" exclaimed Sharn, very shocked. "Doom was the one who realized the cream was poisoned, when he brought the royal emeralds and amethysts to my chamber. He was the one who saved me!"

"And me," Zeean put in. "Jasmine, how *could* you think such a thing of your father?"

Jasmine shrugged again. "Doom is not an ordinary father," she said.

"Very true," said Doom. "And you are no ordinary daughter, I am happy to say. If I had been in your place, I would have thought exactly as you did. We are more alike than we realized, it seems."

He grinned broadly, and Jasmine's tired face broke into an answering smile.

Zeean and Sharn both shook their heads, clearly bewildered by this strange example of family loyalty.

Gers slammed his fist upon the table. "Why do we sit here jabbering when there is a feast to be had?" he shouted. "We are all here now, and my belly is growling!"

Ranesh grinned, and swung a large cloth bundle onto the table.

"Hardly a feast," Marilen said, as the cloth was untied to reveal packets, jars, and nets of glowing fruit. "More a taste of what is to come. I could only bring what I could carry."

As Gers, Gla-Thon, and Lindal began tearing open the nets and packets, Barda grinned at Lief's and Doom's startled faces. "A trading ship has come, it seems," he said.

"Just the first of many, the sailors said," Marilen said happily. "They said that the Bone Point Light has been noticed by all who sail the sea to our west, which they call the silver sea. Soon there will be food in plenty — enough, I am sure, to see the whole land through the winter."

"Marilen was already on her way here when I left to fetch her," Ranesh said, meeting Lief's eyes. "We met not far from Del. She had been missing me, it seems."

He spoke lightly, but Lief's heart warmed for him.

All is well, Lief told himself, as with shouts of delight everyone around him fell upon the delicious fruits, cheeses, dried fish, flat bread, and little spiced cakes heaped upon the table. *My feelings of foreboding were caused by exhaustion and fear, nothing more.*

But still he could not relax. His nerves were tight as bowstrings.

"Father tried to persuade me to change my mind, but I knew my place was here," Marilen was chattering on. "So I put on a garment that Sharn had left in Tora, picked up what food I could carry, and came."

"If only you were Lindal's size," bellowed Gers, with his mouth full. "You could have carried five times as much!"

Everyone laughed. Ebony and Kree looked up from the shred of fish they were sharing and screeched. Even Filli, happily nibbling fruit peel, added his tiny voice to the general din.

All is well, Lief repeated to himself fiercely. *It is over.*

But he knew it was not. And as he bent his head unwillingly, he saw that the Belt knew it, too. The topaz was still shining like a golden star. But the ruby and the emerald were as pale and dull as roadside stones.

There was another burst of laughter around the table. Dazedly, Lief raised his head. He saw that Barda was ruefully displaying his wooden puzzle box, still locked despite the little rods sticking out from three of its carved sides.

"Plainly there is another lock on the fourth side!" cried Manus, holding out his hand. "The trick is in the carving. Let me try it."

"No, let me!" shrieked Zerry. "Bess of the Masked Ones had many such puzzles. I could do it!"

"Oh, no," growled Barda. "This box will open for me, or not at all!"

Disdainfully he poked the box with his finger. His jaw dropped as, with a tiny click, the fourth rod slid outward.

The lid of the box burst open. Out shot a laughing clown face, bouncing on a spring.

Barda yelled and dropped the box. Everyone shrieked in shock, then began to laugh helplessly.

The jack-in-the-box lay on its side on the table, its grinning head nodding foolishly, its tinny clockwork laughter running down.

Lief's skin crawled.

"Why, I spent hours on that foolish thing!" cried

Barda in disgust. "And for what? To have the life scared out of me."

He tried to stuff the clown back into the box, but it would not go, and neither would the rods slide back in place. Clearly this was a puzzle that could be done one time only.

"Barda! Throw it in the fire!" Lief heard himself shouting harshly. His heart was beating like a drum.

"With pleasure," Barda snorted, and tossed the box into the stove. It caught and burned merrily, quickly collapsing into ash.

What is wrong with me? Lief thought desperately. *Why would a harmless toy terrify me so?*

"Oh, that was a fine trick indeed!" gasped Manus, tears of mirth streaming down his cheeks. "The rods hold the lid in place, with the clown pressed down beneath it. One rod removed — nothing. Two rods, three rods removed — still nothing. But when the last rod is removed — bang! Ah, Barda, if you had seen your face!"

He collapsed in fresh gales of laughter, echoed by the whole company.

Lief felt as if he was suffocating. He stood up abruptly and went outside. He sat down on the bench beside the back door and took a few deep breaths of cold fresh air.

The door opened again and Ranesh came out.

"I understand how you feel, Lief," Ranesh said soberly. "After all that has happened, it seems callous to be merry. But Josef would have rejoiced to hear us laugh."

Lief's mind was filled once again with the memory of the frail old man bent over his desk, muttering as he studied the plan of the chapel. And again he had the feeling that something about the memory was wrong, or that there was something about it he did not understand.

Why do I keep fretting over this? he asked himself angrily. *What more is there to understand? Josef guessed that the Sister of the South was beneath the chapel. He was horrified, and tried to contact me, to tell me. The night he died, he was studying the plan of the chapel to make absolutely sure—*

And suddenly Lief's stomach seemed to turn over as he realized that what he had just thought simply could not be true.

Josef could not have been studying the chapel plan the night he died, because the very next day, the plan was in its proper place, in a heavy box high in the storeroom.

Josef could not possibly have replaced the plan in that box. He could hardly walk, let alone stretch up to a high shelf. And if he had asked Paff to return the chapel plan for him, she would certainly have destroyed it.

But if Josef had not been studying the plan, what *had* he been doing?

366

17 - The Trap

Lief's mind was in turmoil. Why had he not remembered Josef's frailty? Why had he not realized that the old librarian must have been
studying something that was already in his room?

Ranesh cleared his throat. Looking up, Lief realized that Ranesh was staring at him, holding out a
stack of paper tied with pale blue ribbon.

"It is the manuscript of Josef's book," Ranesh
was saying. "Josef wanted you to have it. I took it
from his desk earlier, and it seemed right to give it to
you now."

Lief took the manuscript and, to please Ranesh,
untied it. He lifted the top page, bearing the book's title, and looked at the next.

It was not a contents page or an introduction, as
he had expected. It was a tale copied from the *Deltora*

Annals and when he saw which one, he felt cold to his very bones.

The Four Sisters

A Tenna Birdsong Tale from the Deltora Annals

Long ago, on a beautiful island set in a silver sea, there lived four sisters whose voices were as sweet as their hearts were pure. Their names were Flora, Viva, Aqua, and Terra, and they had lived on the island so long that they had forgotten the number of the years.

The sisters loved to sing together, and their voices flowed over the island like a soft, warm breeze by night and by day. Now and then a ship passed by, but to most of the sailors the sisters' song was like whispering leaves, lapping water, drifting sand, and the soft, secret rustling of small animals in the grass. The few who claimed to hear sweet voices were mocked by their fellows. But they knew what they had heard, and never forgot it until their dying days.

It so happened that a sorcerer came to that island, searching for a place to call his own. He heard the singing and hated it, as he hated all things good and beautiful, for although he was still young in years, he was old in wickedness.

He seized the four sisters and imprisoned each on a separate corner of the island. But the sisters still sang to one another from afar, and their song continued to bathe the island in peace and beauty by night and by day.

Maddened with rage, the sorcerer drew his cloak of shadows around him and took up his magic staff. He stormed to each of the island's corners in turn and struck the sisters down, one by one.

First Flora's voice ceased. Then Viva's. Then Aqua's. For a time Terra sang on alone. But when her voice, too, was stopped, the island was silent.

And only then did the sorcerer realize what he had done. For in the very center of the island, hidden deep within the earth, was a vile and hideous beast. Soothed by the singing of the four sisters, the beast had slept for centuries.

Now it awoke, in all its fury.

It rose, roaring, from its bed beneath the earth. It tore down the trees, crushed the small beasts, fouled the spring, and smashed the mountains. It cracked the very rock on which the island rested, and the island began to sink.

In terror the sorcerer leaped into the silver sea. He conjured up a boat with a gray sail marked with red, and sailed away into the east, to find new lands to conquer.

The waves closed over the island and it has never been seen by human eye from that day to this. A few of the sailors who pass that way still claim to hear sweet voices singing beneath the water. They are mocked by their fellows, who hear only the sound of wind and waves. But the few know what they heard, and they never forget it, until their dying days.

Lief put down the second page with a shaking hand.

The Four Sisters . . . You . . . the sorcerer . . . you must stop . . .

Josef's halting words were echoing in his mind. And now they had a new and terrible meaning.

"It is too sad a tale to begin the book, I think," said Ranesh, who had been reading over Lief's shoulder.

"Josef wrote it last," Lief whispered, fighting the rising terror that was threatening to overwhelm him. "He copied it out of the *Annals* and put it at the front of his manuscript so I would be sure to see it at once if anything happened to him. He sent me a note — "

I must see you. Urgent. Fearful news . . .

Lief swallowed. "The volume of the *Annals* was still lying open on his desk when I arrived. The tale was there, in its original form. But I did not read it."

You are the sorcerer. You must stop . . .

Ranesh frowned in confusion. "It is only an old folk tale. And surely Josef had told it to you before?"

If only I had remembered! Fool! Fool!

"His memory of it was hazy," Lief said. "He had forgotten the end. By the time he read it again, for his book, and realized what it might mean, I was far away."

" 'What it might mean'?" Ranesh exclaimed. "I do not understand you!"

Was Josef writing out this tale when Doom came into his room last night? Lief thought. *No.* The Annals *volume was far to his right — too far away for him to see it clearly. The manuscript was on his left, already neatly tied. And Josef was using a ruler. There are no ruled lines upon these pages.*

So Josef must have been working on something else — something that was proof of what the tale had made him suspect.

After Doom left him, Josef must have hidden the proof somewhere close by, Lief thought. *But surely he would have tried to tell me, or Ranesh, where it —*

His heart jolted.

"Ranesh," he said slowly, "when Josef told you he wanted to be buried in his librarian's tunic, what exactly did he say?"

Ranesh stared. "I told you — he could hardly

speak. He just said, 'In my tunic.' He repeated it several times, very urgently, as if he thought I did not understand. But of course I knew exactly what he meant. Joseph had always said he wanted to be buried in the uniform of his office when the time came."

"Was there anything in the tunic pocket?" Lief asked. He had begun to shiver all over.

Ranesh went very still. "I did not look," he said.

Plot . . . treachery . . .

Lief stood up unsteadily and staggered. Ranesh exclaimed in alarm and took his arm.

As Ranesh half-carried Lief back into the kitchen and lowered him into a chair, the talk and laughter around the table abruptly stopped. Jasmine, Barda, and Doom leaped up. Sharn tried to rise.

"Look after him," Ranesh said, and left the room.

Lief was already fumbling in his jacket pocket for the four fragments of the Four Sisters map. Suddenly he was sure he knew what Ranesh would find in Josef's tunic, and he could not wait.

He thrust the Four Sisters tale into Barda's hands.

"We have been tricked," he muttered. "The Enemy took more than the Sisters' names from this tale. He took the idea and twisted it to fit his own purpose. If the *Deltora Annals* had been burned as he ordered — if Josef had not saved them — no one would ever have known."

He pulled the map fragments from his pocket and with trembling hands put them on the table in front of him. "But Josef read it — realized the danger — tried to tell me. Perhaps, at the end, even Paff suspected it."

My Master has many plans . . .

As Barda, Jasmine, and Doom began to read, Lief pushed the edges of the map fragments together. He took one look at the result, and his face began to burn.

. . . evil . . . the center . . . the heart . . . the city . . . of . . .

"Doom, give me your knife," he whispered, feeling for the blunt pencil that he had carried for so long.

Doom looked up from his reading, grim-faced. Without a word, he pulled the huge knife from its sheath and put it on the table.

North . . . to south, east . . . to west . . . lines . . . map . . .

Lief placed the straight edge of the knife across the map and, using it as a ruler, drew a line between Dragon's Nest and the Isle of the Dead. Then he moved the knife and ruled another line between Shadowgate and Del.

Everyone had crowded around now. The tale of the Four Sisters was being passed from hand to hand, and all those who had finished it were staring at the completed map, and at the lines Lief had drawn — the lines that crossed at the place marked *Hira*.

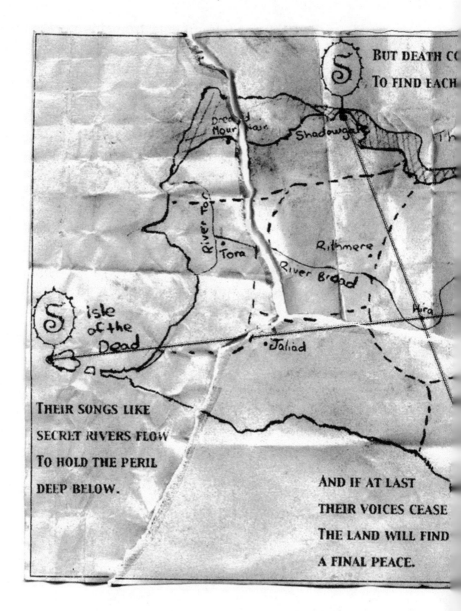

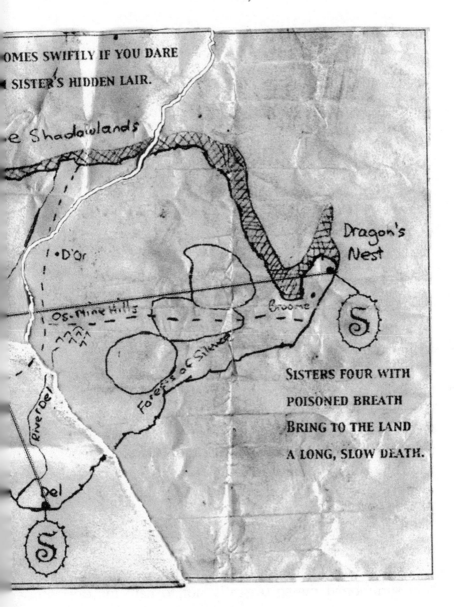

OMES SWIFTLY IF YOU DARE

SISTER'S HIDDEN LAIR.

e Shadowlands

• D'Or

Os-Mine Hills

Forests of Silence

River Del

Del

Dragon's Nest

Broome

SISTERS FOUR WITH
POISONED BREATH
BRING TO THE LAND
A LONG, SLOW DEATH.

Danger . . . fearful . . . here . . .

"Josef did not say 'here,' but 'Hira,'" Lief breathed aloud. "The danger he was trying to warn me of was not the Sister of the South at all. It was an even greater peril, hidden in the center of Deltora. In the City of the Rats."

"I have always wondered why the people were driven out of the city," Doom muttered. "The Shadow Lord could have enslaved them where they were, if he had wished. But now I see. He wanted the city for his own purpose."

"It was the *place* he wanted," Lief said. "The place where the Sister songlines would cross."

Ranesh ran into the room, a paper in his hand. His face looked bleached. His eyes were wild.

"There *was* something in Josef's tunic!" he panted. "It —"

Then he saw the map fragments lying on the table and put his paper down beside them. As Lief had expected, it was a copy of Doran's Dragon Territories map. The positions of all the Sisters had been marked in Josef's handwriting. And between them Josef had ruled the same lines that Lief had just drawn — lines crossing in the territory of the opal, at Hira, the City of the Rats.

Lief pressed his hands together, trying to stop his hands from trembling.

"This was what Josef wanted me to see," he said. "He summoned me so urgently not to help me destroy the last Sister as I thought, and as Paff thought, too, but to *stop* me. He knew that if the voice of the last Sister was silenced, a terror worse than hunger would be unleashed upon Deltora."

"So now we know why the Sister of the South was so easily destroyed," Jasmine said quietly. "With the other three Sisters gone, and the Bone Point Light restored, the Shadow Lord's game of starving us was all but over. He was impatient to spring his trap. He withdrew the last Sister's power, and abandoned Paff to fight on alone."

His face set like stone, Barda read aloud the verse printed on the map.

Sisters four with poisoned breath
Bring to the land a long, slow death.
But death comes swiftly if you dare
To find each sister's hidden lair.
Their songs like secret rivers flow
To hold the peril deep below.
And if at last their voices cease
The land will find a final peace.

" 'Final peace,' " murmured Zeean. And suddenly the words, which had seemed so hopeful, were chilling.

"But Deltora is not a tiny island!" cried Gla-Thon, throwing down Josef's manuscript. "No beast in the center, however terrible, could destroy this whole land!"

377

"You are right, gnome," growled Gers. "Just let it try to invade the territory of the Jalis!"

"The Shadow Lord is not known for idle threats," said Doom grimly. He swung around to Steven, who had remained silent ever since he saw the map.

"We must go at once to the City of the Rats," he said. "The bees and Mellow would be our fastest way. Will you — ?"

Steven nodded shortly. His fists were clenched. His golden eyes were flickering brown. "Our mother's orchard lies at the edge of the Plain of the Rats," he said in a low voice. "Mellow will fly like the wind to defend it."

I will be faster, king of Deltora. And a full moon is rising.

The voice of the topaz dragon filled Lief's mind. The topaz grew hot beneath his hands. He felt Barda and Jasmine close beside him. He turned to Doom.

"You go with Steven," he murmured. "Take as many from here as are able, with every weapon you can carry. We will meet you there."

18 - The Revenge

The dragon flew faster than the wind, its golden scales glittering in the light of the huge, rising moon. The land slipped by beneath it. The first small lights were showing in villages and towns where people sat by their firesides, bathed their children, or prepared their frugal meals, in ignorance of what was happening beyond the safety of their walls.

Flattened against the dragon's neck, Lief, Barda, and Jasmine thought of nothing but holding on. The cold became more intense as they moved inland. The freezing wind buffeted them mercilessly.

We are crossing the border into opal territory. I have broken my vow.

The voice of the dragon hissed in Lief's mind. Defiance and regret were mingled in it, but there was no trace of fear.

If the opal dragon rises, I will explain, Lief replied.

The dragon snorted in grim amusement.

The land below them was flatter now, and more desolate. There were no more villages, no more towns. In the distance, water gleamed.

The bend of Broad River, Lief thought. *We are nearly there.*

His teeth had begun chattering again. The hair rose on the back of his neck as slowly he became aware of a sound rising beneath the rushing of the wind — a deep, ominous rumbling.

The next moment Jasmine screamed, and the dragon's scaly hide twitched beneath Lief's hands.

"What do you see?" Lief shouted. "Jasmine — ?"

And then he saw for himself, and the breath caught in his throat.

Beyond the gleam of the water, something huge was rising — a vast, rounded thing like a hideous reflection of the golden moon.

"By the heavens, what is it?" Barda shouted hoarsely.

The dragon growled, deep in its throat. It flew faster, faster. Now the sweeping bend of the river was directly ahead of them. And they could see, enclosed within the bend, the gigantic, poisonous yellow bubble pushing upward through the ruins of the City of the Rats, pushing the damaged buildings aside as if they were children's building bricks. A few rats were scattering from the ruins, squeaking shrilly as they ran.

Lief stared in terrified fascination as the bubble swelled and grew.

Their songs like secret rivers flow
To hold the peril deep below.

But the Sisters' songlines flowed through the earth no longer. And like the beast in the tale, like the clown in Barda's puzzle box, the Shadow Lord's revenge was rising from its long darkness, for now there was nothing to hold it down.

In a dream of horror Lief saw water beneath him. They were crossing the Broad. And the thing rising from the ruins of the city was still growing, swelling from the earth like a hideous boil.

How close do you wish to — ?

The dragon's voice broke off as there was a thunderous roar from the other end of the plain. Something was hurtling towards them, rainbow colors flashing in the moonlight.

Instantly the dragon plunged earthward in a sickening dive. Lief, Barda, and Jasmine shrieked as the ground came rushing up to meet them and they crashed to a stop. Dizzy and faint, their eyes streaming, they struggled to free themselves from the ropes that bound them.

"Make haste!" the dragon roared. It clawed at the ropes, cutting them through like threads.

The companions fell to the hard ground and rolled aside. The dragon spread its wings, preparing to take off once more.

"No!" shouted Lief. "Do not fight! Be still! Stay on the ground!"

"And let that beast think I fear it? Never!" snarled the dragon, steam hissing from its terrible jaws.

"In Doran's name, I beg you!" Lief cried desperately.

The dragon growled. But it half-folded its wings and remained still.

The opal dragon was almost upon them. It was gigantic — even larger than the dragon of the emerald. The spines on its neck were fully raised. The beating of its wings was like thunder crashing, and the gale of its wingbeats hammered the ground.

The opal on the Belt was burning with rainbow fire. Lief pressed his fingers upon it, and sent his message with all the force of his being.

Dragon of the opal, do not attack! The topaz dragon is here at my wish.

He gasped as the opal dragon's blind, vengeful fury flashed through him like a lightning bolt. Summoning his strength, he tried again.

Dragon, you are blinded by your anger. A great evil is rising in your land — a far greater evil than a dragon who has crossed a border. Open your eyes and see it! In Dragonfriend's name, I beg you!

Again the name of Doran the Dragonlover worked its magic. Lief felt the rainbow dragon hesitate. He felt the battering of the wind on his back ease as the beast wheeled.

He crawled to his knees, looked ahead, and groaned aloud.

The bubble had swelled even more. Its hideous bulk now completely covered the ruined city, and rose as high as the palace in Del.

Lief stared at it in horrified fascination. At the bottom it was the same poisonous yellow as it had been before. But at the top it was paler — paler, tighter, and shinier. As if . . . as if . . .

With a ghastly tearing sound, the top of the bubble split open. A fountain of vile, dull gray liquid, thick as heavy cream, gushed up into the air.

Lief heard the dragons roar. He heard Barda and Jasmine crying out in revulsion beside him. And he heard something else, he was sure of it — the sound of distant, wicked laughter.

The spouting liquid began flowing to the ground, spreading outward in a thick gray flood.

"What is it?" Jasmine shrieked, her eyes wide with horror.

A red-eyed rat, more daring than the others, darted at the gray liquid, perhaps hoping it was something good to eat. The moment the liquid touched it, the rat stiffened and fell, its legs jerking convulsively.

The companions watched, horrified, as the gray liquid covered the rat's twitching body and flowed on, moving very fast. The remaining rats shrieked and ran away from it, scattering outward across the plain.

"It is poisonous," hissed Barda.

"And it is alive," Lief muttered. "It is alive — and growing."

He knew it was true. The thick, gray fluid was making more of itself, and more, feeding on the earth and the air.

There was a blaze of fire as the opal dragon swooped, roaring at the spreading circle of gray. Multi-colored flame seared a great patch at the edge of the flood. The patch stiffened and hardened. The gray mass of liquid on either side of it closed in and flowed on, covering the burned place swiftly, as the rat had been covered.

The opal dragon wheeled and roared again. Again flame seared the moving ground, and again the burned place was smothered in an instant and the circle of gray grew larger.

"We should return to the air, king of Deltora," the topaz dragon murmured, watching its rival's efforts placidly. "The rainbow beast is well occupied. It will not trouble us. And the gray poison is spreading fast. This ground will not be safe for long."

Plainly it was right. The companions scrambled back onto its neck, and in moments were gasping in the cold air, clinging for their lives as the dragon soared upward.

The beast flew a little way across the river, then

turned in the air and hovered. "It is fortunate we did not delay," it commented.

Shivering, Lief, Barda, and Jasmine looked down.

In the few minutes that had passed since the dragon took flight, the place where they had been standing had become a sea of gray. The whole of the land enclosed by the riverbend was almost covered. Driven back to the riverbanks, hundreds of rats had begun leaping for the water, squealing in terror. Other rats were running for their lives across the plain to the north, just keeping ahead of a sweeping gray tide.

The opal dragon was wheeling over the gray sea, blasting it with rainbow fire. But the gray was still increasing, and every moment it seemed to be moving faster.

"Nothing will stop it," Lief heard himself saying.

"The river will stop it," Barda said firmly. "The Plain of the Rats is bounded by water on all sides. And the plain itself is no loss. There is no drearier place in the whole of Deltora."

"Very true," said the topaz dragon, yawning widely. "It is not territory worth saving."

"Would you feel the same if it was yours?" Jasmine asked sharply.

The topaz dragon blinked.

The gray reached the river and began pouring over the banks into the water. And if anything, the water seemed to strengthen it. The gray circle seemed to double in size almost instantly. The rippling water flattened and thickened. Squealing, swimming rats were overtaken and swallowed up.

Barda cursed in disbelief. Jasmine cried out.

The topaz dragon roared and arched its neck. Golden fire poured from its snarling jaws, searing the gray stream spilling over the riverbank below.

But Lief was silent, looking back to the center of the circle.

The collapsed yellow bubble was now hidden beneath a lumpy blanket of gray. The shapes of the ruins of the City of the Rats were visible around it — but only the shapes. Every ravaged building, every fallen tower, every brick and stone, was covered in a thick gray shroud.

And here the gray no longer moved, and no longer shone in the moonlight. It was setting hard.

Lief's nightmare vision slid back into his mind, and his blood ran cold.

Gray, barren land. The skeletons of trees. A gray river, sluggish water thick as mud, with huge gray fish lying dead on the wrinkled surface. . . . Monstrous creatures shrieking in the sky . . .

Not the Shadowlands, but Deltora. He knew that now.

This was a monster they could not fight. The gray tide would continue to spread. It would swallow rivers, forests, and plains. It would cover towns and villages and farms. It would fill the valleys and smooth out the hills.

Nothing in its path would be spared. Death would come equally to the ferocious Sand Beasts and to the gentle Kin, to the flesh-eating Grippers and to the wondrous Lilies of Life.

Some of the gray would age and set hard, turning rivers to sludge, encasing houses, beasts, crops, trees, and people alike in a shell of stone. The rest would move on.

The people who could outrun it would be driven to the coast, to fight over boats or mill helplessly at the water's edge like the rats on the riverbank. Or they would climb mountains and wait, freezing on the peaks, as the gray climbed, climbed . . .

And at last, Deltora, all its variety and strangeness lost forever, would be one great, cold, gray plain.

This was what the Shadow Lord's malice and desire for vengeance had decreed must be, if the king who had been foretold did arise, restore the Belt of Deltora, and rid the land of tyranny.

I never have just one plan . . .

The Shadow Lord knew that this new king would certainly attempt to destroy the magic crystal that was Deltora's last link to the Shadowlands. He knew that, aided by the Belt, the king would be powerful enough to do it at last.

So the crystal was set to reveal the plot of the

Four Sisters as it died. Then the king who had dared to defy the Shadow Lord would learn why his land was starving.

He would learn of the Four Sisters.

And, of course, he would set out to destroy them.

Lief gritted his teeth as one by one the pieces of the plan fell into place.

He had taken the bait offered to him without a second thought. The Enemy had set a trap for him, then dared him, forced him, to walk into it.

Looking back, Lief could hardly believe he had been so easily tricked.

Not once had he wondered why the map showing where the Sisters were had not been destroyed, but had been torn into four parts. Not once had he wondered why each fragment had been hidden with a Sister, to be easily found if that Sister and its guardian were destroyed.

Not once had he considered that the verse placed on the map might have a double meaning.

And not once had he wondered why the stone protecting the last Sister had not been a sober warning, but an insulting dare, almost guaranteed to make him take the last, fatal step.

But now, too late, he saw the reasons for all these things. And he saw that, from the beginning, the Shadow Lord had arranged things so that Deltora would be his, whatever happened.

Anger rose in him — a helpless, white-hot anger.

"It has been the Enemy's pleasure to make us choose unknowingly which way the land would die," he muttered. "If we failed in our quest, the land would die slowly. If we succeeded, death would come swiftly. Either way, the Shadow Lord would win."

And as the last words left his lips, the first dead fish floated to the wrinkled surface of the dying river, and with weird, howling cries, the seven Ak-Baba came swooping in from the north.

19 - Dragon Night

Rage dissolving into numb horror, Lief saw the opal dragon swing to face the shrieking beasts hurtling over the horizon. He felt the muscles of the dragon of the topaz jerk violently beneath him. Then the dragon's neck twisted, and the terrible head turned. Lief was caught and held by the fathomless gaze of a flat, golden eye.

"The Enemy has sensed our attacks on the gray tide, no doubt," the dragon hissed. "He has sent his killing creatures to protect it. He must be using powerful sorcery indeed to defy the power of the Belt of Deltora."

It glanced down at the seared section of riverbank below and snorted. "There is little enough damage. But the Enemy fears dragons, it seems. Even two are too many for him. I must set you and your companions down, king of Deltora. When the pack has finished with the dragon of the opal, it will come for me."

"No!" Lief exclaimed. "There is still time for you to get away from here. Turn and — "

The golden eye flickered. "I would rather die fighting than fleeing," the dragon said. "And I am sick of hiding."

"As the gray tide spreads, there will be nowhere left to hide, in any case!" shouted Jasmine, as Kree screeched wildly, wheeling in the sky above her. "You must keep us with you, dragon! The Belt will aid you — and we can fight!"

"Indeed we can," growled Barda, drawing his sword.

"No!" Lief cried frantically again. "Barda, Jasmine — "

He felt Jasmine's hand close on his, and saw the gleam of Barda's savage grin.

"We know full well that you will not leave the dragon now, Lief," Jasmine shouted. "And we will not leave you. We were together at the beginning of this, and so we will be at the end."

"And if you will take a soldier's advice, dragon, you will not wait to be attacked," roared Barda. "You will go forward and fight beside your brother!"

"That opal beast is no brother of mine," the dragon snarled.

"It is more your brother than the seven Ak-Baba!" Jasmine screamed furiously. "Will you leave it to be torn apart, while you wait your turn?"

The dragon bared its terrible fangs. Its black tongue flickered. Then its eyes seemed to glow.

"Very well," it growled. "Together we will fight beside the dragon of the opal, and together we will die. This battle will be our last. But while we live, we will do to the Enemy what damage we can, for the sake of our doomed land, and for our ancestors, and for our young, who now will never be."

It flung itself forward, streaking over the sea of gray, towards the Ak-Baba.

And as Lief drew his sword and screwed his stinging eyes shut, he saw behind his lids words from *The Belt of Deltora* — words that had always filled him with dread and now had a new and terrible meaning for him.

. . . the Enemy is clever and sly . . . to its anger and envy a thousand years is like the blink of an eye . . .

The book called the Enemy "it." The unknown writer had understood something that Lief himself had never quite accepted until this moment.

However he had begun, the Shadow Lord was now far more — or perhaps far less — than a cruel tyrant who was a master of sorcery.

Long ago, perhaps, he had been a merely a sorcerer, with a cloak of shadows and a boat with a gray sail marked in red. He had felt fear, suffered a bitter defeat, and sailed east across a silver sea to find new lands to conquer.

But if he was human then, he was human no longer. Envy, hatred, and malice had consumed his humanity long ago, burned it away to dust. All that remained were memories.

"He" had become "it" — a force for evil that fed on power, that destroyed and corrupted everything it touched. A force that would never die.

I have many plans . . . plans within plans . . .

How did I ever think that I could defeat the Shadow Lord? Lief thought bitterly. *For a thousand years he has worked towards his goal. And we — we have struggled in his web, blindly, stupidly, repeating the mistakes of our ancestors. In his time, Doran the Dragonlover was called mad. In our time, Josef was insulted and avoided. Over and over again we have ignored the lessons of history . . .*

Learn the lessons of history. . . . Despair is the enemy. Do not let it defeat you . . .

The roars of the dragons were like thunder. The bloodcurdling shrieks of the seven Ak-Baba split the air. Jasmine and Barda were shouting. Kree was screeching. They were battered by wind thick with smoke and the bitter smell of burning hair, dust, and rotting flesh that was the odor of the seven Ak-Baba.

But Lief had ceased to hear, to smell, to feel. His mind was turned inward and his skin was prickling.

For as the memory of Zeean's faint, halting voice had faded away, another voice had taken its place.

. . . the Enemy fears dragons, it seems. Even two are too many for him . . .

The Shadow Lord had thought of everything. But he had not planned on dragons.

Lief opened his eyes. The Ak-Baba had almost reached them. He could see their eyes, like burning pools of madness. He could see their talons, flexed ready to rip and tear. He could see their beaks gaping, their needle-sharp teeth glinting.

He pressed his fingers to the amethyst. He called silently, but with all his strength.

Veritas!

And as he thought the name, more words followed it into his mind. He realized that he was remembering the strange, foreign words that had flowed into him from Doran's soul-stone as he pressed it into the earth.

Veritas hopian forta fortuna fidelis honora joyeu . . .

And suddenly he knew what the words were. Not a sentence, but a list of names. The most important names in Doran's life.

He pressed his free hand to the Belt once more, running his fingers across every gem.

Veritas! Hopian! Forta! Fortuna! Fidelis! Honora! Joyeu! Come to our aid, I pray you! For Doran. For the land!

He felt the dragon of the topaz jerk beneath him,

saw the dragon of the opal turn abruptly, its rainbow eyes blazing.

And then the seven Ak-Baba were upon them — the Ak-Baba were surrounding them, howling like savage wolves, snarling and snapping, claws and teeth ripping and tearing.

They worked as a pack, attacking from all sides, from above, from below. Three or four would distract their enemies by ferocious charges while the others moved in swiftly under the cover of their wings.

They were vicious, fearless, tireless. They bore the scars of countless battles and were filled with ancient cunning. But rarely had they faced two dragons at one time, and never had they faced a dragon aided by swords and the Belt of Deltora.

They screeched with rage as the dragons clawed at them and blasted them with fire. They howled as Lief, Barda, and Jasmine slashed at them, preventing them from closing in. Diving at them from above, as fearless as they were, Kree drove his sharp beak into their necks, their heads, distracting and enraging them the more.

Then one fell — one fell, its throat torn open by a single slash of the opal dragon's talons. Screeching and twisting, it plunged to earth, to be engulfed almost instantly by the gray tide.

The dragons roared in triumph. Lief, Barda, and Jasmine cheered. But the remaining Ak-Baba charged, shrieking ferociously, and the opal dragon's roar became a bellow of agony as the soft underside of its neck was pierced by teeth like needles and claws like sharpened iron.

An Ak-Baba with a speckled head was clinging to the dragon's neck, clinging to it upside down, like a giant bat. Blood flowed from the sides of its gaping beak, dripped over its clawed feet. Howling at the smell of the blood, the other Ak-Baba closed in. In seconds the rainbow dragon was lurching in the air, its body almost hidden beneath a shrieking mass of twisting, snake-like necks and vast, flapping wings.

"Help it!" Jasmine screamed. "Oh, make haste!"

"It is finished," growled the dragon of the topaz. "This is how they end it."

"No!" roared Lief. "Get below it!"

The dragon wheeled and soared beneath the struggling mass of bodies. Now the speckled Ak-Baba was directly above them, its ragged wings wrapped around the dragon's neck, its ghastly body flattened against the dragon's hide.

Lief and Barda hesitated, suddenly fearful that if they slashed with their swords they would fatally wound the dragon as well as the beast attacking it.

But Jasmine jumped upright, balancing on the topaz dragon's neck as lightly and easily as once she had surveyed the Forests of Silence from the branch of a storm-tossed tree. Her dagger flashed as she reached up and plunged it into the back of the Ak-Baba's neck, just below the head.

The vast bird stiffened. It made a hideous, gurgling sound.

"Go!" roared Barda.

Jasmine tore her dagger free. Lief caught her by the waist and held her fast, pulling her down as the topaz dragon sped away. Behind them the speckled Ak-Baba dropped like a stone.

There was no moment of triumph this time. Freed from its clinging tormentor, the opal dragon was twisting in the air, slashing and roaring fire at the other beasts tearing at its body. But its movements were clumsy. It was weakening.

And the topaz dragon was weakening, too. Its enormous strength had been drained by the terrible struggle with the two-faced beast, drained further by the flight to the Plain of the Rats. All over its golden body, old wounds had begun oozing blood.

The Ak-Baba knew it. They could see the beast's uneven wingbeats. They could smell the blood.

Shrieking, they abandoned the floundering body of the dragon of the opal and sped in for the kill. There were only five remaining, but those five were as fresh, as ferocious, as ravenous for blood as they had been at the beginning.

They flew, screeching, through the golden fire and hit the topaz dragon full in the side. It lurched, tilted, lost height, its huge wings beating desperately, its spiked tail lashing. The Ak-Baba pursued it, surrounded it, moved in again.

"This time, we are lost, I fear," growled the topaz dragon thickly. "But let us try to take another of them with us."

And at that moment there was a roar from above them, and the sky seemed to explode in a burning mass of shooting stars. The Ak-Baba scattered, howling in shock. Lief, Barda, and Jasmine cowered against the dragon's scales, coughing in a haze of smoke that stank of singed hair and scorched cloth. And out of the heavens soared the dragon of the lapis-lazuli, wings spangled with stars, starry fire belching from its snarling jaws.

The Ak-Baba wheeled in the air, turning to face it, snake-like necks stretching, beaks gaping wide as they howled in fury. Then suddenly, one was gone, snatched out of the air. There was a sickening crack as its neck broke between vast red jaws.

And as its lifeless body was tossed aside, as the ruby dragon bellowed its triumph and the remaining Ak-Baba shrieked and howled defiance, a ball of emerald fire roared through the smoke haze.

Three of the shrieking beasts dived. The fourth was too slow. The fireball struck. The feathers of its wings burst into flames and it plummeted to the ground, trailing a plume of fire.

Now only three Ak-Baba remained. Through the smoke and fire they could see five vast, glittering shapes, five snarling sets of fangs, five lashing tails. They shrieked defiantly, hovering, weighing the odds.

398

But when there was yet another roar, and a gush of purple flame lit the sky in the west, they twisted in the air and fled.

And the dragons did not follow. For by the light of the great, golden moon they could see the gray tide below. They could see it spreading before their eyes. They could feel its deadening chill. They knew what they must do.

20 - Full Circle

Speechless, Lief, Barda, and Jasmine clung to the topaz dragon as it flew to take its place in the circle of dragons surrounding the gray sea. They watched in wonder as the dragons dropped lower and hovered.

Then, without a word or signal, the dragons roared.

Flame gushed from their jaws. Flame of green, gold, and scarlet. Flame of purple and silver-white. Blue flame filled with stars, and flame that burned with all the colors of the rainbow.

. . . the Enemy fears dragons, it seems. Even two are too many for him . . .

And what of six? Lief thought. Then he changed the number to seven, for he saw the baby diamond dragon gravely hovering beside Veritas, adding her own small, silver-white flame to the fire.

The edges of the gray tide scorched and blackened, and when the circle was bounded by a broad black band, the dragons began moving slowly, patiently inward. Whenever they breathed, they breathed fire, and wherever the fire fell, the gray burned and died. And no dragon moved on while any patch of gray remained.

On and on the dragons moved, their circle tightening, as the great moon rose and paled, and stars filled the blackness of the sky.

Gradually the gray inside the circle grew less, and the black band outside it grew broader. By the time Steven's caravan pulled to a halt on the bank of the clogged River Broad, the people who tumbled out to stare in wonder could see more black than gray.

At last the dragons were so close together that the tips of their wings were touching. Together they roared, and the colors of their fires mingled in a rainbow blaze. And when that last, great fire had died, nothing remained of the Shadow Lord's terror but a vast circle of blackened ash.

In the center of the dark circle the dragons hovered, as if unwilling to end the moment. Diamond, emerald, lapis-lazuli, topaz, opal, ruby, and amethyst, they joined to relish their triumph, grieve for what had been lost, and look to the future.

And all who looked upon that scene were swept by a great wave of joy and wonder. For they saw that

401

the shining wings of the dragons were like the gems of the Belt of Deltora, blazing in the sky.

❋

And so it was that the last plan of the Shadow Lord was undone by the will of Deltora's last dragons, and the kingdom of Deltora was safe.

In years to come, the story would become a legend. The night called Dragon Night would be Deltora's greatest festival of the year, celebrated with feasts, dancing, games, and circles of fireworks from across the silver sea. Children dressed as Lief, Barda, and Jasmine would ride dragons made of painted wood and shining cloth, and at midnight a great bonfire would be lit in every town and village in the land, and Deltora would ring with cheers.

But the people who witnessed that first Dragon Night from the other side of the River Broad were too awestruck to cheer. As it happened, or perhaps because fate had decreed it, every one of Deltora's seven dragon territories was represented among them. For Steven had said that Zerry of the Mere must have his place in the caravan, and Zerry, his eyes dark with wonder, was standing with the rest, for once lost for words.

Lief himself could do no more than silently give thanks. But when at last the dragons settled to the earth, onto the blackened circle they had made, he felt their unblinking eyes upon him and knew he had to speak. And he knew what he had to say.

"My name is Lief," he said, and bowed his head. "Forgive me for using the names that Dragonfriend carried in his heart. I did it for the sake of our land, and his."

The dragons considered. Then they all bowed in reply, even the emerald dragon of honor, if rather stiffly.

"It is not so easy, however," it said. "You called us all at the same time. Now we know each other's true names, as well as yours, for any fool could guess which dragon name is which. This is an evil that cannot be undone."

Lief swallowed. "It cannot be undone," he said. "But perhaps it is not an evil."

The emerald dragon snorted. "To know a being's true name is to give power over that being," it said.

"Then we all have power over one another," said the dragon of the lapis-lazuli pertly. "And I, for one, have no intention of risking your revenge — Honora."

The emerald dragon bared its teeth. "Very wise — Fortuna," it hissed, but said no more.

"What is my name?" squeaked the little diamond dragon.

"Your name is Forta," said Veritas. "Forta — after your mother."

✳

At dawn, three dragons flew into Del—golden Fidelis, scarlet Joyeu, and Fortuna, the dragon of the lapis-lazuli.

403

Fidelis carried Lief, Barda, and Jasmine. Joyeu carried Doom, Lindal, and Manus. Fortuna carried Gla-Thon, Ranesh, and Gers. Gers, his broad face pale as paper, was seen to kiss the ground when the ride was over, but swore till his dying day that he had merely stumbled.

Though it was so early, and though few in Del had any idea of the peril their land had just escaped, the city was alive with rejoicing people. Most had been awake all night.

First, four Kin had arrived from Dread Mountain, their pouches bulging with gems to heal the sick and test the remaining food. Then the city gates had flown open of themselves, and Torans by the hundreds had swept in, drawing carts piled high with food from across the silver sea.

Some yellow notices still blew, trampled and muddy, on the streets. But no one noticed them or cared.

The dragons crouched uneasily together on the palace lawn as their passengers slid from their backs. They accepted renewed thanks gravely, then prepared to depart, for Joyeu and Fortuna felt like trespassers, and Fidelis longed for the hills.

"I hope I may see you again, king of Deltora," Fidelis said. "But I will not come again to Del. The spears and arrows of your friends are not pleasing to me."

Gla-Thon winced, but Lindal lifted her chin.

"I regret harming you, dragon," she said loudly and clearly. "But I believed you were destroying the palace, as once the red dragons destroyed ancient Capra, out of envy for its beauty."

"Indeed?" Fortuna said with interest.

The dragon of the ruby hissed. Its red eyes darkened.

"You have been listening to lies, I fear, woman of Broome," it said stiffly, after a moment's tense silence. "My ancestors destroyed Capra, certainly. But why would dragons envy a small, pink city made of stones? The whole of the east was the ruby dragons' kingdom — a kingdom of land, sea, and sky far more beautiful than a city could ever be."

Lief's throat tightened. He saw at once that the dragon was right.

Lindal stared in confusion.

"The Capricons were most proud of the city they had built," the dragon went on softly. "They planted elegant trees all around it, trees hung with hundreds of little red lanterns. Did you know that, woman of Broome?"

"I have heard of it," Lindal said warily, plainly wondering where this was leading.

"And did you know," the dragon asked, even more softly, "that those pretty lanterns were made of dragons' eggs? Live eggs, stolen from nests while the dragons were away fishing? Eggs sucked dry, then fitted with candles and strung on the trees to make the city beautiful?"

Lindal seemed to freeze where she stood. Lief felt the blood drain from his face. He wanted to bow his head in shame, but he could not look away from the dragon's darkened eyes.

"Three times did the ruby dragons warn that the slaughter of their young must stop," the dragon said. "But the Capricons were proud, and drunk with their desire to add to Capra's splendor. The plunder increased. And so, at last, the dragons stopped it, in their own way."

Lindal wet her lips. "I see now how it was," she said. "I heard only one side of the story, and this led me to judge your tribe unfairly. I beg your pardon."

The dragon stared at her, unblinking. "I accept your apology," it said at last. "And though I refuse to swear an oath that is an insult to my ancestors, I make this promise to you, as friend to friend. I will not harm any human in my land, as long as no human in my land harms me or my kin."

"Thank you," Lindal said humbly. "I can ask no more. And I will tell them. I will tell them all."

✳

One bright morning the following spring, when Deltora was filled with blossom, when bees were drunk with nectar and birds filled the air with song, Jasmine put on a green silk dress, threaded flowers in her hair, and went out to meet Lief on the palace hill.

Hand in hand they were married there, before a crowd the like of which Del had never seen. Barda stood beside Lief. Marilen stood beside Jasmine. Sharn and Doom looked on, and remembered.

Lindal was watching, with a laughing, dancing crowd from Broome. Gla-Thon was there from Dread Mountain, with old Fa-Glin, Pi-Ban who had shared the companions' adventure in the Shadowlands, and the gentle Kin, Ailsa, Bruna, Merin, and Prin.

There were Torans in the hundreds, Zeean at their head, silken robes fluttering like butterflies.

Manus and the people of Raladin were present, their flutes filling the air with gladness. Fardeep the hermit, now once again master of the Games Inn of Rithmere, clapped his hands and sang with Orwen and Joanna, games champions of the Mere. Gers and a troop of Jalis stood proudly with Hellena, Claw, and Brianne, Resistance fighters of the Shadowlands.

All the men and women of the old Resistance were present. All the freed prisoners from the Shadowlands were there. And Zerry, magician's apprentice of the Masked Ones, now chief assistant to the new palace stable-master and wearing his first new suit of clothes for the celebration, made sure that Honey, Bella, and Swift saw everything that passed.

Every friend the companions had made on their travels was present to wish them well, from Tira of

Noradz to Steven and Queen Bee of the Plains, from Bede and Mariette of Shadowgate to Nanion and Ethena of D'Or.

Even Tom the shopkeeper had taken a holiday in honor of the great event, and appeared in dusty finery with his sister Ava on his arm.

And the dragons Veritas, Forta, Hopian, Honora, Fortuna, Fidelis, and Joyeu circled in the sky above.

But for Lief and Jasmine it was as if they were quite alone, for both of them were gaining the dearest wish of their hearts.

In days to come, while the infant Josef slept in a basket beside her, Marilen would write the story of their marriage in the *Deltora Annals*, for she was the palace librarian now. Ranesh had more than enough to do, for Doom had left for parts unknown. Doom wanted to stretch his legs and his mind, he said, and to find out if it was true that a dragon can lay eggs without a mate, if the need arises. He would meet them in Broome in the summer, when Barda and Lindal wed. He knew the celebrations of Broome, he said, and would not miss this one for the world.

✳

And so life went on in Deltora, and life was good.

Barda and Lindal had six children, all of them taller than their parents, and as alike as peas in a pod.

Lief and Jasmine had a daughter, Anna, and twin boys, Jarred and Endon.

And sometimes Doom, home from one of his

many journeys and silently watching the twins at play, would remember two other boys running through the palace gardens long ago. And he would smile.

With Jasmine by his side, Lief ruled the land long and wisely. But he never forgot that he was a man of the people, and that their trust in him was the source of his power. Neither did he forget that the Enemy, though defeated, was not destroyed. He knew that the Enemy was clever and sly, and that to its anger and envy a thousand years was like the blink of an eye. So he wore the Belt of Deltora always, and never let it out of his sight.

Also Available:

Special Edition
Books 1&2